Praise for Erin Nicholas' *Hotblooded*

"Nicholas (*Anything You Want*) is adept at creating two enthralling characters hampered by their pasts yet driven by passion, and she infuses her romance with electrifying sex that will have readers who enjoy the sexually explicit seeking out more from this author."

~ *Library Journal*

"*Hotblooded* is full of emotions, turmoil and passion. But beyond the romance, *Hotblooded* is a story about emotionally healing, finding real love and forgiveness."

~ *Guilty Pleasures Book Reviews*

"*Hotblooded* is a must read romance with hot sensual scenes. The story line is great with a host of wonderful characters... Most highly recommended if you like romances, hotblooded women and small towns. *Hotblooded* is most definitely a repeat read."

~ *Sizzling Hot Book Reviews*

Look for these titles by *Erin Nicholas*

Now Available:

No Matter What

The Bradfords Series

Just Right

Just Like That

Just My Type

Anything & Everything

Anything You Want

Everything You've Got

Hotblooded

Erin Nicholas

SAMHAIN
PUBLISHING

Samhain Publishing, Ltd.
11821 Mason Montgomery Road, 4B
Cincinnati, OH 45249
www.samhainpublishing.com

Hotblooded

Print ISBN: 978-1-60928-795-5
Digital ISBN: 978-1-60928-751-1

Editing by Lindsey Faber
Cover by Scott Carpenter

First Samhain Publishing, Ltd. electronic publication: November 2011
First Samhain Publishing, Ltd. print publication: October 2012

Dedication

To eight of the reasons I love my writing life: PG Forte, Kelly Jamieson, Meg Benjamin, Juniper Bell, Kinsey Holley, Skylar Kade, Kate Davies and Sydney Somers. I couldn't do it without you!

Chapter One

The denim-covered female butt that greeted Jack Silver as he entered the Honey Creek Family Medical clinic made him sure his day wouldn't get any better than this.

The woman—and there was no doubt this was all woman—was on her hands and knees with her upper half hidden beneath the front desk. The frayed edges where the blue jeans had been cut off into shorts brushed against the backs of firm, smooth thighs and Jack found his mood vastly improved as she reached for something, adding an appreciated wiggle to her hips.

"Hello?" he asked just before he spotted the iPod clipped to the waistband of the shorts and realized she had on headphones.

So he decided to wait. He crossed his arms across his chest, leaned a hip against the edge of the front counter and enjoyed the view.

A moment later, she backed up, her hips swaying enticingly. She wore a butter-yellow cotton tank top with her short shorts and he took inventory of the narrow waist, toned arms and shoulders and the blonde hair that hung to mid-shoulder blade from under a red bandana.

The woman pushed back onto her heels, then got to her feet with a dustpan and small broom in hand. She dumped some dirt into a short wastebasket without turning more than a few degrees in his direction.

She exchanged the hand broom for a rag and started singing something about her life sucking, as she started to climb up on the desk. The movement pulled the shorts higher and tighter across her right cheek and he had to shift slightly as things got tighter in his shorts as well.

Once she was up on the desk, he realized that the shorts hadn't really ridden up all that high—they didn't extend very far down her thighs to start with. She stretched up, running the dust rag along the top of the cabinets. The position pulled the tank top away from the waistband of her shorts, exposing a strip of skin that his hands itched to stroke.

Finally she turned to climb down. And saw him.

"Oh. My. God," she breathed, a hand flattening against her chest over her heart.

She wasn't a screamer, he noted. He gave her a smile that he hoped said *Don't worry I'm not a serial killer.* He straightened and she backed up on the desk, pulling the earphones out of her ears.

She was beautiful. The thought seemed to be all that he could really concentrate on for the moment. Her deep green eyes were wide with apprehension, she wore no makeup and she certainly wasn't smiling, but Jack couldn't ignore his basic male awareness of her.

He added *has a gorgeous cleaning lady* to the very short list of things he knew about Brooke Donovan. The fact joined *physician's assistant in Honey Creek, Texas* and *widowed seven months ago.*

"I didn't mean to scare you," he said, stepping forward.

The woman stepped back again. "I didn't hear you."

"The music drowned me out." He couldn't hide the small grin as his eyes dropped to the earphones dangling from her fingers.

She blushed, cringed slightly and said, "Oh, right," softly.

"I was just—" He stepped forward again.

She moved back in response and her left foot slipped off the edge of the desk. She caught herself on the way down, hands splayed on the desk top, left foot on the floor, right still on the desk.

He was beside her, his hand under her elbow in a second. "Whoa, take it easy."

If Brooke thought that she was embarrassed about him overhearing her singing, it was nothing compared to this. And on top of it, *this* hurt.

She wasn't sure which was more painful—the elbows she'd hyper-extended, the left knee she'd jammed, or the right leg she'd stretched far beyond her ligaments' limits. Or, of course, her pride.

She'd stepped back to keep some distance between them and now he was basically plastered against her, his body heat soaking through what little clothing she wore. He wrapped his arms around her as if they were old acquaintances, lifted and turned her slightly to get her right leg on the floor, then set her down again with almost no effort. He released her, but didn't move back much.

"You okay?" he asked.

His chest was only centimeters from hers and she felt his deep voice rumble through her. The fact that he was big had not escaped her notice and having him basically pick her up and put her where he wanted her just emphasized it. It also made it very difficult for her to ignore how much she liked big men. Not big in the sense of having eaten too many Big Macs in his time, but big in the tall, broad-chest, lots-of-muscle sense. Next to her five-foot-five-and-a-quarter inches, he was very tall—at least six-three. And he lifted her as if she was nothing. Which she loved. It went along with the fantasy of the big, strong, alpha man totally taking care of her, protecting her—not to mention taking over and having his wicked way with her whenever he wanted to...

Clearly overcome by the fumes from the cleaning supplies she'd been using, Brooke stepped away from him, needing space. But her knee protested immediately and she inadvertently squawked as she tried to put weight on it. And just like that, he was plastered against her again.

She yelped this time, which wasn't much more sophisticated than the squawk, as he stooped to swing her up into his arms. He took two long strides toward the chair behind the desk and deposited her onto the seat, then knelt in front of her, his big hands sandwiching her knee.

"Where's it hurt?" he asked gruffly.

She thanked heaven for the new razor blades she'd bought that gave an incredibly close shave—and the fact that she'd used one that very morning—as his hands slid over the front and back of her knee. She concentrated on keeping her breathing even. Panting would be hard to explain.

"Um," she answered, staring down at the top of his head. He had brown hair, brown eyes and was extremely good-looking. Some of her favorite qualities in a man. "My knee."

He chuckled. He had a nice chuckle too.

"I figured that. Can you be more specific?" He rubbed his hands over her knee more slowly this time, his eyes coming up to meet hers as he waited for her answer.

She lifted a shoulder, because it was about the only thing she could do with him touching her. The only thing that made any sense anyway.

The heavy drumming in her chest was crazy considering she had no idea who he was or what he was doing there. The soft-sided briefcase he'd dropped beside the desk and the expensive suit and tie he wore gave her some indication, however. He was a sales rep of some kind. He probably had some new fancy equipment to show her.

She felt her face heat as she thought about how that would sound out loud. Then she almost laughed. She'd just bet he had some nice equipment.

Brooke did, however, acknowledge the crazy thumping of her heart, rational or not, for what it was—sexual awareness. Her mama had always said that the women in their family were hotblooded. It was an instinctual, physical reaction Brooke could neither control nor explain. It wasn't, thank the good Lord, like it happened with every man. But it happened more than she liked and each time it hit her—hard.

Of course, the last few times it happened she hadn't done anything about it—

"Miss?"

Brooke jumped slightly as he addressed her. She also hadn't been called Miss in years.

"Yes?"

"Do you have some ice somewhere? For your knee."

Ice—anything cool, in fact—seemed like a really good idea.

"Freezer," she said, gesturing toward the door leading to the break room. She figured she was going to have to work on saying more than one word at a time. But dammit, she was distracted.

He removed his hands and shrugged out of his suit jacket as he stood.

She watched the muscles bunching under the light fabric of his dress shirt, but with some distance between them, her brain slowly kicked on again. “What’s your name?” she asked.

“Jack Silver.”

He disappeared through the swinging door to the back room and she concentrated on breathing but he returned before she got any good oxygen to her brain. Or so it seemed.

He had an ice pack—kept in the freezer for patients with just this sort of injury—wrapped in a dishtowel. He pulled the knot in his tie loose as he came toward her.

“What can I do for you, Jack?” she asked as he squatted next to her. She sucked in a quick breath as he applied the cold pack to her knee.

“I’m hoping you can tell me how to get a hold of your boss,” he said, holding the ice in place as he picked up her shoe and stretched her leg out, propping her foot on his thigh. “I need to talk to her about something.”

She opened her mouth to tell him that she didn’t have a boss, thank you very much, when a brilliant realization struck. He didn’t know who she was. He thought she was— Well, she wasn’t really sure, but it didn’t matter.

She stared at the big hand holding ice against her knee.

He didn’t know who she was. He was a complete stranger. Not from here.

And she wanted to kiss him.

It was a thought completely contrary to what she was used to allowing herself to think. It wasn’t that she never had crazy, it’s-a-really-bad-idea-but-wouldn’t-it-be-great thoughts and impulses. But she was very good at resisting them. She’d had years of practice.

At the moment, however, it was very, very tempting to give in to it and worry about the consequences later.

It had been so long since she'd been spontaneous. So long since she'd had a chance to be. And it would be a long time before she had another chance. That fact reared its ugly head almost daily as she manned the clinic that her late husband had stuck her with in the last place on earth she wanted to be.

The moments were rare when she could crank up the music, put on her comfy clothes and let go. She always did so at the risk of someone finding out and disapproving.

But this guy was a salesman, passing through, on to the next town and the next potential sale by dinnertime. No one would know if she kissed him. Sure, he might talk about it to his buddies at the gym tomorrow or the next day, but no one in Honey Creek would know.

It gave her a little adrenaline rush just thinking about it.

She could French kiss the big, good-looking stranger right here in the clinic, right at the front desk. Just imagining the shocked look on the faces of people in town made her want to do it. She knew the rebellious streak she'd inherited from her mother was some of her trouble here in Honey Creek, but just like telling a dieter they had to avoid cheesecake at all costs, the more forbidden it was, the more tempting she found it.

Just to test the waters, Brooke put her hands behind her on the seat of the chair and leaned back slightly, keeping her elbows straight.

"My boss won't be back for a while," she said. And it was true. The level-headed, do-the-right-thing Brooke she'd turned into over the past few years seemed to have stepped out for the time being.

He glanced up, and she was gratified to see that his eyes

didn't immediately make it past her breasts, which were thrust forward against the soft cotton of her tank top. And, in the spirit of really letting go, she wasn't wearing a bra.

She watched him swallow hard and noticed that the hand on her knee seemed to have forgotten its job as the ice pack slipped to one side.

This was exactly the kind of thing she usually worked so hard to avoid. She'd inherited her mama's looks, body and love of men. She could only assume that her self-control came from her father. She'd never met any of the three men that could have supplied the other half of her DNA, but Brooke sure as hell hadn't gotten any modesty or sense of appropriateness from Dixie. Still, it did do a woman's ego some good to have a man—especially one like Jack Silver, who no doubt had women clamoring and strutting for his attention all the time—give her some good old-fashioned lookin'-good-honey attention.

"My knee is feeling a lot better. You have the touch," she said, her voice a little throaty without even trying. Flirting and teasing were natural for her—another Donovan trait. It was resisting it that had always been the challenge.

His eyes found her face and he gave her a half grin. "So I've been told."

Oh, I just bet you have, she thought, as a little tingle in her stomach responded to that cocky grin. "Are you married?" she asked. If he'd been around as many blocks as she was guessing, he'd know where that question came from.

He definitely didn't react as if the question was odd. "Nope." His hand remembered her knee then, but he let the ice pack slip to the floor and let his palm begin warming the skin as he kneaded the joint gently.

She didn't ask about a girlfriend. She wasn't planning on keeping him, after all, or even compromising him too much. It was just a little kissing. But she most definitely drew the line at married men, no matter how they made her knee feel.

Her skin was quickly regaining its ability to sense heat.

She pulled her foot from where it rested on his thigh, sitting forward on the chair seat.

He seemed reluctant to stop touching her and his hand slid down and around to the back of her calf where it began a slow, seductive stroking up and down.

"Gay?" she asked. Not that she cared. She was going to kiss him anyway. He just might not enjoy it as much as she would.

He laughed and stroked his fingers into the dip behind her bent knee, pressing gently and making heat zing through her.

"No."

She leaned forward until her elbows rested on her knees and her face was less than an inch from his. "You do this kind of thing a lot?" she whispered.

His eyes dropped to her lips and she felt anticipation and awareness shimmy through her. He knew exactly what kind of thing she was talking about.

His breath was hot on her mouth as he whispered back, "Does it really matter?"

Then *he* kissed *her*.

And it wasn't like he was asking permission or testing the waters. It was an all-out assault on her senses. She responded by pressing forward eagerly and wrapping her arms around his neck. There was no reason to hem and haw and waste a bunch of time after all.

His arms went around her waist and he gathered her against him, pressing breasts to chest, pelvis to abdomen. He opened his lips and she followed his lead, straight into the most erotic kiss of her life.

The heat was all-consuming, the desire for more was a pressure she couldn't relieve, and the urge to take her clothes off was unprecedented.

He stroked her tongue with his and her body with his hands. Just the right spots, with just the right amount of pressure, for just the right amount of time to make her limp with wanting and tense with need at the same time. Then his hands went under her, cupped her buttocks and brought her more fully against him as he shifted to fit her against his erection, tipping her pelvis back and forth as he rocked her up and down.

Boy she knew how to pick 'em, This guy definitely knew what he was doing.

Whatever he was selling, she was buying two.

Jack couldn't get enough of her. He wanted to consume her, fill her, possess her. The strength of those foreign sensations shook him.

But not enough to make him let go of her.

In fact, he pressed her closer, relishing the feel of her legs wrapping around his hips, the soft whimpers coming from the back of her throat and the way she arched into him. There was nothing shy and teasing about her. She was blatant about what she wanted—there were no games here, and he found it an incredible turn-on.

Her hands were buried in his hair, clutching and stroking his skull in ways that made him want her hands on other parts of his body ASAP. She was willing, that was certain. Every shift, every lift, every new angle or pressure he tried, whether it was his mouth, his hands or his hips, she responded to with fervor.

He'd been wrong—the day had gotten better after all. A lot better.

Her legs were wrapped around him fully, so she stayed in place as he shifted back, his hands leaving her hips and moving to the bottom of her shirt. He pulled the tank up without hesitation, baring her breasts, and his hands covered them immediately, her hardened tips pressing into the center of his palms. Her breasts were perfect, fitting into his hands as if they were made for petting. She groaned softly as he rolled one hardened tip between thumb and forefinger, and in an effort to make her moan even louder—and because he just couldn't help himself—he pulled away from her lips, lowered his head and took one nipple into his mouth.

Her head fell back and her fingers dug into his scalp. "Oh, yes." But it was more of a husky whisper than a true moan.

He couldn't say that he minded the challenge of trying again for a heartfelt moan. He flicked his tongue over the pert tip, then sucked while his fingers plucked its twin. Her hips rose against him as she shuddered. But still no moan.

He lifted his head and looked up at her. Her eyes were closed and her lips parted as her breaths came in short choppy pants. She rocked her pelvis against him, seeking the relief that he knew he could give her so easily.

But he didn't necessarily want this to be easy. The look of pleasure on her face was good for his self-esteem for sure, but it wasn't enough. He wanted to see ecstasy, bliss, rapture there. He wanted her begging, then as physically fulfilled as any woman had ever been by any man. And he didn't even know her name.

Everything seemed to come to a screeching halt as that thought registered.

He stilled his hands and removed them from the most

perfect breasts he'd ever touched and closed his eyes, pulling in a long, deep breath through his nose. What the hell had just happened? One minute he was rehearsing the biggest apology of his life and the next he was practically screwing the cleaning lady.

Damn. He was used to chaos, but chaos that stayed around him, not in him. That chaos he had control over. He was the commander, the voice of reason, the final decision in the midst of turmoil. He didn't lose his mind like this.

Said cleaning lady pressed against him again and tried to kiss him. He took another fortifying breath and opened his eyes. The first order of business was covering the breasts he was quite sure he'd never forget. The second was getting some space between them. Because when she tightened her thighs around his hips, he couldn't think of one good reason why going ahead with what they both obviously wanted was a bad idea.

He cupped her buttocks and lifted her. "Whoa, sugar," he breathed. "Let's slow down here."

She loosened her grip on his neck and hips slightly and leaned back, blinking at him in confusion. Jack's gaze dropped and then quickly bounced back up to her face. The nipples he'd just been playing with jutted against the front of her shirt and the jolt of desire that shot through him convinced him that this wasn't going to be as easy as just saying no. He wanted her with an intensity he was completely unaccustomed to. He couldn't remember ever feeling the kind of need he felt for the virtual stranger in his arms.

"What's wrong?" she asked, frowning.

He actually smiled at her question. Technically nothing was wrong. Certainly nothing was wrong with the luscious body that was still basically molded to him or with the way she kissed him or with the way she fit against him as if designed for making love with only him.

If he was shocked by his desire for her, he was equally stunned by her corresponding lust for him.

"We're moving a little fast, don't you think?" he asked.

"Do you think this would feel even better if we'd known each other for a while?" she asked, moving her hips just enough to make him sweat.

"So you just want to go at it, right here, right now?" he asked, eyeing the desk next to them and deciding that it would hold up under their weight if needed.

She sighed and wiggled again, her hands against his chest, pushing lightly. It took a moment to realize that she was trying to move away from him. He let her go, telling himself that he was actually relieved when her bottom made contact with the seat of the chair and he could take his hands from her body.

"I should have known it was too good to be true," she said, blowing impatiently at a strand of hair that had fallen over her forehead.

He chuckled at the disgruntled look on her face. "I'm flattered."

"And I'm not," she returned, crossing her arms over her chest. "I finally decide to just go for it and I choose a guy with some morals."

He sighed and got to his feet. He wasn't sure morals were any part of what he was feeling. Crazy. Stupid. A little embarrassed. Like diving right back in? Oh, yeah, all of those.

He ran a hand over his face and determinedly got his mind back on track. "I'm really here to talk to Ms. Donovan. You don't have any idea when she'll be back?"

The woman's eyes widened and she bit her bottom lip as she slowly shook her head.

"Will it be sometime today?" he prodded, frowning slightly at how wary she looked.

She sat up straighter. "No, I'm sure it won't be today. In fact, when I'm done cleaning, I'm locking up."

He huffed out a breath of frustration. Now that his goals for this trip were firmly back in place—helped by the fact that he was resolutely keeping his attention on her face—he was back to wanting to get this thing over with.

"Can you tell me where she lives?"

He didn't want to go to Brooke Donovan's house. He didn't want this to be any more personal than it had to be. This was her place of business and even though her husband had been the primary physician here, Jack figured that it was much less likely to have hints of what was missing and the grief associated than their home would. The last thing in the world he wanted to see was a mantel with some framed photograph of Mike Worthington and Brooke Donovan-Worthington smiling with their arms around each other while on some fabulous, romantic vacation.

"I'm really not comfortable telling a complete stranger where she lives."

The petite blonde got up from the chair, pulled her T-shirt down to meet the waistband of her shorts, again emphasizing the enticing shape of her breasts under the soft cotton, and refused to meet his eyes.

He crossed his arms across his chest. "So, you're completely comfortable having sex with me on the desk, but not comfortable giving me your boss's address?"

She shrugged, still not looking at him and got busy gathering up cleaning supplies and arranging them in a large plastic bucket. "Yeah."

Jack sighed. Why couldn't this be easy? Why couldn't he

just walk into the clinic, introduce himself to Brooke Donovan, tell her he was sorry, give her the check and then get the hell out of Honey Creek and not think about her ever again? But it was just his luck that the day he finally made the decision to come was her day off. It was also just his luck that her cleaning lady was incredibly attractive and not only felt the same way about him, but was brazen in acknowledging it.

Distractions he didn't need. Interruptions in his schedule he didn't need. More things to feel guilty about he definitely didn't need.

He watched her bend to retrieve a rag that slipped from the bucket and found his desire to touch that delectable derriere—and more—not slaked in the least. "Are you afraid I'm going to mention this to her?"

She straightened and looked at him over her shoulder. "To Ms. Donovan?" she asked.

"Yes."

"No, I'm not worried about that." She turned to face him fully, frowning slightly. "But you can't mention it to anyone else."

He saw the tension in her face, even though she tried to seem nonchalant. "I don't know anyone else," he said.

"You don't know Ms. Donovan."

"But I intend to."

She pulled her bottom lip between her teeth and studied him for a long moment. Then she said, "I could give her a message for you. Would that work?"

He pulled a pen from the outside pocket of his briefcase and scribbled his cell phone number on the back of his lunch receipt, then started forward. Then stopped. He hesitated to approach her, feeling for good reason that he might grab her and start right back where they'd ended a few minutes ago. He got only as close as was required to hand her the slip of paper.

Brooke watched him reach out with trepidation. Why couldn't they have just kept on kissing? When she was in the act of kissing him, the kissing made sense. Now that it was over, it seemed a bit unreal—and like a bit of a mistake. Especially in light of his insistence on finding and talking with Brooke Donovan. There was no way she was going to let him know who she was now. Even if he was just trying to sell her something, what had happened between them was so out of character that she couldn't even let a stranger know she'd done it. She took the slip of paper.

"Yes, give her this number and ask her to call me. I have to talk to her before I leave town. It's important."

"You're—" She stopped and cleared her throat and tried for an impassive tone of voice. "You're staying in town then?"

"Until I talk to Ms. Donovan, yes." He seemed irritated. "Can you give her the message right away?"

"Consider it given," she said, wondering what the hell she was going to do.

He wasn't leaving town until he talked to her. Why? She was dying to know why the good-looking stranger was so intent on talking to her. She would have to call him to get rid of him. If she put it off, the chances were very good that he would figure out that Brooke Donovan and the woman he just about had a triple-X encounter with were one and the same. Then she'd have some explaining to do. And she had absolutely no idea what she would say. Without sounding insane anyway.

"You're sure? She'll get the message today?" he clarified.

She looked up at him, impacted once again by the brown eyes staring at her so intently. "I promise."

He just looked at her for several seconds, then stepped forward, grasped her by the upper arms, hauled her up to her tiptoes and kissed her long and sweet, before setting her back on her feet, shouldering his bag and leaving.

She was still trying to catch her breath as the little bell over the front door tinkled happily, announcing his departure.

Brooke waited nearly twenty minutes before calling him. She went home, showered and changed clothes, then sat on the floor in front of her sofa and stared at the number he'd given her. Wow. If he approached his sales quota with the same intensity he put into making out, he had to be the top seller and then some.

Her hands were shaking as she dialed the number. They hadn't spent a lot of their time together talking, so she prayed that he wouldn't recognize her voice, especially on a cell phone. It rang only once before he answered.

"Silver."

"Mr. Silver? This is Brooke Donovan, I—"

"Ms. Donovan, thank you for calling," he interrupted. "I need to schedule a meeting with you as soon as possible."

"Oh, I don't think that's going to work," she stalled, grappling for a good excuse. "I'm very busy. Can't we handle this over the phone?" She was going to say no to whatever he was selling now anyway. There was no way she was going to make a purchase that might require him to be in the clinic to oversee delivery or train them in the use of the equipment. Not that she could afford it—whatever it was—anyway.

"No. I won't take a lot of your time. I'd like to meet tonight. At the diner." There were no question marks in anything he said.

The diner. Brooke shuddered involuntarily. That was enemy territory for her. Even if she wasn't determined to avoid Jack Silver, there was no way she'd go to the diner. "I'm sorry, no."

She heard his heavy sigh on the other end of the phone. His voice had dropped lower and he sounded very tired when he replied, "It's very important. I came from San Antonio today just to see you."

She sat up a little straighter. He'd driven across the state of Texas to see her? He was from San Antonio? No good news came out of the city where her husband had been killed.

Was he a cop? A detective? A collection agent? The significant other of one of Mike's lovers? In any of those cases she couldn't help him.

"What's this about, Mr. Silver?" She didn't have to try to put the tension in her voice when she asked.

"Your husband."

Her eyes slid shut as he confirmed it. She didn't want this, whatever it was. If it had to do with Mike, and most especially something that had cropped up since his sudden and tragic death, she didn't want to hear it. She'd already had three calls like this in the past seven months.

The first had been to inform her of the car accident and Mike's death.

The second had been from the lawyer who had confirmed that she was, indeed, the sole benefactor of Mike's estate. Which amounted to pretty much nothing.

The third phone call had been from Mike's lover who gave Brooke a lengthy and teary confession about how they had been planning to run away together. Their trip had been scheduled for a month from the day Mike died.

Which Brooke had already known since she'd found the confirmation for the airline tickets to Cancun—neither in her name—in Mike's dresser when she'd been looking for black dress socks for the funeral home.

That had been a great day all the way around.

"Mr. Silver, I can assure you that there is nothing you have to say that I'm interested in."

"Ms. Donovan—"

"I don't care if he was involved in mob activity, Mr. Silver. I know nothing about it and that's all I would be able to say even in a court of law. I don't care if there are some outstanding debts in his name. Send the bill to my lawyer. And I don't care if there are six children out there now without a father. The world is a tough place, they might as well learn it sooner rather than later."

Then she hung up on him.

Jack sat staring at the cell phone in his hand and the words *call ended.*

"Son of a bitch." He stopped himself just short of flinging the phone against the passenger-side window of his truck.

This trip just kept getting better and better. Jack parked his truck in front of the only motel in town. It didn't even have a neon sign.

What did he really expect in a town of eight hundred and thirty-two people?

He sighed, swore again, though softer this time, and climbed out of his truck. He'd packed a bag that morning. That had probably jinxed him. He'd had no intention of staying in

Honey Creek overnight, but he knew that he'd never make the nine-plus hour trip back to San Antonio without a break somewhere along the way. Preferably at least a hundred miles from Mike Worthington's widow. Especially after what he'd anticipated being an emotionally draining meeting with her.

But emotionally draining or not, he had been putting this meeting off for seven months and he was finally ready to do it.

So, he was staying. Until he could track Brooke Donovan down in person and tell her he was sorry to her face.

And there was no way he was venturing out in the town. He didn't need a bunch of locals getting curious about who he was or what he was doing there. Lying was much easier in small doses.

Besides, he was only stretching the truth with Brooke.

After checking in and finding his room, he propped two pillows behind his head and settled back as he dialed his brother's number.

Five minutes later, he slipped his shoes off too. His younger brother was in the middle of a lecture and no one and nothing interrupted a Dr. David Silver tirade. Jack might as well get comfortable.

When their dad had died and their mother went into her emotional tailspin, Jack had become the fixer, the guy who got stuff done. David, younger by only ten months, had become everyone's emotional support and cheerleader. Jack was too busy taking care of things to be able to take the time to ask anyone how they were feeling—or to hear their answer. Jack made sure the basics—food, shelter and so on—were handled. David was the one left with a shoulder for their mom to cry on. It didn't really surprise anyone, least of all Jack, that David had become a psychiatrist.

But it could be a real bitch being a shrink's brother.

For instance, the thesis of this particular lecture was the deeper meaning behind the fact that Jack had told neither his brother nor his mother about the trip to Honey Creek. Oh, he'd mentioned the possibility a few months back but had tried to talk himself out of it after both David and Ann freaked out on him.

Jack thought it interesting that David, nationally known expert and acclaimed author in the area of human behavior, didn't see that their reaction to the *idea* of the trip was directly proportional to Jack not telling them about the *actual* trip.

Jack had intended to keep the trip to himself until he was back in San Antonio. But he couldn't avoid calling David once he was laid-over. David was his brother—in spite of the psych degree. They saw each other at least twice a week. Jack couldn't just disappear.

"But now that you're there," David said, his tone resigned. "Do something, whatever, and get out. End it. Tell yourself it's over and as you drive out of town, remind yourself it's finished and you have no more obligation."

Jack didn't comment, because he knew David wasn't done. David had a way with meaningful pauses.

"And Jack," he said a moment later. "Make it really count."

Jack frowned. "Count?"

David sighed. "Whatever you do, make it matter. I know you. If you do something half-assed and not especially significant, you'll never be satisfied. You'll never feel done with it."

Jack squirmed and tried to get comfortable against the pillows. He hated it when David proved how well he knew him. It was actually a little spooky how David could put words to things about him that *he* couldn't even articulate.

He had promised himself he wasn't going to do this, but he

found himself unable—as pathetic as it felt—to refrain from asking his little brother his opinion. "So what do you think about me just handing her a check for the life insurance money?"

"No good," David said without thought. "That's not enough for you. Anyone could do that. Hell, if that was enough you could have mailed it from here with a letter."

Jack gave up on trying to get comfortable against the pillows. He had a feeling he wouldn't be totally comfortable as long as he was on the phone with David—or maybe until this whole thing with Brooke Donovan was taken care of.

David was right. Brooke turning the money down had been a blessing in disguise. It would have been very unsatisfactory to simply hand her a check and then get back in his truck and go on with his life.

"I thought about equipment for the clinic," Jack said. "I thought I could buy something she could use."

What Jack hated even more than David's lectures and eerie insights into Jack's mind was how much he liked having David's affirmation. But he did.

Even at age fifteen when their dad died and Jack had stepped into those shoes as best he could, David had sensed his role. If Jack was more or less the quarterback of the family—deciding what needed to be done and then doing the job—David was the coach with the inspirational speeches and the undying optimism when the team was down by three touchdowns.

David kept them all going emotionally and made Jack think about it when he under-performed and cheered him on when he overachieved. David was also the only person who Jack knew would tell him he was being an ass if he was being an ass and that he'd done well when he'd done well.

Jack needed David's support now more than he could remember ever needing it. To the point of actually asking for it. Which he would have never expected.

But this stuff with Brooke was emotional. The people Jack usually helped were physically sick and injured. He understood what was wrong and could fix it. He also saw poor people, hungry people, homeless people, and he gave them money, food and shelter...or at least a good social worker.

Brooke Donovan was not sick, as far as he knew. She wasn't destitute either.

She was widowed. She was sad, lonely and grieving.

That was David's department.

"The clinic isn't personal enough," David said. "It's nice and she may want it, but it's only indirectly for her. You won't be happy unless whatever it is directly benefits her and makes her happy."

Which was exactly why Jack was still in Honey Creek. He closed his eyes and rubbed his temple. It had to be personal.

Fuck.

"Okay," he said, sitting up. "I'll find something else. Something more. I've got plenty of money to work with. If the life insurance isn't enough, I'll use my own."

David swore—something he generally refrained from—and said, rather calmly considering the expletive he'd used, "You're trying to buy her forgiveness. Just tell her who you are, why you're there and tell her you're sorry."

"No," Jack said quickly and adamantly.

"Jack..."

"For one thing," Jack said harshly. "I don't expect her forgiveness. For another, what the hell good does my being sorry do her?"

"And for another," David broke in. "You can't stand having even a stranger know that you're a regular human being who occasionally makes mistakes."

This was another familiar lecture topic—Jack's hero complex. "Go to hell, David."

"That's fine," David replied, mildly. "Be pissed at me. But you need to acknowledge that this woman may need something you cannot give her."

"That's not an option," Jack said, his voice low and tight.

"Or maybe she doesn't need anything at all."

"How can she not need anything?" Jack shoved a hand through his hair in frustration. "It doesn't matter," he said through gritted teeth. "I need to do this—something—for her."

"This isn't supposed to be about you," David said. "It's about her…isn't it? About making things better for *her*?"

Jack surged to his feet and paced toward the window. "Yes, it's about her. Dammit, David."

"Just explain to me why this is such a big deal. You lose people in the ER sometimes. It happens. You've told me that it's part of the job. They don't all make it. But…" David paused, meaningfully, of course, "…you don't go to all their widows and try to make things better for them."

Jack felt the throbbing build behind his eyes. He couldn't reply right away as he tried to figure out if David was playing shrink or concerned brother at the moment. It was so hard to tell the difference sometimes that the effort to distinguish between the two just increased the pressure between his temples.

"Why can you accept losing patients in the ER but you can't let this guy go?" David asked, his tone gentle but insistent.

"Because." He had to stop and clear his throat. "Because, when I lose them in the ER I know I've done absolutely everything I can. I've always given it the best effort I've got."

"So, then..." David started.

But Jack broke in. "I haven't done everything in this situation. I haven't done anything to make it right."

The pressure in his head lessened a bit as he spoke and his eyes came open. In spite of his pain-in-the-ass tendencies David was giving him the direction he'd needed. His initial plan hadn't turned out as expected and it had thrown him a bit. His heroic efforts were usually right on. Those efforts, of course, primarily occurring in the emergency department. Evidently he wasn't such a natural when he didn't have a monitor telling him the condition of the heart he was working on.

Well, what did he expect? He'd tried to do the minimum here. In the ER he would have never tried to take the easy way out. He went above and beyond. That's what he knew, how he worked. So, he knew what he was going to do now, in this situation.

Whatever it took.

"I'm not coming home until I've done something for Brooke Donovan that, in a brilliant psychiatrist's words, really counts," Jack announced over whatever his brother had been saying.

"Shit," David muttered. Then, louder, "Don't you have to be back in San Antonio at some point in the near future?"

"I have a ton of vacation time," Jack said. He almost never took time off. The ER was where he needed to be.

"Well, remember, Jack," David said, "as a doctor in a huge ER like you're used to, you're in charge of helping hundreds of people every year."

Jack frowned. "Right." He could admit, to himself, that the

draw to the ER was exactly what David had just described.

"I'm just saying, if you have to make a choice here, Brooke Donovan is one life while there are hundreds of lives down here that need you."

Jack groaned. "David, I hate it when you analyze me."

"Then it's a good thing I do it for free," David said cheerily.

Chapter Two

"Hello?"

"Good morning."

Brooke's heart jumped before she reminded herself that the sexy voice on the other end of the phone was the man who had some news about Mike that would do nothing but add to her regrets. And the man seemed determined to tell her whatever it was.

She loved his voice, she thought before she checked herself. "Nothing has changed since last night, Mr. Silver."

If she kept calling him Mr. she could ignore that he was also the man who'd kissed her senseless yesterday.

"I was hoping to change your mind today," he said. "If you would meet me, I could explain that—"

"Would you say that what you want to talk to me about is good news?" she interrupted as she turned her car onto the county road that would take her to the Nelson's farm.

There was a long pause on the other end of the phone and she knew the answer even before he said, "I guess that depends on you. That's something I'd like to talk about."

"So, if it's not something that will definitely make me happy, why would I want to take time out of my day to hear it?"

"It's...important," he finally said.

"Is it important to me or to you?" she asked.

"It's important to me," his voice finally rumbled. "I really need to—"

"No offense," she inserted, though she didn't really care at this point if he was offended. "But I'm barely keeping up with the things in my life that are important to me. I don't really have the time or energy for things that are important to complete strangers."

"I want to help you," he said firmly, undeterred by her statement.

That made her pause. "Help me?" she repeated.

"I know what's going on in your life. You're on your own professionally and personally now. That can't be easy," he pressed.

Brooke could count on one hand the number of people who had offered to help her or acted like they cared about her situation in the months since her husband's death. Her pause had nothing to do with the fact that the man offering to help her was also the star of some rather lusty dreams last night where he *helped* her quite a lot, she insisted as an afterthought.

"I want to do something for you," he said.

He didn't know that he was talking to the woman he'd practically made love to on a desk yesterday, she reminded herself, so the sexual images that sprang to mind at the something he offered were one-sided.

"Why?" she asked, instead of giving suggestions.

He was quiet for a moment. "I'm a nice guy. At least I try to be," he said gruffly.

She pulled over to the side of the road two miles from the Nelson's driveway and shifted into park. Her hands were shaking but she wasn't really sure why.

"Brooke, are you there?" he asked.

She started at his use of her first name. Until that moment he'd been calling her Ms. Donovan. Which kept things nicely distanced between them. But when he said her name, she was instantly jolted back to how it felt to be in his arms, with his mouth doing decadent things to hers.

"Yeah."

"I feel terrible about what happened to Mike. I want to help you out in some way. I have a check for you."

His answer was out of sync with what she'd been thinking and it took a moment for her mind to discard her assumptions and understand what he'd said.

"A check?"

Jack sat on the edge of his bed, his morning coffee churning in his gut as he plodded his way through the conversation he'd resigned himself to having over the phone. At least for now.

He'd tried three times now and still couldn't get the words out that explained his part in Mike Worthington's death. But at least she knew why he was here, mostly, and what he wanted to do for her.

"A check for two hundred and fifty thousand dollars," he said. "It's what's left of the life insurance policy on Edward Movey." He waited a heartbeat for her to recognize the name.

"Edward Movey?" she asked hoarsely. "Two hundred and fifty thousand... But...why?"

"If anyone deserves the money it's you, Ms. Donovan. Mr. Movey's beneficiary wants you to have it." That was the absolute, unadulterated truth.

He could have said, “I’m the beneficiary and *I* want you to have it.” But he didn’t. Couldn’t. Just like he couldn’t say *I caused the accident that killed your husband.*

It probably made him a selfish bastard but he just couldn’t admit his guilt.

Besides, what did he really expect from confessing? Forgiveness? He didn’t deserve forgiveness. Would he feel better? He didn’t really deserve that either.

He was used to fixing things. He didn’t save everyone, but he could always tell the family that he’d done everything in his power. In this situation, he *hadn’t* done everything in his power and Mike Worthington and Jack’s uncle Ed were dead. And Brooke Donovan’s life had been turned upside down.

She was truly the only one left behind. Ed hadn’t been married, had no children, so his passing had affected the bartender at his regular hangout and his poker buddies more than anyone.

But just because no one was blaming him didn’t change the fact that Jack had failed.

He despised that.

He wasn’t used to being anything less than a hero. He spent his days in the ER where he didn’t always win, but where he always fought the good fight and got credit for trying.

Something good *had* to come out of this. He needed to fix it. He needed to fill in the gaps that he’d created for this woman.

“Surely his family could use it or donate it or something,” Brooke said, sounding a bit dazed.

“You are aware Mr. Movey was drunk when he hit your husband.”

He heard her pull in a long breath. “Yes.”

“His beneficiary...his nephew,” Jack said, trying to be as

truthful as possible without exposing himself, "feels that because Mr. Movey's recklessness directly impacted *your* life, perhaps the money can help you with some needs that may have come up since your husband's death."

"The family should consider giving the money to an alcohol education or prevention program," she said. "They could impact a lot of lives that way."

He barely avoided swearing. That sounded great, but it wouldn't be *enough.* He needed his help to be more direct. *This* woman had been affected by *his* actions—or lack of in this case—and he needed to directly help *her.*

Dammit, his brother was right.

"The family has already made their decision, Ms. Donovan. The money is yours."

"I don't want it."

"You don't understand—"

"Yes, I do. Edward Movey's family feels bad about my husband dying and wants to give me money to make it all better."

It definitely sounded lame when she said it like that. But giving her the money had seemed like a decent gesture. And it was easy. Write the check, hand it over, leave town. At least, that's what he'd imagined happening. He let his head drop, resting his elbows on his knees. Of course, if he imagined it going that way, it would go any way but like that.

"Ms. Donovan—"

"Mr. Silver, I'm not taking the money. There's nothing you can say to change my mind."

And she hung up on him again.

Brooke shut her cell phone off to prevent any callbacks and pulled back onto the gravel road to the Nelsons'. She was strangely restless after the phone call. It was really too bad that such a good-looking guy, who could kiss like it was a superpower, was determined to complicate her life.

Two hundred and fifty thousand dollars was a hell of a lot of money.

There was just no way around that fact.

But she couldn't take it. As unbelievable as that was even to her.

A good-looking man that she wanted to sleep with was offering her money.

An exorbitant amount of money.

She was proud of her ability to say no in the face of such temptation.

But she had said no. Emphatically.

If only Walter Worthington could see this. Her ex-father-in-law would never believe she was saying no to both sex *and* money.

But she was not taking help, and definitely not financial help, from anyone. Especially young, hot, single men.

Even if taking the life insurance money hadn't seemed creepy—which it did—she still didn't want any help. She was going to pay her debt to Honey Creek with hard work. Period. Because it would shock and amaze them all.

She had a contract—a stroke of genius on Mike's part—that stated as long as she showed up to staff the clinic every day for two years, Honey Creek would pay off the student loans she'd taken out to get her Physician's Assistant degree. Mike had known how things would go with her and Honey Creek in the case he wasn't there to be a buffer, so the contract read that as long as she showed up she'd have her loans paid. The fact that almost no one came to the clinic for care didn't matter. She was still going to leave Honey Creek debt free in another eight months. In the meantime, she knew it bugged the hell out of Walter for her to even play at running the clinic, so she showed up every day and went through the motions.

The thing was, she didn't want to be here either. She'd agreed to come back to Honey Creek to help Mike out. Again.

And then he'd up and died.

When she saw him in Heaven, he was going to owe her big-time. Heaven better have a Macy's *and* Starbucks.

But for now, she was stuck here. She couldn't leave. She wanted Honey Creek to be shocked and amazed, to know they were wrong about her. They figured that she was the kind of person to get going when the going got tough.

Which was exactly why Walter kept making things tougher and tougher. It had worked with her mother. Dixie had finally tucked tail and slunk out of town.

But Brooke was not her mother.

In any way.

She'd been intent on proving that for years and damned if she was going to let a little thing like Mike's death derail her efforts. She didn't need a man to take care of her. She could handle anything that came her way.

She could also resist the temptation of money, gifts, flattery, hot kisses and even hotter sex. Even with Jack Silver.

She could.

Absolutely.

Brooke eyed her cell phone with trepidation as it lay ringing on her kitchen counter. Only a very few people had this number. But there was one—with a rich, deep voice that made her tingly—who seemed intent on using it. Hourly. And she somehow knew he'd just keep calling back.

"Hello?"

"Hello."

Something warm shimmered deep in her stomach like she'd just swallowed hot cocoa and it was warming her from within. Standing in only her jeans and a bra didn't help.

"Mr. Silver, I presume."

"I'm glad you remember me."

Oh, she remembered him all right. The voice fit him. Big, strong, confident men needed deep, rich voices that would command attention and—with just the right intentional inflection—would pour over and melt a woman like hot fudge over ice cream. Oh yeah, hot fudge was a better analogy than cocoa.

"I need to see you," he said.

"You've mentioned that."

"And I intend to keep mentioning it."

She wanted to offer him a chance to finish what they'd started at the clinic instead of talking about her dead husband, but she knew that would be a huge mistake. In a town where you couldn't even wear new shoes without someone noticing, getting naked with the good-looking stranger from San Antonio would not escape attention.

And that was exactly the kind of attention she was intent on avoiding.

"I can't do it, Mr. Silver."

"Ms. Donovan. I have a large check made out to you, personally. I have no intention of taking it back with me."

She scowled as she shucked out of her jeans. “And I have no intention of ever cashing that check or using any of that money no matter how many zeroes you add.”

“Then let me buy you—”

“I wish you’d just lost the money to him in poker or something,” she broke in. “I *might* take it then.” She’d save it until after her debt in Honey Creek was paid, but she really might spend Mike’s poker money.

There was a moment of silence, then, “A poker loss of two hundred and fifty thousand dollars?”

“That would be a record,” she admitted. “But possible. He was in San Antonio for a big tournament. Well, that and Chris.” Poker was how Mike had met the man of his dreams. The man who he’d been planning to run away with. The man he’d been about to abandon her for.

She took a deep breath and tried to calm her temper. If Mike had left her in Honey Creek the way he’d intended she would have hunted him down and killed him anyway.

An unusual wave of nostalgia and sadness gripped her in that moment as she realized Mike would have thought that was really funny.

God, she did miss him. Her heart wasn’t broken like it should be after losing a spouse but it definitely ached. He’d been one of her best friends. If it weren’t for the fact she really was pissed at him, she’d be even sadder.

“I, um…I don’t gamble,” Jack finally said.

“Well, that’s too bad.” And she hung up on him yet again.

Jack was not used to not getting his way. And he wasn’t about to start getting used to it now.

He pulled the front door to the clinic open with much more force than was necessary. The little bell overhead tinkled merrily anyway, in sharp contrast to the very unmerry mood he was in.

He'd considered leaving town and being happy with the idea that he'd offered to help Brooke and she'd said no. There wasn't much more he could do. She was an independent adult. He couldn't force her to do or think or accept anything she didn't want to.

But he was still here. Because he wasn't satisfied with just offering help. It wasn't his style to let people make bad choices. At least not normally.

Really just the one time. Which he could never forget.

It had been a stormy night seven months ago when he'd used the rationale that he couldn't make a grown adult do anything they didn't want to do. He'd given up arguing with his drunk uncle in frustration and had walked out of the house. Less than thirty minutes later, Ed had gotten into his truck and driven off, with his blood alcohol level twice the legal limit.

Jack could still smell the rain that had hung in the air that night. The cold, damp air had surrounded him, seeping into him, as deep as his heart. It had followed him all night—a frigid, oppressive reminder of all of the things he could not change: the weather, for one...and the fact that his uncle and an innocent man were dead.

Jack's eyebrows pulled together. He could, however, change some of Brooke Donovan's circumstances. He was going to help her whether she liked it or not.

He pulled himself from the past and stopped at the front counter, looking around the deserted clinic. He had a moment of déjà vu. It wasn't the lack of patients or staff, or the furniture or any other triviality that came to mind, however. The only thing he could see, hear, taste or feel for a moment was the woman he'd nearly taken on the front desk.

The physical release he'd denied himself yesterday with the sexiest woman he'd ever kissed was doing nothing to improve his mood.

Maybe he'd run into her again. If so, he didn't think he could walk away a second time.

And this time, he was sure as hell going to get her name.

"Hello?" he called out.

"Be right there!"

The voice came from down the hallway where he assumed the treatment rooms to be. He felt his pulse quicken. He and the maid hadn't spent much time conversing yesterday so he wasn't sure he'd recognize her voice. He knew he'd recognize her scent though.

"Hi."

Stupidly, he felt his heart sink as a Hispanic woman dressed in scrubs emerged from a door down the hallway and came toward him carrying three cardboard boxes. She was beautiful, but she wasn't the woman he'd been dreaming of.

But maybe this was Brooke Donovan.

"Hi," he returned, carefully putting his smile in place.

As much as his body begged to differ, he didn't need to get laid. He needed some absolution. At least, he needed absolution more.

"Can I help you?"

The woman drew close enough for him to read *Carla* on her name tag. Damn.

"I sure hope so," he said, using his good-ol'-boy Southern Texas drawl. He leaned onto one elbow on the counter. "My name's Jack Silver. I came to meet with Ms. Donovan."

"Well, lucky Ms. Donovan," she said, looking him up and down blatantly, but with a smile that told him that flirting was like blinking for her—something that she did without thinking.

This was more like it. He was charming, dammit, and knew how to talk women into almost anything. Brooke Donovan was perhaps an exception, but he was determined that was only temporary.

"Well, thank you, ma'am," he returned, wishing he had a cowboy hat to tip to her. He didn't understand women's attraction to cowboy hats but he knew it was real and was not above using it to his advantage. Or anything else for that matter.

Speaking of which...

"Let me help you with those." He stepped forward and relieved Carla of her armful of boxes.

"Thanks." She led the way behind the counter and pointed for him to put the boxes on the countertop near the copy machine. "Sorry, Brooke's doing house calls until eleven."

"House calls?" he repeated. "Seriously?"

Jack glanced around. This was the second time in as many days that he'd been in the clinic when it was basically deserted. "Does she always come in at eleven?"

Carla shrugged. "She comes in when she needs to."

He frowned at that. This was a medical clinic. She was the medical provider, the only one in town. Her supervising physician came out of Amarillo. So how could she not be here? What if there was a medical emergency for God's sake?

"What if I was going into anaphylactic shock?" he asked before he could stop himself.

Carla didn't look concerned about the possibility. "I'd page her and start treating you per her instructions until she got here."

He played with the idea of faking something just to get Brooke in front of him. He was sure he could do a convincing job with many illnesses. But it probably wouldn't make her any friendlier with him when she found out it was a hoax.

Carla eyed him up and down. "I'll be glad to check you out for hives and such. But you look pretty danged healthy to me."

He chuckled. "No hives. I'm good."

"You sure? I mean, you could slip your shirt off for just a minute to be sure."

He laughed at that. "You Honey Creek ladies sure are friendly."

Carla seemed intrigued by that. "Who else have you met?"

"Just your cleaning lady." And that was all he was going to say about that.

"Our...cleaning lady," she said nodding slowly. "Right. You found her friendly?"

He shifted as his body remembered just how friendly. "Yes. Very...sweet." God was she sweet.

"Well, good," Carla said, watching him with an expression he couldn't label. "I didn't realize Brooke had a meeting scheduled today."

"I took my chances and just showed up."

She laughed. "That's probably not going to work for you. Brooke doesn't like surprises."

"Then maybe you can help me."

"Well, let's hear what you've got."

"I've got a bunch of money and I want to spend it on Brooke."

Carla looked at him for a long moment. Then she asked,

"Did you obtain this money legally?"

He grinned. "Yes."

"Are you asking anything in return? Medical care, votes...sexual favors?"

She winked at him.

His grin grew. "No, I'm not. It's free and clear."

She sighed. "Hm, too bad."

"I'm flattered."

She smiled and rolled her eyes. "I was thinking more for Brooke's sake. Not that I'm not fully dedicated to helping this clinic however I can," she added with another wink.

"Thanks." But his smile was a little forced this time.

For Brooke's sake echoed in his head but he kept his mouth shut on the questions that threatened to fall out. It was a weird comment to make. Especially about a woman who had lost her husband only a few months ago. But he let it go. Completely. He was not curious about Brooke Donovan. All he cared about was leaving Honey Creek with a clear conscience.

"My shrink says I'm addicted to being the hero."

Carla's eyes scanned over him. "You're built for being a hero, Jack Silver." Her eyes returned to his face. "You any good at it?"

He nodded. "I am."

"You got a tight fittin' superhero outfit with a cape?" she asked. "'Cuz that I'd like to see."

He laughed. He liked Carla. "No. I'm a bit more understated than that."

She shook her head regretfully. "Too bad" she said with a grin. "So hero-boy, what do you need my help with? I'm just a mortal, remember. Unless line dancin' and grounding teenage boys are superpowers—then I might be in your league."

"How many boys?"

"I'm a single mom of four. Youngest is twelve."

He whistled. "Lady, you are so far beyond me on the hero-scale, it ain't even funny."

They stood smiling at each other, feeling their growing camaraderie.

"Okay, here's the deal," he said. "I have two hundred and fifty thousand dollars for Brooke, and she won't take it."

Carla didn't say anything for a few seconds, just stood watching him. Then she moved to the desk behind her, opened the top right drawer and pulled out a bag of peanut butter M&M's. She undid the twist tie at the top of the bag and shook a few candies out into her palm. Then she held the bag out. He opened his palm and she poured a small pile into it.

She munched on two M & M's for a moment. Finally she asked, "A quarter of a million dollars?"

He nodded.

"Just like that?"

He wanted to laugh. Right, just like that. Piece of cake. No big deal. If she only knew the torment that had preceded this decision.

"The money is the life insurance from the man who hit and killed her husband." And God knew Jack wasn't keeping any of it. "His family wants her to have it." All true enough. He didn't need to mention that he was a part of said family. Or that he had spent two weeks talking the rest of said family into the idea.

Carla looked at him and chewed on her M&M's for a moment. "Nope." She shook her head finally. "She won't go for that."

He huffed out a frustrated breath. “No kidding.” He threw a few M & M’s into his mouth and chewed glumly.

“Yeah, you mentioned that she won’t take it. You talked to her?”

“Finally. I was persistent.”

Carla smiled. “That’s a good place to start with Brooke.”

“Yeah, well, it pretty much ended there too,” he said with aggravation.

“She won?” Carla looked like she was trying to hide a grin.

He raised both eyebrows. “I’m here, aren’t I? She won’t win until I give up. Which won’t happen.”

Carla dug in the bag for more candy. “Why’s it matter so much? Take the money and go home.”

“I...” He stopped and regrouped, considering his words carefully. “This is especially important to one of the man’s nephews.”

“The family doesn’t need the money?”

“No.” They definitely did not need the money. Jack’s brother did very well for himself and Jack’s mother was dating a wealthy investor and was very well taken care of. The rest of the family was fine...and had long ago distanced themselves from Ed and his alcoholism. Ed had no children and his two wives had preceded him into eternity. The only life left in tumult was Brooke Donovan’s.

“They don’t *want* the money either?” she asked.

He shrugged. “Not really.” His mother and brother’s aversion to Jack coming to Honey Creek wasn’t about them wanting the money, or about them not wanting Brooke to have it. It was about them wanting Jack to stop being obsessive about Brooke having the money.

Carla dug in the bag until she found a red M & M. She

popped it into her mouth. “What can I do?”

He bent his knees so that he was on eye level with her five foot two inches. “Help me spend this money on Brooke. I’ll do anything.”

She tipped her head to one side. “Anything?”

He hesitated. “You want me to take my shirt off, don’t you?”

She laughed. “A little,” she admitted. “But I have something else in mind.”

“Brooke, you’re here!”

Carla, the clinic nurse and Brooke’s only true friend in Honey Creek met her with a huge grin as she stepped through the front door and into the empty waiting room.

“Hi,” Brooke said slowly, taken aback by the exuberance of the woman she’d never known to be exuberant. Ever.

“Isn’t it a great day?” Carla asked brightly.

“Okay,” Brooke said. She hadn’t really formed an opinion of the day yet.

She headed for the back room. She needed a cup of tea before she could delve into what was going on with her friend. “Any patients?” she asked as she pushed the swinging door open between the front of the clinic and the back break room.

“Sorry.”

Nothing. Brooke glanced at the clock. She sighed. During graduate school and her time in San Antonio at the free clinic she would have paid for down time where she could sit, drink tea and read romance novels. Now she went through at least two thick novels a week and she was almost sick of her favorite tea.

She stepped into the back room to get her cup and tea bags, but froze in the doorway, the door swinging back and bumping her in the rear end.

"Um, Carla?"

"Yeah?"

"What is that?"

She felt Carla come up beside her. "That is the cappuccino machine." She said it with obvious affection in her voice.

Brooke stared at the polished silver appliance. Well, it would solve her tea boredom.

"It's ours?" she asked.

Carla lifted a shoulder. "Yeah."

"I don't remember ordering it," Brooke said mildly. She started toward the monstrosity.

Carla spoke when Brooke was halfway across the room. "Jack bought it."

She froze. She pivoted slowly back toward Carla. "Jack?"

"Jack Silver. The guy who was..."

"I know who he is," Brooke interrupted. "What is he doing buying a cappuccino machine for us?"

"He said you wouldn't take his money so he thought he'd get us something we need instead."

"We need a cappuccino machine?"

"Hey, you don't have four kids, but I know *I* need a cappuccino machine." Carla gazed fondly at the appliance.

"What else?" Brooke crossed her arms and regarded the other woman with narrowed eyes.

"What do you mean?"

"I mean what else did he buy for us? I know he didn't settle for just a coffee machine."

Brooke wasn't sure how she knew, but she did. She had a feeling Jack Silver wasn't the type of guy to do anything partway. He went all the way, and then some.

"It's not just a coffee machine," Carla protested. She crossed to the machine and began preparing herself another cup.

"Carla, what else?" Brooke asked firmly.

Her friend sighed. "Okay. Computer equipment and software. It's supposed to be delivered tomorrow."

"I can't take this stuff from him."

"Why not? He's loaded."

"He's loaded?" Brooke asked. "How do you know that?"

"I can just tell. Doesn't he seem loaded?"

Brooke didn't really want to think about that, or anything else related to Jack Silver. She'd spent far too much time thinking about him already. And wasn't that just what everyone would expect anyway? She had to keep her mind on her work and the clinic, not the good-looking, single guy passing through town. At least, she assumed he was single. Like it mattered, she thought with a roll of her eyes. It certainly wouldn't slow the speculation if he was married.

"Seriously," Carla went on, having to raise her voice over the noise of the machine as she steamed her milk. "He's just got...something, don't you think? I mean, sure he's good looking. Really good looking. But he's also just—" she paused in the midst of rotating the carafe, "—so *there*. He's pretty hard to say no to."

"I managed it," Brooke pointed out just as loudly, increasingly annoyed by Carla's observations about Jack. Even more because they were true.

"Well, you didn't really," Carla said with a smile, shutting the steamer off. "I mean he still managed to give you the money…indirectly."

Brooke wasn't sure what to say. But it certainly wasn't going to be an acknowledgment that Carla was right. "That's only part of the money he wants to give me." No way that thing cost two hundred and fifty thousand dollars.

Carla abandoned the cappuccino for a moment, planting her hands on her hips. "Why won't you take it?" she demanded.

"I can't. You know that."

Carla looked at her, her expression exasperated and sympathetic at the same time.

"I'm right," Brooke insisted. Walter wanted to believe, and wanted to convince everyone else—including Brooke—that she was nothing without a man taking care of her. Like her mother had been. "Everyone is expecting me to bail. I have to stick this out. Do it the hard way if I ever want to feel like I proved something."

Carla nodded slowly. "I know."

"So, you understand why I have to turn it all down." Brooke moved toward the door. "I have to do this on my own. In every way."

"But—"

"I have to," Brooke said firmly.

Carla didn't argue, but she was looking at the cappuccino machine sadly when Brooke glanced back.

"For the record," Carla said, "you don't have to do it all on your own. I'm in this with you."

Brooke turned back. Her throat felt tight. "Thanks, Carla."

That was nice. But Carla came with the clinic. Her job was secure no matter who provided the medical care and there would be someone after Brooke. Someone who patients would actually come to see. Walter and the rest of the City Council wanted medical care in Honey Creek. They just didn't want Brooke.

"Did Mr. Silver mention what company he ordered the computer from?"

Carla sighed. "Yeah." She touched the silver side of the cappuccino machine lovingly. "They faxed an order confirmation a little bit ago. It's in my top drawer. I was saving it for Jack."

"Thanks." Brooke found the paper right away and went to her office to make the call. A woman answered after a two-minute hold period. Brooke explained the situation and that she wanted to cancel the shipment.

"I will have to inform the gentleman who placed the order of this...development." The woman's tone was icy.

"Oh, I hope you do," Brooke said sincerely.

She disconnected the call, leaned back in her chair and propped her feet on the desk. Maybe Carla would even bring her a cappuccino while she waited for Jack to show up.

She couldn't avoid a face to face with him any longer.

"Is she here?" Jack asked Carla as he strode through the front of the clinic.

"Oh, yeah. In fact, I have a feeling she's been waiting for you."

He couldn't help the smile. "She figured I would come?"

"I think so." Carla pointed down the hall toward Brooke's office. "I'd knock before you go in."

"Of course."

He did knock, but he didn't wait for her to invite him in.

She was sitting behind her desk, a pair of glasses balanced on her nose and a thick paperback book open in front of her.

She pulled the glasses from her face and shut the book, turning it over so he couldn't see the front, and stood all in one fluid motion.

"Mr. Silver."

His body reacted before his brain fully caught up.

She was dressed in black slacks, a white button up shirt, her hair pulled back into a severe twist, so it took his mind a few seconds longer to process the fact that Brooke Donovan was, in fact, his cleaning lady.

And then it made sense.

Kind of.

His reaction was surprisingly strong. It was more than a male appreciating a beautiful female. It was more than a man recognizing a woman he wanted. It was like every cell in his body was remembering hers all at once—how her lips felt, how her breasts felt, how her legs felt wrapped around him like he was a life preserver and her ship was going down.

He stopped in front of her desk, not sure what to say or do. Perhaps asking if he could taste the sweet skin just below her ear wasn't appropriate but it seemed to be all he could concentrate on. "I'm sorry the computer system isn't what you wanted. The new system will be here in the morning."

"It better not be," she protested. "I don't want anything from you."

He didn't think that was entirely true. He thought there were some things she wanted as much as he did. And he wasn't opposed to reminding her of that given half a chance.

"That's not an option."

While giving Brooke *things* wasn't his ultimate goal—and

wouldn't be ultimately satisfying as David had pointed out—he needed to be around long enough to find out what she really needed. Carla had assured him that if he bought Brooke some outlandish thing she would confront him face to face. It was pure coincidence that the most unusual thing they could come up with was something Carla was dying to have.

That was just the first step anyway.

The second step was, well, to hang around as long as necessary to figure out a way to satisfy them both. And he didn't even mean that sexually. Much.

It was strange how quickly he was adjusting to the fact that the two Honey Creek women he'd been obsessing about were one and the same.

In fact, Brooke's insistence about not seeing him made more sense this way.

He wondered if the stain of pink on her cheeks was about something more interesting than ire. Embarrassment? Arousal?

He liked that idea. And he liked the realization that he'd won round one—they were face to face. He wasn't worried about round two either. Or the entire battle.

There was no way she had a better reason for declining his help than he had for giving it.

No way.

He took a seat in the chair in front of her desk. He crossed one ankle over the opposite knee and leaned back, casually. "I'm glad to see at least you're enjoying the cappuccino."

He looked pointedly at the large mug on the corner of her desk.

She followed his gaze to the steam rising from the creamy brown liquid. And she blushed.

Somehow, Jack held back his smile.

She took her seat again, folding her hands primly on the huge calendar on the surface of her desk. Primly wasn't a word he would have ever associated with the woman he'd met yesterday and it bugged him that it fit today. She might look all buttoned up and serious right now, but he knew that she could let go.

"Carla brought that in to me."

"Pretty good, huh?"

Brooke laid her glasses to one side and leaned onto her desk on her elbows. "I'm not going to let you buy me a cappuccino machine, either."

"Actually, that was more for Carla than you. But that's just a detail." He shifted and perused her office instead of concentrating on how much he hated that her shirt was buttoned nearly to her throat and her hair was pulled back.

He couldn't pinpoint why—because it was ridiculous for him to even imagine that he knew her—but this look didn't fit. Sure, the first time he'd met her she'd been without a bra—he had to shift again to try to get comfortable in his pants—but there was something more bugging him about her appearance today. She seemed...uncomfortable. And it couldn't be because of him. At least not entirely. Could it?

Her office was incredibly dull.

The ivory walls had only her framed degrees to break up the monotony. The windows were hung with very plain off-white blinds and no curtains. Her desk was at least thirty years old and the chair older. One glaringly bright black metal lamp illuminated the workspace while fluorescent bulbs shone from above. The chair he sat in was hardly comfortable, though he gave every pretense of being totally at ease.

"Nice office," he commented, looking down at the gray carpet.

She frowned. “It does exactly what it’s supposed to do—give me a place to do my paperwork and make phone calls.”

“You need a decorator.”

“I need one less cappuccino machine.”

He smiled. He could tell it irritated her, but he did it anyway. In fact, the smile grew as her frown deepened.

“You can’t send the cappuccino machine back. It’s been used.” His gaze dropped to her cup.

She watched him for a moment. Then she pushed back from her desk and stood.

“I don’t need a fancy office. I’m hardly ever here.” Then she swept around the edge of her desk and out her office door, like a queen promenading at a ball.

He got to his feet, somehow enjoying all of this more than he should. He found her a minute later at the front counter.

Carla handed her a slip of paper even as the nurse gave Jack an apologetic shrug.

Brooke dialed the phone and stood listening, ignoring Jack. Or at least pretending to.

“Purchasing, please,” Brooke said into the phone. It only took a moment to connect evidently, because she then asked, “I have a cappuccino machine, model number 77896. I need to know the total price of the machine, including delivery to Honey Creek.” She glanced at Carla who took a sip from her own cup. “Rush delivery I assume,” Brooke added. She gave the address of the clinic and then waited again.

He moved in behind the counter and leaned against the edge of Carla’s desk. “She’s going to try to send it back?”

Carla shrugged. “She just asked me to get the model number off the machine.”

He raised his voice slightly. “I promise you, if that

cappuccino machine disappears, I'll offer you another job Carla. No one should have to work for such a stingy boss."

Brooke gave no indication that she'd heard him. She studied the numbers on the front of the phone instead of looking at him or Carla.

"Yes," she said a moment later. "It was delivered today." She paused again, listening. "Okay." She scribbled something on the slip of paper with the machine's model number. "Thank you very much."

Jack continued to sit next to Carla, waiting to see what Brooke would say next.

She said nothing. Instead she started dialing again.

"Hi, Ashley. This is Brooke Donovan."

Jack straightened away from Carla's desk. Who was Ashley?

"I'm fine, thank you," Brooke said, smiling slightly. "Ashley, I have some really good news. I'm going to be sending a donation on behalf of a Mr. Jack Silver. The check will be for two thousand, three hundred and forty-four dollars and sixty-one cents. Will you let Mary know?"

She paused and listened, then said, "Oh, no, he doesn't want any thanks at all. In fact, he'd prefer to keep his name out of it entirely."

Jack couldn't help his smile. The check amount was the exact cost of the cappuccino machine, including delivery.

He wanted to shake her, and to laugh, all at once. The urge to laugh overpowered the other in the end.

She looked at him as if she was questioning his sanity. "There, that's taken care of."

"Who's Ashley?" he asked.

"A volunteer at the Mary Elizabeth Girls Home."

"Never heard of it."

"It's a home in San Antonio where pregnant teens can live until they deliver their babies. I did pro bono work there while I went to school, then started a job with them just before I moved back here."

He stared at her, surprised and fascinated and certain those were not good things considering the circumstances. "Did you clean the place or give medical care?"

"Whatever needed to be done at any particular moment. Like here," she said, meeting his eyes without flinching. "I'm really good at...lots of things."

He responded, probably exactly as she'd expected. He was suddenly very warm, very aware of her, and very impressed. That was the closest they'd come to talking about yesterday and their initial meeting and she'd definitely taken the upper hand.

"So we're keeping the cappuccino machine?" Carla asked, her eyes bright.

Jack took a deep breath, but couldn't wipe the smile from his face.

"Yes, we're keeping it." Brooke didn't break eye contact with him. "I'm not a complete witch."

He didn't even try to protest her misinterpretation of his comment. He just kept grinning broadly.

"I'll be in my office," she told Carla who had just moved to answer the ringing phone.

As Brooke turned away, Jack could have sworn he saw a faint smile on her face.

Chapter Three

Brooke didn't even make it five feet toward her office.

"We've got a situation," Carla announced, hanging up the phone and striding toward the door that led to the garage where the clinic's pickup was stored. "Amanda Cartwright fell down the steps at the post office."

It took Brooke two seconds to switch gears and change directions. It took Jack only one.

"When?" Brooke asked, following Carla—and Jack—out.

"Five minutes ago."

Jack held the truck door open for her and then climbed up onto the front seat beside her.

"Any other details?" She frowned at Jack as she was forced to slide to the middle toward Carla.

"Laura didn't think her water broke or anything, but I guess she's carrying on loud and clear about her ankle hurting."

Laura Clark was the postmistress in Honey Creek. She'd likely been too scared of Amanda and a potential lawsuit to get close enough to truly check things out.

"She's pregnant?" Jack asked as Carla sped through a stop sign.

"Thirty-three weeks," Brooke answered.

Carla tore around the next corner, throwing Brooke up against Jack.

He was solid. As she knew intimately. She'd certainly pressed enough of herself against enough of him to know that. And she wanted to be against him more. Which was the stupidest idea she'd had in a long time. She didn't think he'd mind but that definitely didn't make it any smarter.

There had been a heat between them in her office. Even as he was clearly stunned to find out who she actually was, it was as if memories from their first meeting were zinging back and forth telepathically. She remembered his mouth, his hands, his...well, everything.

Her cheeks heated and she fought the urge to fan herself.

"Any problems with the pregnancy so far?" Jack asked.

She forced herself to concentrate on their conversation. Pregnancy, Amanda, fall. She shook her head. "Nothing really. She complains a lot, about every ache and pain. But she's very healthy, as is the baby."

Not that she'd know firsthand. Amanda went to an OB/GYN in Amarillo for her regular pregnancy checkups. For her routine, minor complaints she would only see Mike. Not just because Brooke was Dixie Donovan's daughter and the Cartwrights never associated with anyone they deemed to be beneath them, but because Amanda hated Brooke.

And it wasn't just rivalry dislike. It was outright hatred.

"Is this her first pregnancy?" Jack asked.

"She has a set of twins who are three."

She wondered at his interest and was going to ask him when they pulled up in front of the post office.

A small but concerned crowd was gathered around the front steps in spite of the fact that it had been sprinkling on and off all morning. A little rain wouldn't stop good gossip. Brooke excused her way through the circle of people that stood three-deep where Amanda sat on the top step. She was holding her stomach with one hand and her head with the other.

Brooke concentrated on being straightforward and businesslike as she knelt on one knee in front of Amanda and put the stethoscope into her ears. She needed to keep her mannerisms, tone and eye contact steady and confident. She could get through this. In spite of the command performance in front of an audience. The most important thing was Amanda's unborn child.

"Are you feeling any contractions?"

Amanda looked dazed as she looked up. "No."

Brooke braced herself as Amanda realized who was in front of her.

"I didn't want them to call you."

Brooke's flinch was internal only. She switched to her firm but gentle I'm-the-boss-here tone of voice. "We have to be sure the baby is okay. We can deal with everything else later."

She actually pulled back as Brooke leaned forward with a blood pressure cuff. "No."

"Amanda." Brooke tried her best to ignore the crowd around them witnessing the denunciation. "Right now your baby's health depends on you cooperating with me." She reached for Amanda's arm a second time.

"I'll be fine until I can get to Amarillo," Amanda insisted.

Brooke didn't reach for her again. Instead she sat back on her heels, still at eye level with the other woman, and changed strategies, starting her assessment with questions instead. "What happened?"

Amanda didn't answer her. She simply stared at Brooke

defiantly. After a few seconds, Laura Clark, the postmistress, stepped forward.

"She was flipping through her mail and missed the top step. She slipped down all three steps with her right foot and twisted her left ankle behind her. She sat down hard on the second step there."

Brooke looked at Amanda with renewed intent. "What kind of pain are you having?"

Amanda focused on a spot over Brooke's shoulder.

"Looked like she was doin' the splits," Laura volunteered.

Brooke's concern mounted. "Amanda, this could be serious. Where are you in pain? Your water didn't break?"

Amanda sighed as if the weight of the world was resting on her shoulders. "No, my water didn't break," she said impatiently. "I would know if my water broke. Nothing is wrong. The baby is fine."

"We have to check you out." Brooke got to her feet, through with this ridiculous arguing. So Amanda was holding a grudge. Fine. She could be jealous and petty at the clinic on the exam table as well as she could right here. "Let's go. Carla's got the truck ready."

"I'm not going with you." Amanda crossed her arms over her rounded belly, looking a great deal like a pouting three-year-old. "I want someone else to check me out."

"There is no one else." Thunder rumbled overhead while Brooke struggled to hold onto her calm façade. She felt like a storm was mounting inside her as well.

She had no tolerance for this spoiled girl who was no more mature regarding their relationship now than she had been at eighteen when Brooke ran off with—and married—her steady boyfriend.

“I’m all you’ve got,” Brooke informed her, meeting Amanda’s eyes directly. “I can help you. But you have to cooperate.” Brooke signaled to Carla to call for the helicopter even as she was speaking to her stubborn pseudo-patient. “We’ll arrange to transport you to Amarillo from the clinic after I examine you and make sure you and the baby are safe to travel.”

“No.” Amanda turned to face Brooke, her eyes narrow. “My father will take me. I don’t need you.”

“Amanda—”

“Enough.”

Brooke turned as Jack stepped forward, bent, hooked Amanda behind the knees and tipped her into his arms as he stood.

“What are you doing?” Amanda shrieked.

“I’m afraid I must insist that you be examined here before going to Amarillo,” Jack said, striding toward the passenger side of the truck. Carla scrambled to open the door.

“Who are you?” Amanda challenged.

“Jack, really…” Brooke started after them. She recognized that he was trying to help her, but he was making things so much worse.

Jack deposited Amanda on the front passenger seat. “Doctor Jack Silver.”

Brooke stopped abruptly at the curb, unable to make her legs move any closer to the truck.

Jack slammed the door, but the window was down and Brooke heard Amanda ask, “You’re a medical doctor?”

Brooke watched dumbly as Jack motioned for Carla to toss him the truck’s keys.

Was he kidding? Surely he wasn’t… He couldn’t be… Why wouldn’t he have told her?

Brooke was balanced precariously between anger that he'd kept the information from her and an overwhelming feeling of relief. Someone was here who could take control of the situation. He could help Amanda, and Amanda would let him. The baby would be okay.

"Yes. I'm an emergency physician." Jack climbed into the driver's seat.

"I'd like to see some identification," Amanda told him in her all-too-familiar superior tone of voice. She folded her arms across her chest.

Jack reached into his back hip pocket as he started the ignition. He handed his ID to Amanda and looked at Brooke. "Get in."

She didn't want to, but she didn't have any better ideas, so somehow Brooke made her feet move and she joined Carla in the backseat of the extended cab.

They arrived at the clinic three minutes later and Jack carried Amanda through the front doors and into the first exam room.

Carla got busy trying to reach Amanda's husband but Brooke was right on Jack's heels. This was her clinic and technically, like it or not, Amanda was her patient. She couldn't just abandon the whole situation to a virtual stranger, even if he did have a medical degree.

"You have a monitor?" he asked.

"Right here." She'd retrieved the machine on her way to the exam room.

"Get it on her," he said shortly.

Brooke was already pressing buttons and readying the

straps and monitor pads. She began placing the electrodes that would read the baby's heart rate and monitor Amanda's blood pressure and any contractions.

"Once I see the baby's numbers, I'm going to have you change into a gown so I can check you for fractures, abrasions and so on," Jack said to Amanda.

"I'm fine."

"I insist." He said it firmly and finally Amanda nodded.

Before he could say another word, Brooke placed a clear plastic mask over Amanda's nose and mouth and started a gentle flow of oxygen. It was routine. The reducing-Amanda's-ability-to-talk effect was just a bonus.

Brooke crossed the room as Carla came in. "The helicopter's going to be delayed because of the cloud cover. As soon as it's safe, they'll call."

Brooke took the chart from her as Carla told Amanda, "Your husband is in Amarillo. He's wondering if he should just stay and meet you there."

Amanda nodded.

"I'm sure Diane is on her way down here. Why don't you meet her out front and keep her occupied until we finish the examination?" Brooke suggested, flipping the chart open and making notations. Diane, Amanda's mother, was high-strung in the best of circumstances. In this case, she would be distracting and would only add to the already elevated tension. "Then she can go with Amanda on the trip to Amarillo."

Carla agreed and headed for the front.

There were a few moments of silence in the room, but for the gentle beeping of the monitor. Brooke tried her best to ignore Jack, who seemed to be watching every move she made.

Finally his voice broke the relative quiet. "Can I take a

look?”

She glanced up at him from the chart she was still writing in. When she realized he was talking to her she asked, “At what?”

“The chart.”

“I’ve got it covered.” She wanted to put him in his place. But she wasn’t sure what that place was. He was a physician. She was a physician’s assistant. But this was her clinic. He was a visitor. All she knew for certain was that he was taking over and making her look bad.

“Blood pressure readings?” His voice was laced with impatience.

“One fifty over ninety-six,” she recited.

She caught his frown and knew that it wasn’t for her. He didn’t like that high of a number for Amanda and the baby.

“What has she been running?” he asked, evidently forgetting for the moment that he was irritated with Brooke.

She paused and glanced at Amanda who had her eyes closed, her hands protectively cupping her stomach. “I, um...I don’t know. She’s followed by an obstetrician in Amarillo.” Brooke didn’t add that for her first pregnancy Amanda had happily seen the local doctor. Because the local doctor wasn’t Brooke.

Thankfully, Carla came back. “Diane is here. Doris and Helen came along and are keeping her distracted. They were getting their hair done together.”

Suddenly the monitor beside the bed began beeping. They stepped toward the display at the same time. Amanda was contracting.

“Amanda, I need you to breathe deep and slow,” Jack said.

She opened her eyes and looked at him.

He kept his voice and tone steady and calm. "You're having a few contractions. They're not very strong and are far apart right now, but I want to do a brief internal exam. Your water is still intact, but I want to be sure you don't have any tears or bleeding and that you're not dilating."

Amanda didn't look pleased with the suggestion. She pulled the oxygen mask to one side. "Can't I just go to Amarillo now?"

"No," he answered resolutely. "We need to be sure you and the baby are stable first. We'll move you as soon as it's safe. Would you be more comfortable if Brooke did the exam?"

"Why in the hell would I want her to do it?" Amanda asked sharply.

Jack's eyebrows rose and Brooke's cheeks flushed.

"Because she's a woman. And you know her."

"She's not touching me," Amanda declared, her voice rising...along with her blood pressure.

The monitor signaled as much and Brooke and Jack both looked toward the monitor, then at each other.

"You will not touch me!" Amanda snapped at Brooke, seemingly oblivious to the monitors and their meaning. "I know you would love the chance to hurt me and this baby."

Brooke was as shocked as Jack looked.

"Amanda," she gasped. "I would never hurt you or your baby. I'm a professional. Our personal past has nothing to do with—"

"No," Amanda interrupted. "Mike always loved me. You knew it. When you moved back to Honey Creek you knew it was only a matter of time before he came to me."

Brooke didn't know what to say to that. For one, it was ridiculous. Not just because Amanda was one of the reasons Mike had agreed to marry Brooke. But also because, Amanda was even less his type than Brooke had been. They were both women, but Amanda was also a bitch.

Brooke frowned. "I don't really think—" The monitor's beeping intensified and she stopped.

"Well, this is not your chance for revenge," Amanda vowed, her voice low and menacing, but still clear in spite of the frenzied beeping of the monitors. "Stay away from me."

Brooke sighed. Now she was just getting mad. "You—"

"Brooke," Jack interrupted, coming toward her. "Can I see you outside?" He didn't wait for an answer but took her arm firmly and steered her out of the room.

"Carla!" he bellowed.

"Yeah?" the nurse called from the end of the hall.

"Go in and monitor Amanda," he said in a clipped tone.

"Sure thing." Carla hurried past with wide eyes. But she didn't dare say a word.

Once the door was shut behind Carla, Jack turned to Brooke and spoke gently, but firmly. "I want you in there and I know you want to help, but you saw how she reacted. I can't risk getting her so worked up. She's at least two weeks short of being safe to deliver."

Brooke looked at him for three long seconds, feeling equally stunned and irritated. "You can't honestly believe that I would let my personal feelings get in the way of patient care."

He cocked his head toward the exam room door. The monitor's beeping had quieted some. "Let me guess," he said. "Amanda was Homecoming Queen, right?"

"And Prom Queen." Brooke propped a hand on her hip.

"And you were..."

She wanted to ask him if he meant before Dixie Donovan's big unveiling or after. Before she was blamed for her mother's sins and extravagance or after. Before Mike decided that she was the solution to all his problems—and worth a monthly paycheck for four years—or after they discovered their perfect plan was flawed.

Either way she was…

"Not the Homecoming Queen," she finally said impassively.

"Okay." Jack held his hand up. "There's obviously a history between you two. I want you to know that my decision to ask you to leave is not about your professional abilities. This is purely about Amanda's reaction. My first concern at this moment has to be her and that baby."

He was absolutely right. But this was Honey Creek and it was always personal here. "I—"

"Jack!" Carla's voice reached them through the door. "I need you in here!"

"Damn." He muttered. He pinned Brooke with a hard look. "We need to talk later." He twisted the doorknob and pushed the door partway open.

"I can—" she started.

"Brooke," he interrupted as he stepped through the doorway into Amanda's room. "I'm sorry, but you just can't be in here."

The door shut behind him. She stared at the oak grain thinking how appropriate it was. She was always on the outside in Honey Creek.

Though the same was clearly not true for Jack Silver.

Her shoes hit the pavement with a steady *whop, whop, whop*, and Brooke tried to lose herself in the rhythmic sound, the feel of the damp, cool air on her face and the burning fatigue of her muscles. It was dark and she knew it was supposed to rain again, but she hadn't been able to stay inside any longer. She'd tried to lose herself in her medical journals, then television and finally a favorite romance novel. Nothing worked. Her thoughts kept returning to the clinic where Jack Silver, virtual stranger, had become a hero and she'd been once more banished to the outside. So, if she couldn't escape her thoughts, at least her emotions would drive her through a good workout.

After about an hour, Amanda's contractions were under control, her blood pressure was steady, if a bit high, and her other vitals were good. The weather had cleared enough that the helicopter could make the trip and Amanda and her still-unborn child were airlifted to Amarillo Memorial. They were both in good condition and Amanda was expected to go to full-term but remain on bed rest in the hospital. Which was perfect. There she could be waited on hand and foot much as she was everywhere else, but at least the hospital staff would get paid for it.

Brooke felt bad about the thought almost before it was fully formed. Amanda was spoiled but she hadn't always gotten her way. Brooke had seen to that. She had stolen the love of Amanda's life. It had been his idea, but that didn't change the fact that Amanda had been crushed.

As raindrops began to fall, Brooke turned uphill and pumped her arms harder, pulling her already tired body up the last incline before home. Trying to escape the memories, the mistakes, the regrets. She had more immediate problems anyway. Like the fact that she'd been thrown out of her own clinic.

That news was certain to get around.

Thunder rumbled and she ran harder, pulling against the

friction of the pavement. She had every right and reason to be in that examination room. Okay, being Amanda's friend was out of the question, being voted Miss Congeniality or Ms. Honey Creek wasn't going to happen. But if someone was bleeding from the head and needed someone to save their life? Then she was the one for the job. She knew more than anyone in town about what to do in medical situations, emergency and otherwise.

Well, everyone except for Jack, she acknowledged with a frown.

He couldn't even just be a physician. He had to be an emergency physician. Wasn't that just typical of how things went for her within these city limits?

She heard a vehicle approaching and took a few steps closer to the sidewalk, out of the way, but the black truck slowed down beside her.

"I've been looking for you."

She nearly groaned. The last person she wanted to see right now.

"I'm busy."

"It's starting to rain," Jack pointed out.

The drops were falling faster now, soaking her hair and clothes. "No kidding."

The truck continued to crawl along next to her.

"We need to talk," he said. "I've been trying to find you."

"I went for a run."

"Obviously."

"And I'm not done yet." She picked up her pace.

Of course, he was in a truck. He stayed right beside her.

"I don't want to wait."

"Too bad." She was getting winded trying to talk while running. She decided to quit trying to talk.

"I want to apologize. And finish the conversation we started in the hallway. Let me give you a ride home."

She said nothing and kept her pace steady.

"Brooke—"

Just then a loud clap of thunder boomed above them, followed by a blinding flash of lightning and the clouds split, dumping a cosmic bucket of water down on them. She was drenched within seconds.

Of course.

She stopped running, wiping water from her eyes as she turned her face upward. The rain was cool and refreshing...and a nice distraction.

She didn't want to hear Jack say he was sorry for how things went today. He couldn't be sorry in the sense that he'd done something wrong. It was more that he felt sorry for her. And she hated that idea.

Brooke could admit, if only to herself, that she was mortified he'd witnessed Honey Creek's princess rejecting her help.

She continued walking, letting the rain pour over her, trying her best to ignore the man in the truck beside her. He was stubborn, she knew too well. But he was getting way too close to things she didn't like to think about, not to mention talking about with a man she didn't know all that well. Or really at all. What she knew about Jack could be summarized in four words—great kisser, pushy, physician.

"Brooke, get in the truck."

"No."

He swore and suddenly the truck lurched forward then

swerved several feet in front of her, blocking her path. She calmly altered her route and continued. He got out of the truck and stepped in front of her, hands on his hips. He was also drenched within seconds, his hair plastered against his forehead, his eyes flashing like the lightning overhead.

Jack had experienced more frustration since meeting Brooke Donovan than he'd ever felt in his life. She was stubborn, and strong...and beautiful, even wet.

Her long hair was swept away from her face where she'd pushed it back out of her eyes. Tiny rivulets of water chased each other over her cheeks and down her throat. Her light blue T-shirt was plastered to her body, emphasizing curves that Jack remembered all too well. He'd dreamed about those curves.

He'd been too frustrated and worried by the time he'd seen her jogging along the street that he hadn't paid attention to her long, tanned legs beneath the short running shorts—but now he took a moment. She was clearly a regular runner, her body trim and toned. Suddenly, he felt more supportive of her finishing her workout before their talk.

"Get out of the way," she said, obviously exasperated. "I don't want to talk."

"Too bad," he said, mimicking her earlier words.

"You can't make me talk to you." She planted hands on her hips as well, clearly in challenge.

"You might be surprised what I can make you do." He was pleased by the way her eyes widened, with surprised curiosity and maybe a few memories.

"I'm not..." She stopped and cleared her throat. "I'm not going anywhere with you."

He wondered about the throat clearing for a moment. She

seemed distracted.

"You need to get out of the rain," he told her, stepping forward.

"I like it."

"You'll catch a cold."

She looked at him as if she couldn't believe what he'd just said. "You're a doctor. I'm sure you know colds don't come from being outside in the rain."

He narrowed his eyes. "Get in the car."

"I thought you were a salesman, you know," she said suddenly.

"And I thought you were the cleaning lady."

"You could have told me who you were the very first time we met."

"Likewise." He watched her try to argue that point in her mind and then fail. "And I wasn't here as a doctor, so it wasn't relevant."

"Well, I wasn't in the clinic as a physician's assistant when you showed up yesterday."

Yesterday. He didn't need to try hard to conjure nearly every detail of yesterday. "I wasn't looking for a physician's assistant. I was looking for you."

"I wasn't in the mood to talk to anyone looking for me."

"So you lied."

"I intentionally misled you," she corrected. "There's a subtle but important difference."

He snorted. "Okay, that's fine. The fact is I wouldn't have even been there today with Amanda if you'd just told me who you were upfront. We could have had everything taken care of by now."

"Right. And if you'd just take 'no, thank you' for an answer you also would not have been there today with Amanda."

Which brought them effectively back to the reason he'd come looking for her. Well, the reason other than the fact that he couldn't get her out of his mind.

"Listen—"

She interrupted his intended apology. "I assume you didn't tell Carla that you were a doctor either. I'm sure she would have told me."

"I just met her and—"

"I must have looked like an idiot not knowing you were a doctor, not asking for your assistance."

He hadn't intended to step in at all. But his instincts as a physician had kicked in when he saw her getting nowhere. The patient had been his first concern.

"You didn't—"

"Contrary to popular belief, I do realize I'm a P.A., not a physician. I realize that there are times when I should defer to a doctor. But I didn't know there was a doctor around. I was trying to handle the situation the best I could considering I thought I was on my own."

He needed to apologize. He wanted to apologize. Well, not exactly. He wasn't good at apologies. But he wanted her to feel better. And she would, if she would just shut up.

"I—"

"You also shouldn't have thrown me out of that room. I know she was getting agitated, but I need to establish my role here in town. You're not going to be here next time. And I'll need to be able to take control."

"I didn't—"

"But now you're the big hero. Carla said that's your thing.

Well, I'm so glad you got to show off today and stroke your ego a bit. Those women were fawning all over you after Amanda was stabilized and her mother activated her gossip phone tree. You'll probably have casseroles coming out of your ears tomorrow. But this is my medical practice, in my town. This isn't about you, Jack."

Dammit, he wanted to say he was sorry. He didn't want casseroles or applause or thank yous from a town of strangers. He wanted to hear how he could help Brooke, what he could do for her, how he could be *her* hero. He wanted to hear that she was going to be okay. Dammit. If she would just shut up.

There was only one option.

"I know what you're thinking," she continued. "That maybe I deserve the way Amanda feels about me and that I—"

He stepped close, cupped the back of her head, pulled her forward and covered her still-moving mouth with his.

Brooke stiffened in surprise, but she did stop talking. In fact, it only took a second for her lips to shift gears and begin kissing him back. With enthusiasm.

She'd been thinking about this all day. Which pissed her off because even when she was mad at him, she wanted him. When he'd come barging into her office, when they'd been arguing about the cappuccino machine, even in the midst of him making her look bad, she'd wanted to kiss him.

There were clearly some things that were genetic after all. Wanting inappropriate good-looking men was evidently one of them.

She considered pulling back, but then Jack's other hand cupped the side of her head and brought her in until her breasts pressed against his chest. He deepened the kiss, tipping his head to one side and opening his lips.

And there was no way in hell she was moving anywhere but closer.

She responded, following his lead, parting her lips, gripping his biceps and going up on tiptoe to get closer. He welcomed her body more fully against his, widening his stance to keep his balance as she pressed against him.

He traced her bottom lip with his tongue and she felt a surge of heat sweep through her. The hand against her cheek left her face and dropped to the curve of her right buttock, where he lifted her, bringing their pelvises even. She wrapped her arms around his neck and her right leg around his waist. She wasn't sure who groaned first at the intimate contact. He turned and walked her back toward the truck until her back was against the driver-side door. Then he pressed more fully into her. She dug her fingers into his hair and met his tongue with hers.

The truck door was becoming slippery with the rain and Brooke could tell he was struggling to hold her where he wanted her. Finally, after she slid twice, he pulled back, took a gulp of air and let her slide gently to the ground.

She gazed up at him, dazed. Regretting the lack of contact already.

He grinned at her, then wiped some of the water away from her cheeks. "Now will you let me apologize?" he asked.

She licked her lips. "No. But you can do that again."

He paused only two seconds before acting. He braced his hands on the side of the truck on either side her head, bent, and touched her lips once more.

This was a softer kiss, more exploratory than passionate.

They didn't touch other than their lips. Her arms were at her sides, palms flat against the truck door. He kept his body back, away from hers. She'd *felt* him the first time, now she *tasted* him. A minute later, the sound of car tires splashing through water broke through her haze of pleasure. Panic raced through her instinctively and she jerked back. Hands splayed on Jack's chest, she pushed hard. He obeyed the pressure and leaned back, just in time for a car to drive past, its headlights glancing over them.

"Dammit," she muttered.

"What?"

"Someone saw us."

He frowned down at her. "So what if someone saw us?"

"Now it will probably be all over town."

No one would be surprised, of course, which was the entire problem. She shouldn't even spend time alone with Jack, not to mention kissing him, and definitely not in public, for God's sake. What had she been thinking? She hated that even this moment with him—this incredible moment—could be ruined in this town.

"So?" he asked again.

She sighed heavily. "You don't understand." But she suddenly had the urge to tell him all of it, just to see if maybe, possibly, he could understand just a little bit.

His eyes widened and he spread his arms. "Obviously. Explain."

She pulled her bottom lip between her teeth, just watching him. Could she?

He leaned in slightly. "Does it have anything to do with Amanda?"

Damn him and those intense eyes that seemed to see inside her. Brooke bit down a little harder, keeping herself from saying anything…or everything.

"Your husband?"

Jack was a stranger. She still wasn't entirely clear why he was here. And he was driving her nuts. She wasn't going to confess anything to him.

Suddenly she straightened. "I'm really tired. I'm going to head home."

She started walking briskly down the street in the direction she'd been jogging.

He reached out for her just in time to grasp her wrist, abruptly halting her retreat.

"Oh, no you don't." He tugged, bringing her stumbling back to him before he spun her. "I want some answers. What the hell is going on with you and this town?"

She wouldn't meet his eyes, but she stood still. Not that she had much choice with him holding onto her.

"You don't want the money, you were avoiding me like the plague after almost stripping down with me, now this blowout with Amanda—"

"They hate me, okay?" The words tumbled out before she could press her lips together. She risked looking up in time to see his frown. She sighed again. "And I'm a mess. It's a long story."

"They hate you?"

She nodded, feeling stupid.

"And when you say 'they', you mean Honey Creek?"

She nodded.

"All of Honey Creek?"

The whole situation was stupid. She didn't want Jack to see this side of her. She didn't want him asking questions, wondering, formulating opinions—because opinions in Honey Creek never went her way. A surge of indignation hit her. "Meaning, what did I do to deserve it?" she asked, her tone instantly defensive.

"No. Just that... There must be a reason—or a perceived idea," he added quickly.

"There's a reason all right," she said bitterly. "Walter Worthington."

Jack finally dropped her wrist and wiped a hand across his face, clearing his eyes of the rain. "Your father-in-law?"

She realized she shouldn't be surprised that Jack knew who Walter was. Jack seemed to know far more than she wanted him to.

She wiped her cheek, hoping that he wouldn't realize there were tears mingled with the raindrops. "I don't want to talk about Walter." She squared her shoulders. "I want to go home."

"I'll take you."

"I'm going home to take a shower and then go to bed."

"That's fine. We can keep talking after you've showered and are more relaxed." He started walking toward his truck. "Have you eaten?"

The word tenacious didn't do him justice.

"Are you coming?" he asked when he realized she wasn't following him

She let her head fall back, the raindrops refreshing on her face. She was exhausted, physically and mentally and it was suddenly overwhelming. This conversation needed to be over. Being vulnerable with Jack from weariness, and because he was an amazing kisser, was a bad idea. She didn't want to say anything she might regret later. Better to do something—preferably something distracting—rather than confess something she couldn't take back later.

She went for blunt—and, hopefully, diverting.

"Unless you're planning to join me in the shower and bed,

you're not invited."

He retraced his steps quickly, stopping directly in front of her. His voice dropped low. "After that kiss we just had, I wouldn't say things like that unless you mean them."

In spite of her knees going weak, she raised her chin, and hoped Jack wouldn't notice that she swallowed hard. "And during the whole thing I don't want to do any talking except the dirty kind."

She could see the heat in his eyes even as he chuckled. "Only during? What about before? You know, to get things going?"

She felt her cheeks color slightly and knew that he noticed. It was a fun, if dangerous, game they were playing. But she was going to be the one to end it. If it went any further, and he did come home with her, she might as well go to Walter's office and say, *you were totally right about me.*

"I'm going home. Alone," she added, with a pointed frown at him.

"I'm not going to let you walk home, soaking wet, when I have a perfectly good, dry truck right here," Jack said, letting his exasperation show.

"There's no need to—"

"Enough." He put up a hand. "End of argument. Get in the truck."

"But I—"

"I'm not asking."

"I just—"

He sighed, then stepped forward, bent at the waist, grabbed her hips and carried her up and over his shoulder as he stood.

"Jack!"

"I'm giving you a ride home."

She didn't even try to fight him. What was the point? He placed her unceremoniously in the passenger seat and slammed the truck door. She watched him with raised eyebrows as he slid in behind the wheel.

"Where to?" he asked.

She pointed ahead. "Up this street."

He shifted into drive, but didn't start forward. He turned to look at her. "Why won't you let me give you anything?"

It was an abrupt shift in topic, but she knew what he was talking about. The stupid check.

"Why are you being so stubborn about it?" she returned.

"It's important."

She watched him in the dim lights from the dashboard. Finally she sighed. "It's more important that I prove to them that I'm not what they think I am. I have to do this on my own. And I have to do it well."

He said nothing as he drove slowly up the street.

"It's right here," she said, pointing to the gray brick ranch with the wide driveway and perfect lawn three doors down from where they'd been standing.

He looked from the house to her, then back. "This is your house?"

"Yes."

"Oh," he finally said sheepishly.

She grinned but hid it quickly. She crossed her arms. "I told you there was no need to give me a ride."

He shifted the truck into park in the driveway and turned, sliding his arm along the back of the seat. "I'll remember that you're the type to say I told you so."

"Completely the type," she agreed.

"Me too."

She gave a little snort. "No kidding."

His expression suddenly became solemn and she had the strange impression that he wanted to kiss her again. He didn't give any specific indication of that, it was more just a feeling. She watched him take a long, deep breath.

"Goodnight, Brooke."

She smiled softly. He wasn't going to push anything, in spite of her earlier wantonness.

"'Night."

She pulled on the door handle and slid from the high seat.

It was absurd how pleased she was that he waited and watched as she let herself into the house. The door swung open and she turned and gave him a little wave. Then she made herself go in rather than watching him drive away.

The shower in his room was hot, but that was about the only convenience the small bed and breakfast could offer that he needed at the moment. They took the breakfast part of their title seriously and offered only the one meal a day. Not even a vending machine.

Which was what took him back to the diner that had provided his lunch and dinner since he'd arrived in Honey Creek. Not that he minded, exactly. Vi, the owner and head chef, was a fantastic cook and had any number of hilarious stories. The menu was full of homemade meals and he could stay for a month without eating the same thing twice. Except for the hash browns. He could eat Vi's hash browns every day.

"Hey, Jack, was wonderin' when you were gonna git here," Vi called out as he walked in.

"Hey, Vi."

"Lasagna night."

"Perfect."

He took a seat at the front counter and gratefully accepted a glass of iced tea from Lila, the waitress that worked the dinner shift every night.

"That's straight up, now," she told him with a wink.

He saluted her. She'd already learned that he didn't like sweet tea.

"Hey, Doc, heard you're a bit of a hero."

He swiveled on his stool to find Will Parson, one of the local ranchers standing behind him, grinning around the wad of chewing tobacco in his bottom lip. He'd met Will during his first meal in Honey Creek. People around here didn't leave strangers strangers very long.

"Hero?" Jack repeated. "How's that?"

"Heard about Amanda." Will hooked a hand in the back pocket of his blue jeans. "Everybody heard."

Jack wondered if the man was going to just spit his tobacco wad on the floor of the restaurant. "I was just doing my job, Will."

"Oh, no, son," another voice protested. A stout, gray-haired man stepped forward. He lacked the denim that was part of the typical dress code in Vi's place. He wore khaki slacks and a dress shirt that looked as if it had been paired with a tie at some point in the day. He reached a hand toward Jack. Jack shook it as the man said, "I'm Amanda's uncle Ben. Ben Cartwright. I told everyone what really happened."

For Jack, emergency medical situations were a regular part of his day. He was surprised to find every eye in the restaurant—and there were several tonight—was suddenly on him.

"My family doesn't know how to thank you for helping Amanda and her baby."

"You're welcome, Mr. Cartwright. But as I said, that's my job."

"Where're you from, son?" Will asked.

"San Antonio."

Will and Ben looked at each other and then back at Jack in surprise. The rest of the café continued to be silent. "What brings you out here?"

Damn. In the spotlight and confronted with the one question he didn't want to answer. "Brooke Donovan," he finally said, opting for as much of the truth as possible.

That drew even wider-eyed stares. "Brooke?" Will repeated.

"That's right." Jack couldn't put his finger on it, exactly, but he felt defensive. Thinking of Brooke's comment that everyone hated her here he felt himself bristle.

"But...why?" Ben asked after a few seconds of stunned silence.

Jack squared himself up with the man. "What do you mean *why*?" As if it was so unbelievable that a man would drive a thousand miles for a woman like Brooke. She was gorgeous, smart, sassy and funny—when she let her guard down. She even had a sweet side. He hadn't seen much of it but the glimpses he'd gotten made him want to see more.

Any man who knew his ass from his ankle wouldn't think twice about driving across Texas to see Brooke.

"Why would you come all the way across Texas for Brooke Donovan... Unless..." Ben seemed to come to some kind of understanding without Jack's input. "I see. You knew Brooke in San Antonio? Did you know her husband as well?"

Take it easy, Silver, Jack reminded himself. Maybe he was just imagining the sinister tone. It would make sense that Jack was visiting if he had been a friend of Brooke's and Mike's from their time in San Antonio.

"Actually, I knew of her husband. I came out here to..." he thought fast and his mind landed on the one thing he had managed to do since coming, "...make a donation to a charity Brooke supported back in San Antonio." He hadn't meant to make the donation to the Mary Elizabeth Girls Home but he'd been more than happy about it once he'd Googled it. Brooke Donovan was full of surprises. She'd been listed on the website as one of the medical practitioners and volunteers. She was also listed as a major donor.

"A charity?" Ben looked at Will with obvious confusion. Jack was glad for the first time that all the attention was on him. They clearly didn't know this very intriguing piece of information about her. "Brooke worked at the Girls Home in San Antonio. They give a home to pregnant girls who want to give birth to healthy babies and then put them up for adoption, but who don't have the resources to take care of themselves properly or to find good homes."

Jack watched Ben's face carefully. The man went from puzzled to almost impressed. But then he swung toward the rear booth. "I didn't know..." he started.

"She couldn't get a job anywhere else," a deep bass voice from that back booth interjected.

Jack turned toward the voice and saw a very tall, distinguished-looking man rise from the farthest table.

If Jack thought Ben's clothing didn't fit in Vi's, this man definitely stuck out in a tailored dark gray suit and deep maroon tie. His silver hair was cut and styled perfectly and Jack knew somehow that a farmer's cap hadn't spent much time on that head. The man was poised, confident, and commanded the attention of the crowd completely.

"Excuse me?" Jack said.

"She was given the position at the home as a favor to my son," the man said, approaching Jack as he pulled the suit jacket together and buttoned it.

"Your son?" Jack repeated.

"Dr. Michael Worthington," the man answered. "You said you knew of him."

So this was Walter Worthington. Brooke's father-in-law.

The man reeked of money—cattle and oil, Jack knew—and self-importance. Jack suspected that Walter had located his ranch in Honey Creek where he could own half the town and influence the other half, rather than compete with the other millionaires in places like Lubbock or even Dallas for the title of big shot.

Jack straightened from his stool slowly. Even at his age, Walter had the build of a linebacker, but Jack was no slouch. His six-foot-four-inch frame put him about two inches above Walter, a fact that Jack fully intended to use. Not that this was going to get physical. Still, it was good for Walter to know that Jack had confidently faced a lot worse things in the ER than a cattleman with too much money and ego.

"I know there are a number of physicians in San Antonio who admire your daughter-in-law a great deal," Jack said, again able to speak the truth. His Google search had quickly expanded to Brooke Donovan-Worthington and had pulled up articles about events and fundraisers she led where several San Antonio physicians were quoted, as well as some human-interest stories about girls from the Girls Home.

"Ex-daughter-in-law," Walter corrected. "And I'm sure they said that. Professional courtesy and all that. Especially if you were a…friend of Brooke's?" He said it with a slight question at the end.

Jack certainly wasn't offended by the insinuation that he and Brooke had been involved beyond a collegial relationship. She was an amazing woman. Except that she'd been married. Walter's tone suggested that he was questioning both her and Jack's morals in that regard and that offended him. In fact, Walter Worthington pretty much offended him in general.

"I'd never personally met Ms. Donovan until I came to Honey Creek. But she has in impressive reputation."

It was immediately clear that that was the wrong thing to say.

"Oh, of that I'm certain," Walter said with an arrogant smile. "You should watch yourself, son, you might find out how she earned it."

Stunned by the man's blatant attack on Brooke's character, Jack started to lean in as he opened his mouth, but the other man went on.

"Before he died, my son was Honey Creek's primary medical practitioner."

Before he died. My son. Oh, God. Jack felt his chest tighten in spite of his dislike for the man.

Jack had inadvertently affected Walter's life too. Walter had lost his son.

His research had told him that Michael Worthington was also survived by his parents, but it was quite clear that they didn't need any money, so he'd written them off as unimportant to his trip to Honey Creek. Of course, his trip to Honey Creek was supposed to have been one day and involve nothing more than handing over a check. And now that he knew Brooke it seemed that he couldn't focus on anything but her. Still, no matter how pompous he was, Walter had been forced to attend the funeral of his only child. That wasn't right.

Then—fortunately for Jack's conscience anyway—Walter spoke again.

"Of course, Brooke had to tag along. No matter how often I asked him to leave her in San Antonio." Walter chuckled and looked around the room as if he was just kidding.

But Jack, and everyone else he was sure, knew Walter meant it sincerely. He faced Jack as he said, "But it won't be long until Brooke will no longer be able to practice medicine here even if we wanted to seek her care."

"How's that?" Will asked.

Jack was amazed to see he was still chewing on the same wad of tobacco.

"Well, correct me if I'm wrong, Dr. Silver, but as only a Physician's Assistant, Brooke is unable to practice without a supervising physician. Dr. Cunningham is taking an early retirement effective...why—" Walter looked down at his watch, "—I believe effective tomorrow."

It took only a few seconds for Walter's words to sink in. Jack nearly expected to see a light bulb illuminated over his head. Walter Worthington, of all people, had just given Jack the answer to his situation with Brooke. Not to mention the perfect way to bring Walter himself down a peg or two.

"There's just one little detail you are obviously not aware of," Jack interjected. Strangely, his comment had the same effect on the surrounding conversations as Walter's had. Everyone instantly shut up.

Walter gave him a bland smile. "What's that, son?"

Jack hated being called *son.*

"Ms. Donovan will be able to practice tomorrow, and for a long time after that. I'm Ms. Donovan's new supervising physician."

There was a surprised silence of nearly five seconds. Walter Worthington, of course, regained his voice first.

"I thought you were just passing through," Walter said, his eyes narrow.

"Well, everyone is so nice and friendly here," Jack said, "I thought I'd stay awhile."

He slid back onto his stool and pivoted to face the counter. "But you know, Lila, I've had just about enough conversation and socializing for one night. How about you wrap that lasagna up for me to go?"

"Sure thing, kiddo." Lila was grinning as she tore aluminum foil from a roll and wrapped Jack's plate. "You just bring that plate and silverware back 'round tomorrow, honey," she told him.

"Great. See you then." Jack stood with his plate and faced the room, almost tripping over two little old ladies who had sidled up—somehow with a walker and a cane in tow—behind him.

"Dr. Silver? I'm Maddie Conner and this is Emma Petersen. We were hoping you would be able to squeeze us into your schedule tomorrow. My arthritis is killin' me."

He smiled down at the woman who was a good foot and a half shorter than he was even before age had bent her spine. "Of course. I've always got room for sweet ladies like you."

The tiny woman and her friend both blushed and giggled. Actually giggled. He grinned and lifted his head to address the whole room. "If anyone else has anything they'd like to see me about tomorrow, I'll be in the office eight to five. We'll be doing free blood pressure checks all day," he added as the thought occurred to him.

First and foremost, they needed to get people in the door. They would deal with Brooke's reputation and history as it came up. Perhaps it wouldn't be as big of a problem as it seemed now with Walter holding court in the most public gathering in town.

As he faced the room full of relative strangers, he realized that he'd been thinking about *we* regarding him and Brooke.

He supposed it made sense. He'd come to help her and he'd found a way. A way that would truly make an impact. Being her supervisor, getting patients into the clinic, being the buffer between her and her father-in-law, maybe even keeping Walter in check to some extent, was better than anything he could buy her. He'd even find her a great supervising physician to take over when he had to leave. Someone who would appreciate her fiery independence but who could cushion things a bit for her here—without her knowing it, of course.

He smiled and waved with one arm as he headed for the front door. "See y'all around."

The little bell above the door tinkled as he stepped out into the night. The clouds that had doused him and Brooke earlier had cleared out and the stars shone like silver glitter spilled on black velvet. He took a deep breath. The night suddenly seemed fresh and bright.

Chapter Four

"Good morning!"

The enthusiastic greeting seemed to hit Brooke in the face the next morning.

Carla was placing three large, steaming mugs on a small tray in the back room.

"Hi." Brooke definitely felt grumpy this morning. Likely due to the restless night she'd had thanks to dreams of hot kisses in summer rain showers. She also didn't have any home visits scheduled today, so she was stuck in the clinic.

Brooke pulled her locker open and set her purse inside. Then she stopped and turned toward Carla. She realized what was puzzling her. "Are you humming?"

"What?" Carla swiveled toward her and Brooke saw the powdered sugar donut in her fingers.

"I asked if you were humming." Brooke crossed her arms and watched Carla closely.

"Oh, yeah." Carla giggled. "I guess I was."

Brooke arched her eyebrows suspiciously, but Carla was already leaving the room with tray in hand. Still humming.

Brooke frowned as she faced the mirror and brushed through her hair. Pulling it to the back of her head, she twisted it and then secured it up with a large black clip. One tendril escaped, tickling her ear and she gave a disgusted sigh, unhooked her hair and repeated the process. She pulled tightly on the twisted mass and dug the clip deep into the thickness. She winced as one plastic prong jabbed her scalp. Just to be completely sure it wouldn't move, she gave it two good squirts with the extra-hold hairspray.

She met her eyes in the mirror and pressed her lips together. She knew what it was like to love a job, to look forward to work every day, to feel rewarded by what she did.

This wasn't it.

A deep breath, one more pat to her hair and she decided to go get her day over with.

"Good morning, Amy." She greeted the young part-time receptionist as she stepped into the front of the clinic.

"Morning, Brooke." Amy turned from the copy machine with a smile. "How are you?"

Brooke hesitated and then mentally chastised herself for doing so. She was fine, great, wonderful. She was. "I'm great. How about you?"

"Oh, yeah, I'm definitely great." Amy's smile was almost as bright as Carla's had been.

Brooke ignored the strange response and glanced around the empty waiting room. "Is Karen Matthews running late today?" she asked, putting on her professional air.

"No, she and Christopher were actually here at a quarter to eight."

"Where are they?"

The phone rang just then and Amy reached to answer it, saying hastily, "Room three."

"Thanks."

The door on room three was open halfway and Brooke

could hear low voices as she approached.

"Good mor—" She stopped in the doorway abruptly. The first sight to meet her eyes, and the only thing in the room to register, was that the denim of Jack Silver's blue jeans fit better than any pair of jeans really should.

She remembered the feel of that denim against her inner thighs last night as they...

Frick. She had to stop doing that.

He turned toward her, his smile warm. "Hi, partner."

"Good morning, Brooke," Karen Matthews greeted with a happy smile. "How are you?"

"I'm...great," Brooke insisted.

What is he doing here? Partner? What's going on? Several thoughts seemed to trip over each other as they ran through her head. A dominant thought quickly overtook the others though: Be professional. Be cool. Don't show you're surprised, pretend to be completely aware of everything that's going on.

"We're just about done." Jack pivoted away from her again and bent to put his face on level with the one-year-old patient, Christopher. "Right?"

The little boy giggled and bopped Jack's nose with his chubby fist. Jack only grinned.

Brooke decided that she needed to say something and decided to concentrate on her patient and his mother, as they were the only things that made sense in the room at the moment. "The ear symptoms have cleared up?" she asked.

She noted that Jack seemed to be getting along wonderfully with a little boy who, to the best of her knowledge, had never giggled in her presence. Or even smiled. Christopher was a shy child and was often cranky due to the chronic ear troubles and respiratory infections that he battled. At least, she always contributed his irritability to his illness. Suddenly, with the charming Dr. Silver in the picture, she wasn't so sure.

She blocked the sound of Christopher's happy squeal as Jack's fingers found ticklish ribs and concentrated on Karen's answer. "Yes, he's doing much better. He's not sleeping very well but Dr. Silver has given me some great ideas to try for that."

Is that right? "I'm glad. I hope they work."

"If not, let me know," Jack chimed in. "My aunt raised seven kids altogether, so I'd be willing to bet that she's got some tricks. I'll give her a call if you need some more help."

Karen's grin was quick and bright. "I'll do that."

Brooke turned to exit the room. The whole situation had her flustered. "Well, I just wanted to stop in and see how things were going. I'll let Dr. Silver finish up with you then."

Once back in the hallway, Brooke drew a steadying breath. She had another appointment in twenty minutes and she needed some answers. Mostly, how could she get rid of Jack? Soon. Before she did a hell of a lot more than kiss him up against his truck.

The minute Jack stepped from the exam room, Brooke grabbed his sleeve and jerked him down the hall to her office. She shoved him inside, then stepped through and shut the door.

"What are you doing here?"

God she looked good. He wanted to kiss her. Rain or not, frown or not, he wanted this woman in a crazy, never-before-experienced way.

"I'm here for you, Brooke."

For just a moment, her gaze dropped to his mouth and it was like he could read her mind—and he liked all of it. His body tightened with anticipation of all the things they were both thinking and he felt himself lean forward.

"Ah, dammit," she whispered just before she rose on tiptoe, her hand went to the back of his neck and she met him halfway into the kiss.

She beat him to the moan by a millisecond and he pressed closer, one hand cupping her jaw, the other on her hip. In sync they opened their mouths, moved closer to the door—her backward and him forward—and met the other's tongue and pelvis with their own.

Damn this was good. Better than it had ever been. Something he'd never get enough of. It was amazing that this was Brooke Donovan and he—

Fuck. He jerked back. This was Brooke Donovan. He was giving himself a break on the make-out session the first day because he hadn't known who she was, but when he'd almost taken her on a public street against his truck he had definitely known who she was, and now he sure as hell did.

He couldn't fucking kiss her. It was that simple. He couldn't do anything else either, but there was less risk of doing those things if he resisted putting his mouth on her—anywhere.

He was here because her husband was dead. Because of him. He was here to make things right in her professional life. He was here to help her.

He. Couldn't. Fucking. Kiss. Her.

"Stop, slow down." His breathing was ragged and the look on her face did nothing to cool him down. She wanted him. As badly as he wanted her. She'd been an equal in that kiss in every way.

He still couldn't kiss her.

"What's wrong?" she asked, pressing her lips together and settling back on flat feet.

"I just..." *Can't want you like this, can't have you like this, can't stop thinking of you.* "We're in the middle of your office."

"We're actually against my office door."

He smiled in spite of the tension—sexual and otherwise—in his body. "Still seems not quite the right place for this."

She sighed and straightened her blouse. The one that he wanted to unbutton, completely. Or maybe just rip open. The damned thing made her look so uptight, so in contrast to the woman who had been giving as good as she got against that office door.

It annoyed him for some reason.

"Fine. But if we're not kissing, I'm going to yell."

"About?"

"Why are you seeing my patients?"

"They're sick," he offered. Then, seeing her raised eyebrow, he held up his hands. "Okay, sorry. I'm trying to help you out."

"You seriously think that this is helpful?"

Well, after yesterday with Amanda... He tipped his head slightly and shrugged. "Yeah."

"How?" she asked. "How is this helpful?" But before he could answer, her eyes widened. "Are you here because you don't think anyone will let me treat them?"

He opened his mouth, but she interrupted again.

"Forget it!" She spun on her heel and jerked the door open, then stomped down the hallway. "You don't know me. You don't know anything about—" She didn't even finish her sentence before the swinging door into the back room closed behind her.

A few seconds later, Jack followed her. As she'd expected.

"Brooke, listen," he said the minute he was through the doorway.

She was in the midst of putting on her white lab coat, but she was ready for him. "What are you doing here?"

"I'm here to help."

"So you keep saying."

She buttoned the coat up the front, smoothing it over her plain black skirt. She needed to be even more put together, composed, buttoned-up literally and figuratively with Jack around. He flustered her, made her do things she didn't want to do, made her forget where she was and what she was trying to be—or not to be, as the case may be. He was dangerous. He had the ability to make her turn into everything she was afraid of—a wanton hussy who'd do anything for the man who made her feel...like Jack made her feel.

She wanted to scream. There was more in life than sex. There were other amazing feelings and experiences. There were other things—chocolate for instance, and liquor—that could give her the high kissing did.

But damned if she'd ever tasted anything that could outdo Jack Silver kissing.

So she needed everything she could find to put him off, to remind herself that poise and serenity were superior to chaos and excitement.

No matter what her mother had taught her to the contrary.

She put her hands on her hips, trying to think of something scathing to say.

"Why do you wear that damn thing?" he asked suddenly, gesturing toward her jacket.

She glanced down at her clothing. She didn't have to explain anything to him. "Because it's...professional."

"It makes you look uptight," he told her bluntly. "Uncomfortable."

He reached for her hair, grasped the large clip and opened it. Her long hair cascaded from the top of her head, settling around her shoulders.

"Hey!" Her hand flew to her head.

"Doesn't this thing give you a headache?" he asked, holding the clip up in front of her face.

"No." Well, it did sometimes, but... She was so...flustered with him touching her that every thought vacated her mind. She wanted more. All he did was unfasten her hair and she wanted his hands all over her.

Good God. She'd been attracted to men before. But never like this.

"You need to loosen up. You need to seem more approachable."

"I'm approachable," she said, knowing that she was lying at least a little. Generally speaking, she didn't want the people in Honey Creek approaching her. Living her little hermit life—except for the people who accepted her and sought out her medical care—was working for her. A little less than a year to go.

But Jack certainly had no trouble approaching her. And she welcomed it, even when he was driving her crazy.

Her gaze dropped to his lips and she swallowed hard.

"Brooke." His voice had dropped to a husky rasp and he lifted a hand to run his thumb over her bottom lip. "You're hot and sexy and passionate one minute and the next you're cool and crabby. What the hell is going on with you and this clinic?"

This clinic. Those two words succeeded in breaking through the hot fog that surrounded her when he was this close. This clinic was the last place she could give in to any type of temptation. The entire town was watching now that Jack was here, coming to the clinic, so obviously gorgeous and sexy and yummy. They were expecting her to jump into bed with him—or rather pull him into bed with her. And though she really wanted to do it, she couldn't. The sex would be amazing, she was sure, but proving the town of Honey Creek wrong would be more so.

Probably.

Well, maybe.

No, it wouldn't. But it would be worth it.

"You've been here for two days. How can you tell if I'm approachable, or not?" she asked him, pulling away and letting her exasperation show, hoping it covered the desire that had to be easy to read on her face.

Donovan women were known for being hotblooded—and blatant about it.

"Karen told me that Christopher is scared of you," he said.

"Christopher?" she repeated, thoughts of the sick little boy effectively cooling her off for the time being. "He's scared of me? Why?"

"Karen just said you're so businesslike when you come in. And the coat and everything. He's intimidated. Frankly, I would be too."

"I'm wearing the coat now and you don't seem very fucking intimidated," she said.

Jack's eyes widened at her language and, if she wasn't mistaken, the corner of his mouth curled up. "No, intimidated isn't what I'm feeling for you, you're right. But I do hate that coat."

She took a deep breath in through her nose, focusing only on the irritation she felt and not the tingles. “So, why are you here again?” Her tone was calm, but she knew he was aware of the temper she was trying to keep in check.

“To help you.”

“And insulting me is helpful how exactly?”

“I’m going to help you make this clinic successful.”

Oh, no he wasn’t. Hell no.

For one thing, she didn’t want anyone’s help with anything. Second of all she didn’t want this clinic to be successful. She was here temporarily to fulfill her contract. Period. She crossed her arms and lifted her chin. “I don’t need your help.”

“So you’ve been telling me since I got to town.”

“When are you going to start listening?”

“When you don’t need help anymore.”

She stared at him for several ticks of the clock. Then she said tightly, “I am perfectly capable of seeing the patients scheduled today. That’s the nice thing about having a small caseload.”

“That’s why you should let me help. Let’s build this up, do some renovations maybe, get some—”

“You think we should renovate.” Really? He wanted to put up curtains or something? That’s what all of this was about?

He lifted a shoulder. “Just make it feel a little warmer and friendlier.”

“You think people aren’t coming in because of how we painted the waiting room?” Not that she loved the waiting room either. It was boring and, okay, cold. But that wasn’t why she could hear crickets up there.

“New paint can’t hurt, can it?”

“We’re not repainting.”

He waited until she’d brushed past him.

When her hand was on the swinging door he said, “Fine. But that still leaves one issue un-attended to.”

Don’t ask. Keep walking. Leave. But she asked, “What issue?” anyway.

“The issue of you needing a supervising physician as of...let’s see...oh, yes. Today. Right now.”

She stood stock still at the door for several long seconds. Then she turned.

Even once she faced him again, she didn’t speak right away. Finally she asked simply, “You?”

He grinned, clearly pleased in spite of her lack of enthusiasm. “Yes. Me. You need a supervising physician to practice as a physician’s assistant. I’m a physician. It works perfectly.”

She frowned at him. “How did you know I needed a supervisor?” But she held up a hand as the answer came to her. “Carla.” Clearly her nurse—and *former* friend—had filled Jack in on the fact that Dr. Cunningham was retiring and that there was no replacement yet. The patients on the schedule today were the last ones she could see until someone stepped up to supervise her.

She hadn’t been exactly pushing for that supervisor. All she had to do in this clinic was show up. Patients or not. Supervising physician or not.

So what if that bugged her a little? So what if she was a little bored, knew she was wasting her time and knew there were patients she could be helping? It wasn’t like they were going without medical care entirely. They had to drive an hour but no one was dying. And she didn’t want to get attached.

She'd gotten attached in San Antonio and then had to leave. It had been hard on her patients and on her. She wasn't going through that again. Especially here. She wasn't staying even if she did get attached and that was that. Better not to have to say any tearful goodbyes.

He nodded. "She confirmed it."

Brooke rolled her eyes. "It's amazing the topics that come up over cups of cappuccino. I'm so glad we got that machine."

He smiled widely. "Anyway, you need me."

He shouldn't seem so pleased by that. And she needed to get her imagination in check. She couldn't go off on pornographic daydreams every time he said the word *need* or *help* or *take* or...

She shook her head and asked, "So you think you're going to be my supervising physician?"

"Yes."

"What about your real job?"

"Leave of absence."

"Indefinitely?"

"No." But he didn't elaborate.

She studied him for a moment, considering the information.

"You don't know what you're getting into," she finally said, simply, but honestly.

"I'm not worried."

She sighed. "I know. But you probably should be."

Brooke felt as if she'd been frowning for a week. Actually, it had only been six days. Six days since Jack Silver had inserted himself into her business, in more ways than one.

He'd also inserted himself in her dreams. But at least in those he was naked and quiet—pretty much—and did what she told him to.

In the clinic, not so much.

She stepped into the hallway on her way to her office just in time to see Jack duck into an exam room and shut the door. She immediately turned on her heel and went to find Carla.

"Who's Dr. Silver with?"

Carla looked up from the copy machine. "Mrs. Perkins came in early. She said her head was killing her and Dr. Silver offered to take her. I didn't think it would be a problem." Carla stood and watched Brooke for a moment before adding, "Is it?"

Brooke wanted to shout, *Yes! Of course it is!*

Jack was great with the patients. Really great. And there were more and more of them to be great with all the time. He was actually increasing their business. Dammit.

But she kept her professional poise, as she had for the past week, and shook her head slowly, lest she look insecure. "Of course not. I just wanted to follow up on her new medication. Maybe I'll stick my head in..."

"I gave him her entire history and he reviewed her meds before he went in with her. I'm sure Jack's got it under control."

Brooke bristled slightly at Carla's defense of the man she had known only for a short time. "You just met him. And Mrs. Perkins doesn't know him. I hope she's comfortable with him seeing her."

"She's female and not dead. I'm sure she's enjoying him quite a lot. In fact," Carla went on, "*my* head is starting to hurt a little." She put her hand against her forehead and grinned.

"Very funny." Brooke glanced down the hall at the closed

exam room door that hid Jack and one of her favorite patients from her view. Fine. "I'll be in my office doing paperwork."

She knew that she could not pull off a smile at the moment but she could feign indifference and disappear into her office until her next patient came in. She held herself tall and tight as she passed exam room three. *Do not give it a second thought. Walk on past. Do not stop and listen at the door.*

But the exam room door opened just then and Brooke could hear Thelma chatting with Jack about her prize-winning cherry jam that came from her very own, beloved cherry trees.

Brooke stopped and pasted on a smile. "Thelma, how are you?"

The older woman gave her a warm smile in return. "Oh, Brooke, I must say that you did a good job."

Brooke was pleased. "The medication is working?"

"Oh, yes, that too. I meant you did a good job in picking Dr. Silver...I mean, Jack." The woman turned to pat his arm affectionately. "He's just wonderful."

Brooke forced her smile to remain for her patient's benefit. But it was tough when she really wanted to glare at Jack. This wasn't about bringing patients into the clinic or making her look bad. This was about him stealing one of the very few people she actually enjoyed in this damned town. "I'm glad to hear that. I'm sorry I wasn't able to see you, though." She shot a glance toward Jack, but he was busy giving Thelma one of his charming smiles.

"Oh, honey, don't you worry about that. Jack is wonderful."

You already said that. Brooke gritted her teeth as she took the older woman's arm and began escorting her to the front. "I'm sure that all the compliments are making him feel right at home." Unfortunately.

"Well, I hope so. I would really love to see him stick around too."

"Too?" Brooke echoed.

"Oh, everyone in town is talking about him and what to do to keep him here," Thelma told her.

Of course they were.

They came to the front desk and Brooke patted Thelma on the shoulder. "You take care. Please call me if you need anything at all." She resolutely stood between her patient and Jack, childishly thinking that by separating them physically she could help dissolve the bond that had clearly already formed between them.

Jack ruined that idea instantly. Leaning around Brooke, he squeezed the woman's arm. "Bye, Thelma."

"Bye, Jack." The seventy-six-year-old's voice sounded as enamored as a teenager with a crush.

Brooke held her smile for Thelma even though she could feel warmth emanating from Jack, who still stood close behind her. If she jerked her elbow back suddenly she would connect directly with his ribs.

"What a nice lady." Jack's voice was so close to her ear that Brooke jumped.

She turned immediately, taking a step back to put some space between them. "Yes, she's very nice."

"She thinks a lot of you."

He was not simply looking at her—he was studying her. Why? What was he looking at her for?

"I've known Thelma for years. We have a very nice relationship." She studied him right back. Would he pick up on her not-so-subtle hint that he was butting in where he was not welcome?

He didn't even blink.

Those big, gorgeous chocolate-brown eyes just watched her. And her skin started getting warm. And tingly.

How did he do that? It had to be intentional. Because when he did it she got all distracted. Which worked well for him considering he was generally distracting her when she was mad at him. And when he did it she wanted to kiss him. Which also seemed to work well for him since he had yet to push her away when she did it.

Finally he spoke, though his voice was husky when he did. "Well, then you'll be glad to know that she's doing much better. I adjusted her medication a bit and she's coming back to follow up with me next week but I think she'll do fine after that."

Husky, sexy voice or not, Brooke felt her eyes narrow. Dammit. Thelma was coming back in to see him. He had adjusted the prescription Brooke had given Thelma without consulting her. Was he really this dense or this rude or this arrogant? Or all three? Brooke opened her mouth just as the bell above the front door tinkled.

"Oh, Brooke, I almost forgot these." Thelma was panting slightly as if she'd just walked from her car very rapidly. "I had a feeling today would be a good day."

Brooke groaned inwardly. Not in front of Jack. "Thanks, Thelma."

"What do you have there?" he asked, leaning around Brooke again to peek at the plate Thelma held.

Brooke barely resisted the urge to stomp on his toes.

"Sweet Blessings," the older woman said with delight.

He was so close his sleeve brushed Brooke's and she pulled away, shooting another glare in his direction. He calmly ignored both the irritated look and her obvious adverse reaction to his nearness. Probably because of all the previous proof she'd given of how much she liked his nearness.

He tipped his head to look at her and Brooke stubbornly refused to look back. "Sweet blessings?" he asked.

She ignored him. "Thanks, Thelma. I appreciate it," Brooke said.

Thelma squeezed her arm and smiled.

"Thelma, I have to know, what are Sweet Blessings?" Jack asked.

The older woman turned her attention to him. "I made that up." She grinned, with an actual twinkle in her eye. "They're cookies, but like a lot of things in life, there's more to them when you look harder."

Brooke risked a glance at Jack, but he wasn't looking at her. His full attention was on Thelma, and he looked intrigued.

"Give me an example," he said, gesturing at the plate in Brooke's hands.

Thelma seemed giddy and Brooke couldn't help but smile fondly at the older woman. But she braced herself for Thelma's explanation. Brooke liked Thelma's cookies and she loved the reason behind them. But it was obvious that this wasn't the first plate of cookies Thelma had brought to her. What if Jack didn't get it? What if he thought it was silly?

"These are chocolate cookies," Thelma started. "They're made with semisweet chocolate, because none of us are purely sweet all the time."

She winked and Brooke felt Jack smile. She wasn't sure how she managed that without looking at him, but she knew he was smiling.

Thelma took a cookie from the plate and held it up. "And see, these are crispy on the outside, but," she broke it open and showed them the gooey chocolate middle, "they're soft and mushy inside."

Brooke bit the inside of her cheek. Whether she was going to laugh or object she wasn't sure. This wasn't even slightly subtle. She wasn't sure how Thelma knew that there was tension between her and Jack. She also wasn't sure why Thelma wanted Jack to know Brooke had a soft side. Jack was her co-worker. Sort of. But co-workers didn't need to know each other inside and outside. The outside was enough. More than enough. Just like everyone else in Honey Creek, Jack only needed to see the "crispy" outside. The crusty outside kept the mushy stuff inside. Where it belonged.

He chuckled and took the cookie. "I'm partial to soft and mushy insides."

Brooke couldn't help looking at him then. Good grief, how could he make that sound so nice and...sexy.

He bit into the cookie. "There's mint in there too," he said with some surprise.

Thelma nodded. "There's more to it than what you assume."

Okay, enough already. Brooke took the plate of cookies and set them on the counter. "Tell you what." She took Thelma's elbow and turned her toward the door. "I'll come over the next time you bake. We'll have tea. And then I won't have to share the cookies with Jack." She glanced at the man who had already taken three.

Thelma frowned slightly. "You haven't been to my house in such a long time."

"I haven't had a reason," Brooke said, referring to the fact that Thelma always brought the cookies right to her at the clinic. "Now I will."

It took Brooke several seconds—several seconds too long—

to realize how her words sounded to Thelma.

"Well, if you get a chance then," Thelma said, pulling open the front door.

"Thelma, I just meant..." Brooke said, scrambling to think of a way to explain what she'd meant. But the bell tinkled over the door, signaling Thelma's departure.

Brooke rubbed at the throbbing in her left temple. She was going to have to make it up to Thelma somehow. She turned and almost bumped directly into Jack as she moved toward her office, lost in thought. She looked up, startled that he was standing there so close.

"You do realize that she brought you *cookies*, right?" Jack asked, holding one up.

She took a deep breath. "Yes, I'm aware."

"And that's a *nice* thing to do?"

She gritted her teeth. "Yes."

"Just making sure," he said with a shrug. "Hard to tell when you treat everyone as if they're out to get you."

Brooke wasn't sure how long the silence hung over them. She was stunned by Jack's words. How dare he say something like that to her? He didn't know what he was talking about. And who cared what he thought anyway?

The problem was, Brooke cared. She didn't want anyone thinking that she was cruel and she especially didn't like the idea that Jack thought less of her. She was professional, honest, responsible, capable...any number of adjectives that she was proud of and strove for each time with each patient. Cruel was one word she never wanted to hear linked with her name.

"Brooke, you okay?" Amy asked from her desk only a few feet away.

Brooke glanced at her. “Fine.”

“You need another pencil?”

She looked down at the pencil in her hand. There was actually half of a pencil in each hand. She had snapped it right in two. She tossed the halves into the wastebasket near her foot. “No. I'll get a pen.” She turned away, ignoring Jack, unable to think of an appropriate reply to his impertinent statement.

“Amy, did Dr. Martin call yet?” Jack asked.

Brooke was relieved he was letting it go.

He still leaned against the counter and Brooke tried to block him out of her mind but it was nearly impossible. He filled a room and drew attention like no one she had ever known.

It's because he seems so comfortable. He seems to actually like it here.

Brooke shook the thought off as if it was a pesky bug buzzing in her ear. Who cared if he liked it here? He could have it—the clinic, the town, the whole shebang.

She yanked the drawer open and began digging for a pen. She threw objects out of the way of her searching fingers without even registering what they were. Jack would never have said something so uncaring to Thelma. He wouldn't have forgotten to visit either. Brooke jerked a pad of paper out of the way. Where were all the blasted pens?

Amy moved away from her desk toward the counter where Jack reclined, laid-back as ever. Brooke tried to ignore them.

“Not yet. Do you want me to interrupt you when he does?” Amy asked cheerily.

“That would be great, I really need to talk to him. You're the best,” he said.

Brooke looked up in time to see Amy beam at him and the

quick wink she received in return. Brooke kept her groan silent. Did every female in Honey Creek have to think he was the best thing since cheesecake? Surely one person with ovaries—past or present—could find him less than amazing. She slammed the drawer shut hard enough to attract Amy's and Jack's attention.

She smiled sweetly and made her tone of voice mild. "I can't seem to find a pen."

Jack gave her a funny look as he withdrew a pen from his back pocket and held it out to her. He said nothing.

"Thanks," she muttered. To the rescue, as usual.

"Oh, by the way, Mrs. Gerpkin brought this over for you," Amy said.

Brooke turned back and watched as Amy retrieved a small package wrapped in bright red shiny paper from her desk. Brooke knew that Mildred Gerpkin's arthritic hands would surely have bothered her while wrapping the package, but it seemed that no sacrifice was too large for Jack.

"No kidding." He accepted the parcel with a smile. "What for?"

"There's a card." Amy stood resolutely by his side as he tore the card from the piece of tape securing it to the box.

Just then the phone began ringing. Brooke continued to observe Jack under the pretense of reviewing the four-month-old inventory checklist she had dug from one of the drawers in her search for a writing utensil. The phone rang again. Then again. Brooke turned to stare at Amy, waiting for the girl to move even an inch in the direction of the phone. It rang again. Finally, Brooke realized that Amy didn't even hear it.

She rolled her eyes as Amy exclaimed over the handkerchief Mildred had embroidered with Jack's initials.

She stomped to the phone and grabbed the receiver.

"Honey Creek Family Practice."

Jack and Amy did turn their attention to her then and, to avoid yelling at them, Brooke angled her head slightly to study the hanging plant in the corner of the waiting room.

"May I put you on hold for a moment?" she asked the caller. Upon hearing an affirmative answer, she punched the red hold button on the phone and held the receiver toward Amy. "Mr. Delphini needs to schedule an appointment." Mr. Delphini who hadn't been into the clinic for seven months. Coincidentally.

"Oh, sure." Amy moved instantly toward the phone, sliding carefully around Brooke as if fearful of getting too close. The girl immediately removed the caller from hold and proceeded to greet him graciously under Brooke's watchful eye.

"Want a cookie?" Jack asked her, pulling her attention away from the flustered girl. He held the plate of cookies from Thelma toward her while he popped one into his mouth.

Brooke frowned. "Not really." She began walking toward her office.

"Too bad," he said around chocolate mint cookie. "Might sweeten up that attitude a bit."

Brooke froze. She tried to convince herself to just go to her office and forget about the whole thing. For some reason, he was baiting her, but she had more self-control than that. Jack Silver's opinion did not matter to her—as much as that might surprise him.

In the end, she couldn't do it. She couldn't just ignore the second blatant dig in one morning. She swung around and glared at him. "Do you have something you would like to say to me?"

He straightened and regarded her intently. Finally he said, "Yes, as a matter of fact."

"Then just say it."

"I'm not really sure I should. It might upset you." He settled one hip against the counter and crossed his arms.

She crossed her arms as well. She wondered how she could feel defensive with the gesture while he just looked casual. But then, Jack always looked casual. It was one of the things she was beginning to dislike most about him. "I've been upset since you got here."

He looked at her for a long time before saying, "I see. All right. What I was going to say is that it's no wonder people are driving to Amarillo."

She stared at him. He really thought she cared? He really thought she wanted to try to change that?

Well, screw him.

Especially since there was a niggling little voice in the back of her mind saying he was right.

He couldn't be right. She didn't want to want this clinic. She didn't want to want anything to do with this town.

And until Jack Silver showed up, it hadn't even occurred to her that she might.

She pulled her arms tighter against her stomach, pressed her lips together and took a deep breath.

"Dr. Silver, I think we should talk in my office." The words were a little gruff but she managed.

He glanced over to where Amy sat, pretending to be absorbed in a magazine.

"We have patients coming in," he said.

"You started this."

His eyes roamed over her face and then, at last, he seemed to make a decision. He gestured toward the hallway. "By all means. After you."

Brooke hardly waited for Jack to close the door behind him. "What you don't seem to understand is that I don't care if people are driving to Amarillo."

He didn't reply as he locked the door, then turned slowly to face her.

She frowned. "You're locking the door?" she asked.

"Yes."

"Why?"

He moved farther into the room and she crossed to her desk and stepped behind the chair, putting it and the desk between them.

Well, good, she should be nervous. This hot-and-cold, Jekyll-and-Hyde thing was ridiculous and he was going to end it. This clinic could be booming if she'd let a little of herself show. If she'd smile, laugh, let her hair down, people would see that she was sincere and sweet and smart. That's all most people needed in their doctor.

He came to stand right in front of the desk. "Because we're going to have a talk that I want to keep between the two of us."

"Why?"

"Because everyone else in town thinks I'm nice, but I'm not sure you will when we're done here."

She raised an eyebrow and crossed her arms. "I already don't think you're nice. No worries about ruining that impression now."

He didn't believe that for a second. "So are you a good friend of Tom Dawson's at the sporting goods store?"

She frowned. "Not really."

He wondered if she had any friends besides Carla but that was probably a conversation for another time. "I just thought maybe you had a deal with him since he's doing such a good business selling long underwear and thermal socks to your patients."

She rolled her eyes. "Right. Because I'm so cold. Ha, ha. Very clever."

In spite of the eye roll, he saw some pink in her cheeks and he hoped that her temper was heating. He was sure that she could prove how wrong he was about her frostiness with a few scorching words. He wanted to lay it all on the line. Here and now. It was no longer about defending Thelma or reprimanding Brooke about her attitude in the clinic. Now he wanted her mad.

He wanted to see some emotion in place of the distant, superior façade she kept so firmly in place while in the clinic. He wanted true emotion, open expressions, without hesitation or restraint. He wanted the woman who yelled at him, then kissed him like an erotic dream.

Jack jumped in before she could speak, intent on getting some type of emotional reaction from her—anger, tears, hysterical laughter—whatever she would give him.

"You never smile here at work, you act defensive all the time and you look at everyone like you've never even heard the word trust. Everything is sterile with you and I don't just mean the bandages. Your expressions, your tone of voice, your manner is all so reserved. It's like you don't have any feelings."

He thought that maybe her lip trembled but she got it under control instantly if it had. She gripped the back of the chair and shook her head. "You wouldn't understand. Not everyone has it as easy as you do. I guess I'm just not as charming as you are."

"It has nothing to do with charm. It's about treating your patients like people. It's about realizing that there is more going on inside of them than whatever illness or injury brought them into the clinic. I know that you understand this stuff. You were all about taking care of people at the Girls Home. What's going on here?"

"Nothing." She said it firmly but her eyes would not meet his as she answered. She was staring at the clock on the front of her desk instead.

"Do I make you uncomfortable?" He prayed that she would deny it.

"No."

He felt the relief spread through him swiftly.

"You make me crazy."

He blinked. He made her crazy? What did that mean? He felt a grin begin to stretch his lips. Crazy could be a positive thing. In many ways, Brooke drove him crazy as well.

"Good crazy or bad crazy?" he asked.

She frowned at him. "Crazy as in I'd like to shake all of that cockiness and charm right out of you. Crazy as in you make me want to scream. Crazy as in I hold my breath every morning waiting to see you."

He felt his grin widen. He liked the idea that Brooke was anxious to see him each morning. He liked the idea that she woke up thinking about him. Maybe she even dreamed about him at night once in awhile...

She obviously noticed his smug smile because she rushed to amend the statement. "I hold my breath waiting to see what trouble you've caused me before the day has even started."

Well, maybe it wasn't that she was dreaming about him but he was still getting to her. He rounded the corner of her desk and didn't stop until he was close enough to make her visibly squirm. He could have counted the number of eyelashes that framed her now-very-wide eyes. "I'm not trying to cause you trouble. I want to help you, but I can't help you if I don't know what's going on."

"Nothing is going on." She took a deep breath. "You just frustrate me when you don't respect my space."

"Oh, your space." He moved closer and put a hand on the chair back next to hers. She didn't move away but he could tell she was tense. "You think that I'm stepping over some boundaries, is that it? You've got these walls built up pretty high and wide, don't you?"

"I mean with my patients—"

"I have to tell you." He moved closer yet, able now to catch the faint scent of her. "Being close to people isn't such a bad thing. It just takes some getting used to." He lifted a hand and touched the tip of her hair that lay against her left shoulder.

Her intake of breath was quick and sharp and he was pleased that he was having an effect. Maybe he was just irritating her or maybe he was breaking some dumb rule of etiquette she had in mind, but at least it was a reaction.

"Now are you uncomfortable or crazy?" he asked softly.

Her hair was even softer than cashmere. Jack rubbed the very end between his thumb and forefinger. He watched her swallow hard twice, without blinking.

"Um..." she said hoarsely.

He was close enough that he could easily bend and kiss her. He shouldn't. He knew that. He'd feel guilty about it later if he did. But it seemed the only time she was real, the only time she let go, the only time she truly gave into emotions was when it was with him. Physically, for sure. She let herself go in their kisses. Yes, they were hot and erotic, but he could feel that she was all there somehow. And she let go emotionally with him. When she was mad or frustrated she let him know. No one else got glares or sarcastic remarks or even hints of temper. With everyone else she was cool and poised all the time.

He loved that he could get her to react when no one else did.

And he intended to do more of it. It wasn't healthy to keep all that emotion inside. Whatever it took, he'd get Brooke thawed out.

He moved his hand from the strand of her hair to the top button on her blah navy-blue blouse. Watching her face, he unbuttoned it with one hand. "Or both uncomfortable and crazy?" he asked as the top of her shirt came apart.

She pulled in a long, deep breath. "What are you doing?"

"I'm getting to you." He leaned in next to her ear. "Aren't I?" He unbuttoned the second button.

She closed her eyes then and shook her head and he pulled back to look at her. Without opening her eyes she said, "I'm unhappy."

Jack frowned. That wasn't the response he'd been hoping to get, that was certain. He made her unhappy? Him touching her made her unhappy? Or maybe his presence in general? He couldn't quite accept that one, not with her breath still coming more rapidly than it should and her inability to look him in the eye as she formed coherent thoughts.

"You're unhappy because...?"

"You're making things...complicated."

He knew the feeling. Things had certainly been complicated in his life since Brooke Donovan showed up in it. But things here with the clinic didn't need to be complicated. She just needed to show everyone the warm, funny, passionate side he'd seen.

"Complicated can be good." It at least meant something mattered.

"Jack, I'm aware that—"

"Come on, Brooke, cut the formality." He was tired of watching her swallow her first reactions. "Tell me off if you want to. Kiss me if you want to. Slap me, rip my shirt off, tell me to go to hell—whatever you're feeling, just do it. Stop making everything so proper and unemotional."

She took a deep breath and looked directly into his eyes. She exhaled all at once.

"Fine. I hate how you came barging in here and took everything over. I hate that you can make everyone love you and trust you without even trying. I hate that you are so comfortable here after only a few days while I feel like an outsider in my own hometown."

She said it all in one breath and then stood, rapidly inhaling and exhaling, watching him, waiting for his reaction.

Jack was fascinated with everything from the raised volume of her voice to the flush in her cheeks. "That's more like it. How do you feel now?"

"Better." She sounded as if she resented the fact.

"You should always show your true emotions. You shouldn't close yourself up. People can tell when you're holding back and it's hard for them to trust that. You don't have to have all the answers or be happy all the time. Just be real."

"You want real?" she asked. "You want me to just do what I want, whatever I'm feeling, no worries about consequences?"

"I think you should do what makes you happy."

She licked her lips and nodded, her eyes on his. "Okay. You asked for it." She shrugged out of her jacket and let it drop to the floor behind her. Then she leaned in, wrapped her arms around his neck and put her lips against his. "Why is it whenever you're within five feet of me I want to kiss you?"

Ah, consequences.

"Five feet? Hell, girl, I can't be in the same town without wanting to kiss you." Then he sealed his mouth over hers.

The moment she stroked her tongue along his, he put both hands under her butt and lifted her, turned, kicked her chair out of the way and set her on the edge of her desk. His fingers went back to the buttons on the front of her shirt and quickly freed them all, spreading the blouse open before pulling back to look at her.

"Every time I see your hands on someone else, I remember the way they felt on me that first day," she said breathlessly. "Every time you take a drink from your coffee cup I think about how your mouth felt on my nipple. Every time you..."

"Jesus, Brooke." Jack pulled in a sharp breath as need sliced through him. He was wound so tight that another word or two from her and he'd be a goner. "You have to stop that."

She leaned back, the white satin of her bra hugging the curves that he remembered too well.

"You're the one that wants me to make it real, wants me to say what I really feel." She gave him a naughty smile. "This was your idea, remember?"

"I remember. And I love that this is what you really want deep down."

She smiled and it was the first time he had seen a truly confident smile from her. She knew just what she was doing to him and she knew that she was good at it. Very good at it.

"I want something deep all right."

The woman was going to kill him just by talking.

"The door is locked," she reminded him. "No patients for a while. You can help me with all this tension and emotion and need."

He couldn't fight this. He needed to have her need him.

Even if it was only sexually, the idea of giving Brooke something—like a nice hard orgasm right on top of her desk—was something he couldn't resist. He leaned in and rubbed his jaw against hers. "You need me, Brooke? There's finally something you're going to let me give you?"

"What do you think?" She turned her head and kissed him, full and wet and wanton.

But he had to hear it. "Tell me," he said raggedly, pulling his lips from hers. "Tell me what you want."

She had a wicked gleam in her eye as she turned on the desk and lay back. "Make this desk my favorite piece of furniture ever."

Her blouse was spread out around her, her nipples pressing against the soft satin of her bra, her skirt hiked up on her thighs. He leaned in over her. "Tell me how. Exactly."

"I want your mouth on my nipple, your hand up my skirt, your finger in my—"

He kissed her before she could finish the thought. He didn't actually need her instruction beyond that point—thank you very much. She was clinging to him when he lifted his head. He looked down the length of her body, on display for him on her desk. It was the most gorgeous sight he'd ever seen.

He reached to push her lamp and pencil holder out of the way. As he slid a coffee mug to the side as well, he noticed it was still half full of room-temperature cappuccino. His second favorite flavor in the clinic—next to Brooke's skin. The idea to combine them seemed natural.

He reached and dipped his index finger into the liquid. With his wet finger he traced a trail from the valley between her breasts to the waistband of her skirt, then bent his head and followed the path with his tongue. “God, I love cappuccino,” he said huskily.

She chuckled softly, her hand in his hair holding him close. “If you’d told me we were going to use it like this I would have been all for it from the beginning.”

“And this is just the start. This is going to be your favorite beverage in the world when we’re done.”

He hooked his index finger in the waistband of her skirt and tugged it down to reveal her belly button. Which had a dark red gem in it. He stared, then lifted his eyes to hers. “A pierced belly button?”

“Surprised?”

He thought about that. Was he surprised that Brooke Donovan, the woman who could go from ice cap to inferno in under a minute, had a sexy secret? Not in the least. “It fits.” He dipped his finger in the cappuccino again and then let it drip from his finger to her belly button, wetting the stone before bending and sucking it clean.

Her back arched and she moaned, further fueling his desire. He wanted to hear a lot more of that.

“Unhook for me,” he said.

She reached to free the hooks on her bra. The satin cups fell away revealing the breasts he’d been thinking about for days. They were firm, the tips tight, begging for his touch.

Without taking his eyes from her, he dipped his finger again, then ran the pad of his finger around her right nipple. As she arched closer, his eyes went to her face, wanting to see her eyes as he wet the nipple itself. Desire colored her cheeks, her eyes slid closed and his name escaped her lips on a breath.

Making himself go slow, he lowered his head and took the nipple in his mouth. At first he teased with light flicks over the tip, but in response to her sounds he increased the pressure and finally sucked, pulling all the sweet coffee from her and finding the skin underneath was even sweeter.

Her fingers tangled in his hair, holding him closer. "More, Jack. I need more."

She needed more. From him.

He was happy to oblige.

He kissed his way down her rib cage to her stomach, pausing to paint another stripe of cappuccino along the edge of the white satin panties just barely revealed when he pulled her skirt down. His tongue followed that edge as his hand slid over her skirt to her bare thigh, then between her thighs.

Her legs parted and she arched closer to his hand. "Jack."

He loved the sound of his name from her. "You sure?"

She gave a half chuckle, half sob. "God, yes. Please."

The skin on her inner thigh was as silky as her stomach and he paused to stroke his hand up and down a few times. She shifted restlessly and he could feel the heat emanating from only a few inches higher. Drawn to that heat he slid higher, until his middle finger contacted hot, wet silk.

A sharp breath hissed from between her gritted teeth and he smiled. "You really sure?"

"If you stop now," she said tightly. "You haven't even begun to see cold and bitchy from me."

Desire for her, fueled by how much she obviously wanted him too, tightened his gut and his erection swelled, but he actually chuckled softly. "Well, can't have that. It would be bad for business." Before she could reply, he slipped his middle finger under the edge of her panties and into the hotter, wetter silk underneath.

She gasped and he couldn't have stopped for all the money, fame and gratitude in the world. He slid his finger out, then in deep again, before adding a second. His thumb found her clit and he circled, then pressed. Her neck arched and her hands gripped the edge of the desk. Her breasts bounced softly as she met his fingers' thrusts and her lips were open with the deep ragged breaths she took.

There was no ice queen here, no question about what she was feeling in this moment.

His other hand took her nipple between his thumb and finger, plucking and rolling. "Tell me what you need, Brooke." *Say it's me, say that I'm what you need.* The thoughts were clearly lust inspired, but they were loud and impossible to ignore. He wanted her to need him. Only him.

"More. Harder," she gasped.

He gave it to her.

"Need looks good on you," he told her huskily.

"Not as good as satisfaction looks," she managed.

He increased the speed of his thrusts. He wanted to rip open his fly and really satisfy her, but this was good. Really good. He was doing something just for her, in the most personal, intimate way.

Unable not to, he bent and kissed her and she came as his tongue met hers.

Several seconds later, far too short a time, he slipped his fingers from her. Unable to help himself, he sucked the taste of her from his fingers, watching her the entire time. Her eyes widened and she squeezed her thighs together at the sight.

He wanted her. More than he could remember wanting another woman, ever. He loved making her burn, making her respond, making her need, when it seemed nothing and no one else could do that.

She suddenly sat up, swinging her legs over the edge of the desk and reaching behind her to re-hook her bra. Then she shrugged into her shirt and combed her fingers through her hair—that wasn't just loose now but was completely disheveled. And incredibly sexy.

"And now you've built this clinic up to the point of having patients scheduled this afternoon so you have to go back to work." She pulled her shirt together and pushed him back so she could slide off the desk. "Too bad about that, because I think I'm going to head to my house. For a shower."

She was teasing him. He couldn't believe it. He wouldn't have believed Brooke Donovan would tease—especially sexually.

But he loved it. Because he loved how self-assured she seemed, and he loved that smile. Maybe part of him felt like he shouldn't be kissing her—or more. But maybe this was something even more he could give her, something she needed. Not just an orgasm or the feeling of being wanted, but the ability to let go, take what she wanted, not worry about consequences.

That had been the word she'd used before—consequences. He didn't know what that meant exactly but maybe she was talking about sex, letting go, getting wild. She'd been without her husband for months now, she was stuck in a town where she obviously had some issues. That might be what this whole thing was about for her—she needed to feel comfortable and confident about something, with someone.

If this was the solution, he'd happily help her as often as she wanted him.

He caught her arm as she tried to slip past him and brought her up on tiptoe so he could kiss her again. Then he said, “Anytime you feel the need to express how you really feel, you just let me know. I’ll be there for you.”

She took a shaky breath as he let her go, but said nothing as she started buttoning up. She left first. It took Jack a few extra minutes to be able to leave her office without embarrassing himself.

Chapter Five

It was really hard to avoid a guy who was dead-set on finding you. Especially in a town the size of Honey Creek. Especially when he "worked" at the same clinic she did.

But there was no way Brooke could face Jack.

Even two days later, her face—and the rest of her body—heated remembering what had happened in her office. What she'd let happen.

What she'd made happen.

That was the worst part. She could claim she'd been swept up in the moment, too overwhelmed by him to think straight, that he'd seduced her, swept her off her feet...forced her. But that was as far from the truth as she could get and her memory—which insisted on replaying every single detail of the time in her office with Jack—wouldn't let her forget how she'd kissed him, how she'd been the one to lay back, how she'd had plenty of chances to say no or stop, how he'd asked if she was sure and she'd threatened him if he stopped.

But he hadn't stopped. Not at all. And she now couldn't walk into her office, look at a cup of coffee or even hear his voice without her heart racing, her nipples tingling and her panties getting wet.

This was so bad.

She was every bit the slut she'd always feared she was. That everyone had always known she was.

And that she wanted to be again. And again. And again.

So avoiding him seemed the best option. The only option, frankly.

Yesterday she'd seen her home patients and she made the obligatory stop at the clinic—but only after Jack's truck was gone for the day. Then she'd found a cup of cappuccino on her desk with a sticky note that said, *I prefer cold cappuccino now too.* Which had made her hot.

She'd had three messages on her phone. The first had said, "We need to talk. Or better yet, let's not talk and just do more of what we did in your office." Which had made her hot. The second said, "I'm a big fan of naked and wet but you can't possibly still be in the shower." That had also made her hot. The third said, "I'm trying to respect your space but I will come to your house. And you know you won't lock me out."

He was absolutely right. But thankfully he hadn't shown up. So far.

He couldn't. That big black truck in her driveway would be more than conspicuous and it would stay all night. Which would ruin everything she'd been working on. She was sure she wouldn't care until the morning, but still…

So today she was determined she wasn't going in to the clinic at all. Not even to the back room—with that huge cappuccino machine that made her breathe hard just looking at it. She'd texted Carla and told her she was in the back parking area. Carla could come out and fill her in on anything that she needed to know, give her any messages, and then Brooke could get out of there before she saw Jack…or vice versa.

Not that there was anything she really needed to handle. Jack was there.

For better or worse. And apparently indefinitely.

Of course after getting what he'd gotten from her the other day, with really very little effort on his part, it was no surprise he was staying around. In fact, he had every reason to believe there was even more where that had come from. Hell, they'd been arguing leading up to her being half-naked and panting for him. What could he possibly do to *keep* her from getting naked with him?

She sat in her car behind the clinic but Carla didn't poke her head out and after nearly five minutes Brooke turned off the ignition with a sigh and slunk toward the back door. Why she was slinking she couldn't really say. She knew Jack was likely seeing patients and even if he wasn't, there were no windows in the back room.

She slunk anyway.

At the door, she pulled her phone out but it still showed no return message from Carla. Dammit. She pulled the back door open a few inches and peered inside but saw no one.

Hoping the ringing would be louder than the text-message signal, Brooke dialed Carla's number. It started to ring—both in her ear and in the back room. Scowling, she stepped into the room and looked around. Carla's jacket hung on the hook by the door, her cell phone obviously in the pocket.

Brooke snapped her phone shut. "Dammit."

Then she slunk toward the door leading to the front of the clinic. If Jack was in with a patient she could catch Carla quick and then get out before he saw her.

But as she neared the door she heard voices. One definitely male. She hoped it was a patient but even with the door open just a crack, she knew it was Jack. Only his voice could make tingles erupt head to toe.

She was equally frustrated and thrilled about that.

In spite of herself, she liked being a woman with Jack. That sounded dumb, even in her head, since she was obviously a woman with everyone—but with Jack she was a *woman.*

Part of her liked having adrenaline rushes when she saw him, liked the tingles he created, liked feeling sexy and wanted and powerful. She hadn't felt any of that in a long time. And in the past, when she had, she'd really tried to suppress it. She and Mike hadn't had a traditional marriage in any sense of the word, but they'd had a deal that kept them both from getting too serious with anyone else.

At least that's what she'd thought.

In the past several years, she'd had a few brief, superficial relationships, but she never let herself get involved emotionally and never allowed herself to really let go.

It was good that she hadn't met Jack before this because it was damned hard, seemingly impossible even, to not let go with him.

Common sense said that she should be able to enjoy all of this with Jack. She wasn't married, he wasn't married, they both wanted it and no one was getting hurt.

She wanted to enjoy things like orgasms on her desk in the middle of a work day. She wanted to grab him and give *him* an orgasm on her desk in the middle of a work day.

But she wouldn't.

Because that was something her mother would have done.

Dixie never did anything as ordinary as date a man. She never simply sat on the couch and watched TV with someone. She never had a relationship where they went on picnics or just held hands or talked for hours on the phone or spent Sunday morning in bed laughing and reading the paper.

No, she did things like give blowjobs in the backseats of

limos or in storage closets at parties. She used her phone to send explicit text messages and pictures to her lovers in the middle of business meetings. She did occasionally have sex in a bed, but if the desk was the closest thing, she'd definitely make it work.

Strangely, Jack was the first guy to make Brooke understand her mom in that regard. Dixie had claimed to be unable to help herself.

With Jack, Brooke got that.

After all, how could she be expected to resist a guy who could give her an orgasm so easily—and so well—and who constantly claimed to want her to be happy?

Yeah, well, she'd been happy yesterday.

If she were honest, she'd admit that in general she was feeling less I-hate-it-here than she had prior to his arrival. There was a little flip in her stomach on her short drive to work in the mornings. She found herself smiling more often. And she almost wore red shoes one day.

Almost.

But that was closer than she'd come in a really long time.

She was leaning over the back counter writing a note to Carla when Jack came into the room. She didn't see him enter, but she felt him. It seemed from the very beginning she was incredibly aware of him.

She turned and crossed her arms. Not sure what to say, she waited for him to speak.

"Good timing. I've got an hour between patients," he said, heading for the cappuccino machine.

"Good timing for what?"

"More self-expression."

He gave her a wicked grin she couldn't help but respond to.

He wasn't going to tiptoe around anything—big surprise. He was going to jump right in to how things were between them. "How do you know I haven't been expressing myself like crazy at home on my own?" she asked.

He set his cup down and strode toward her. As he crowded close she didn't move but to tip her chin up to meet his eyes.

"Are you thinking of me when you're expressing yourself?" he asked huskily. He didn't touch her but she felt like every inch of her skin was anticipating it.

She was thinking of him every second of every day, it seemed. She could give him that much. Plus she was sure that imagining her pleasuring herself while thinking of him would cause that amazing flame to flare in his eyes. She loved that.

"I'm thinking of you and your fingers when I'm driving my car, Jack. Of course I think of you when I'm using my vibrator."

She hadn't actually gotten her vibrator out lately, but if she did, he'd be the star of the fantasy for sure.

He gave a little groan and started to lean in to kiss her. There was no lock on this door, which made that a really bad idea.

She'd known coming to the clinic would end up with her doing something stupid—like going down on him in the back room.

"Guess what?" she asked, changing the subject quickly.

He raised an eyebrow. "What?"

How could that even sound sexy?

"I think we should repaint." She'd been thinking about it since he'd suggested it, not as a way to bring more patients in, but for her. And Jack and Carla and everyone else who actually spent time in the clinic. There was no denying that the clinic was cool and boring and uninviting. She didn't care if patients came in because of a change or not but why shouldn't the people who spent most of their time there enjoy it?

He leaned back, realizing that her idea didn't include fewer clothes. But he smiled. "Wow, where'd you come up with that idea? It's brilliant really."

She rolled her eyes. He was so cocky. "So I'm going to need some of that cash you seem so intent on getting rid of."

It was probably stupid, but she'd also gotten the distinct impression that using the money was a big deal for Jack. He'd backed off, hadn't mentioned it lately, but she still knew it really mattered.

"Just let me know what you need," he said.

She needed a bunch of stuff that involved him taking his pants off. But she didn't say that. Mostly because Carla came in right then.

"Hey, Brooke," she greeted as she too headed straight for the cappuccino.

She smiled at her friend, not sure if she was glad her near confession to Jack was interrupted or not.

"Have you heard from Ken Bickford?" she asked Carla.

"Yep, just called and said he'd be here tomorrow right at eight." Carla turned with a full cup. "What's he coming for?"

Ken was a general contractor in Honey Creek and was someone Brooke could have an actual conversation with. "We're repainting."

"Repainting what?"

"The clinic."

"Outside or inside?" Carla asked.

"The whole thing. Both. All of it. The outside's going to be yellow."

Carla blinked at her. “Yellow.”

“Yep.”

“Do I want to know what the inside’s going to be?”

“And,” Brooke said, ignoring Carla’s question, “I’m ordering couches to replace the waiting room chairs, and we’re going to put in new carpet and use floor lamps instead of the fluorescents. And each exam room will be different. I want to do one in turquoise, one coral, maybe another purple and put colorful rugs over the tile floors. What do you think?”

Carla just stared at her. Brooke glanced at Jack, who was smiling and sipping cappuccino.

“I was also thinking of moving the cappuccino machine up front and putting in a small coffee bar in the waiting area,” she said.

Carla’s face actually lit up at that. “Really? Like with lattes and mochas and biscotti and stuff?”

Brooke had no idea. She was flying by the seat of her pants with this whole thing. She’d been to coffee bars, of course, but had never really paid attention. She didn’t know what it took.

She was a lot more excited about the comfy couches and pretty coral paint on the walls in room three.

“Of course. The whole bit,” she said.

But then reason seemed to sink into her nurse’s consciousness. “I’m all for a coffee bar, but what does it have to do with a medical clinic?”

Who cares? This was her space and she should enjoy it. Screw normal, screw conservative, screw trying to impress anyone. “Jack thinks we need to repaint to make the clinic successful. And really, what’s a friendlier color than yellow?”

“You said that?” Carla asked Jack.

“Sure, everyone knows that yellow clinics do better than

any other color," he said.

Brooke didn't look at him, but she did smile.

"You do realize I think you're nuts," Carla said.

Brooke wasn't sure which of them she was talking to.

Carla went off to make some phone calls and Jack said, "Tell me, Ms. Donovan, would you say that you're prone to overreacting?"

She smiled serenely. As a matter of fact, she *was* prone to overreacting. "You think yellow is too much?"

"It was the purple that got me."

She smiled. "Maybe I'll let you pick one of the colors."

"Great. And, if painting doesn't work, we can always hope someone eats too much biscotti or scalds their tongue on the coffee so we can showcase our medical care along with our chai tea."

"Oh, chai tea. I'll have to add that to the menu."

They stood grinning stupidly at each other and Brooke was literally reaching for him and he was literally leaning closer, when Carla called for her from the front.

"Hey, Brooke, can you come up here for a minute?"

She took a deep breath and reluctantly pulled herself from the cocoon of intimacy that seemed to wrap itself around her and Jack so easily.

Carla. Work. Right. "Sure."

She stepped through the swinging door and froze.

The three bouquets of flowers were so big that the delivery man was mostly hidden behind the arrangement of roses he now held. Brooke stood with her mouth hanging open. Besides the vase of roses, there was also one of tiger lilies and one of a variety of wildflowers. They were all stunning.

After he set the roses on the counter the man handed her a card.

"Have a great day, ladies," he said with a little salute.

Brooke handed the card to Carla.

"What's this for?" the nurse asked.

"Well, they sure aren't mine," Brooke said. Though she was jealous. They were gorgeous and romantic and she'd never had anything like that ever happen to her.

Carla didn't hesitate, but ripped the envelope open. Then gasped. "Brooke, they are for you!"

"Not funny." Brooke frowned at her friend.

"They are," Carla insisted.

Brooke crossed her arms. "How do you know?"

"Because the card says, 'Dear Brooke'."

Brooke frowned but dropped her arms. "It does?"

"Yes." Carla grinned at her.

"What else does it say?"

"Your desk is my favorite piece of furniture too."

Brooke's cheeks heated. She was stunned. Jack? He'd sent her flowers? A boatload of flowers?

Carla waved the card back and forth. "What'd you do to deserve this?"

Brooke opened her mouth to say *nothing*, but Carla's comment sunk in just then. "Oh, my gosh. Help me get these into my office!"

She swept the lilies and wildflowers up while Carla, thankfully without question, took the roses. Brooke hurried to her office and deposited the vases on her desk. When all three bouquets were safely out of public sight she sighed.

"You okay?" Carla asked.

"I just don't want any questions or rumors," Brooke said. She knew Carla understood.

"Okay."

"Will you tell Jack to come in here?" Brooke asked.

Carla gave her a wink. "Sure thing."

And it was that wink that summarized all of Brooke's fears.

If the thought occurred to her friend, Brooke could only imagine what thoughts and scandal everyone else would come up with.

And they'd be true. Very true.

It seemed to take him forever to get to her office. Brooke heard Jack's voice even before he made it to her door. She stepped out of her office to find him halfway down the hall answering some question for Carla.

She strode up to him, pushed him into the nearest exam room and shut the door behind her.

"What are you doing?" she asked.

"What do you mean?" He gave her a little grin as if he knew exactly what they were talking about.

"The flower garden that showed up five minutes ago."

"Did you like them?"

"Well, yes, but...you can't send me flowers," she exclaimed.

"Evidently I can." He propped his hip on the corner of the exam table and looked smug.

"What I mean is, it's not a good idea. It will cause problems."

"Like what?"

"People will talk. They'll think we're involved."

"What's wrong with that?" He frowned now.

"It will confirm their belief that I sleep with every guy who comes to town."

"Brooke—"

"Seriously, Jack," she said. "Thank you. They're beautiful, but you can't do stuff like that." Which sucked, because she really liked them. She liked that he'd sent them. She liked the whole damned thing.

"Is that also a no to the date I haven't even asked you out on yet?"

"It's a—" She stopped as his words registered. "You were going to ask me out on a date?"

"Yes."

"Really?" She couldn't ignore the thumping of her heart. A date. With Jack. Dammit, why did he have to be so...tempting?

He smiled. "Really."

"Why?"

He rolled his eyes. "Because I want to spend time with you."

"But...we can't." She regretted those words almost more than any others she'd ever spoken. "My goal here is to show them that I can be a responsible, professional and respectable member of the community."

"Pure and chaste, honest and true?"

She heard the sarcastic tone to the question, but she paused and considered the words. "Yes," she said finally.

"That's really too bad."

She looked at him, admittedly suspicious. "Why did you send me flowers? You could have just asked me out and we could have had this conversation."

"Have you ever gotten flowers before?" he asked.

"No." How did he know that?

"Well, I think every woman should get flowers from an admirer at least once."

"You're an admirer?" she asked softly, touched in spite of herself.

He stepped close and looked down at her, a strangely gentle look in his eyes. "Yes, I'm an admirer."

Her heart tripped and she was at a loss for words temporarily. He was an admirer. He'd sent her flowers. He'd wanted to ask her on a date.

So this is what this feels like.

She smiled. "Thanks, Jack."

"Should I ask you for that date now?"

She hadn't wanted anything so much in a very long time. Maybe not ever.

The sadness was surprisingly sharp. Brooke had to press her lips together to stop the trembling before she said, "No."

She couldn't believe she was turning Jack down. She had more willpower than she thought. But she had to get away from him before she threw her image and reputation to the wind.

She was at the door when he said, "If I really thought you didn't want to, I'd stop asking."

Turning slowly she narrowed her eyes. "But?"

"You do want to."

"Based on what? The scene in my office yesterday? I'll give you a hint, Jack, you don't have to buy me dinner or flowers to get more of that."

He pushed off the table. "That's good to know. Because I definitely want more of that. And I'm glad you said that so you know when I keep asking it's because I want more than that."

"That's stupid," she told him bluntly. "You're leaving. Why would I want to get involved with you?"

"Because it's gonna be the best you've ever had."

The promise in his words sent shivers down her spine. She had absolutely no doubt that he was right.

"I'm positive the sex would be amazing," she assured him.

"Not just the sex." Though he certainly didn't deny they were going to do that too. "All of it. Every minute, every bite, every laugh, every kiss. And yes, every orgasm."

As in, more than one. Her heart was racing and she couldn't remember wanting anything as much as she wanted to date Jack Silver. She wanted to strip him down, pour cappuccino over every inch of him, and then ride him until they both couldn't move. But she also wanted to date him.

"In that case, there's no way we're dating. Or kissing—anymore. Or having sex."

"That's stupid," he informed her.

"Look, you don't get it." She sighed. And she really didn't want to explain it. There was one near sure-fire way to turn him off of this. "Basically, if we date, or have sex, or both, we're going to have to get married."

He just looked at her, then nodded. "So this is like painting the clinic yellow—an overreaction so that you don't have to admit that I have some good—amazing even—ideas."

"Actually, that's not what this is. I absolutely can't—will not—have an affair with you."

"You're a grown woman. You're not married, you're—"

"The town slut."

He blinked at her, obviously taken aback.

"That's right. That's how I got Mike. That's how I got everything I've ever had. At least according to this town."

Jack stepped toward her. "Surely you're blowing this out of proportion."

She stepped back, away from him before he could touch her. "Are there patients waiting?" she asked.

"No."

"Then come with me." She pivoted on her heel and headed for the door, not even pausing to see if he was following.

"Where are we going?" he asked. But he started after her.

"On a tour."

"Of what?"

"Honey Creek."

"Why?"

She stopped and turned so suddenly he practically knocked her over before he could stop.

"Because you don't know what the hell you're talking about."

"What..." he started but she'd already turned and stomped away again.

"Where're you two goin'?" Carla asked with her usual perkiness as they passed the desk.

"To the house," Brooke said, her attitude anything but perky.

Carla looked startled and turned her eyes to Jack. He could only shrug. He didn't even know what house. Not to mention why. Well, besides the bit about him not knowing what the hell he was talking about, of course.

"Page us if anything comes up," Brooke told the nurse as

she continued on past the desk.

"Okeydokey," Carla said brightly, but she gave Jack a sympathetic grimace as he passed her.

He considered digging in his heels and refusing to go farther with Brooke until she explained. But curiosity won out. Whatever she was going to show him had to be interesting if nothing else.

Brooke didn't say another word as they got in the car and drove out of the clinic's parking lot and headed west.

Three miles outside of town, Brooke turned right onto a white crushed-rock road. Honey Creek was not a large town, and Jack had been sure he'd seen all of it in his few days in town. He'd been wrong.

The road was actually a private drive, he realized when what he assumed to be a huge house materialized at the end of the drive. A very unique house.

But mansion was a much more accurate word.

It was a three-story rectangle, but four huge cylinder shapes broke the structure up into four sections. All of the windows—and there were a lot of windows—were huge and...round. None of them were covered with draperies of any sort.

Not only was it enormous, but it was also...well...pink.

Carnation pink. Little-girl-birthday-cake-frosting pink. Barbie pink.

Brooke parked in the circular drive in front of the twelve steps that led to the front door and Jack whistled low.

"Nice," he said mildly.

"Thanks."

He glanced at Brooke. She was staring at the house with a mixture of contempt and sadness.

"It's yours?"

"Sort of."

"Meaning?"

She sighed and faced him. "It was my mother's. I lived here until I went to college. She gave it to me when she went to Vegas."

"But you don't live here now?"

"Hell no," she said sharply. "I hated living here when I had to. I have a choice now."

"It's…"

"Atrocious."

"No," he said carefully. "The color is…unusual. But the house is beautiful."

"Well, now you can see where I get my tendency to over-react." She glanced at him. "And why over-the-top gestures from others make me nervous."

Okay, maybe he'd overdone the flowers, but he'd loved it. It wasn't clear to him how he knew she'd never had flowers from a man before, but he'd been thrilled to find out he was right.

He stretched an arm across the back of the car seat, stopping just short of touching her. "Tell me the story."

There had to be a story behind this house. And Brooke's disdain.

"You want to know how my mother could afford this house."

He shrugged. "I have no idea what your mother did for a living. How do I know if she could afford it or not?"

"She could." Brooke sighed. "Unfortunately."

He didn't say anything, wanting her to go on, afraid she wouldn't, but unwilling to push.

"My mother moved me here when I was sixteen," she said finally, her gaze on the house again. "She brought me here to make a better life, to give me a fresh start." She laughed derisively. "But she built this house. Can you believe that?"

"It's a nice house," he said again.

"Yeah, I had a suite all to myself. Bathroom, living room, bedroom. I thought it was cool, until I found out she did it to keep me out of the way. Not to mention the pool, the home theater system, my own convertible, the best clothes…" She trailed off as if exhausted. "Not exactly the way to lay low and blend in."

"Your mom didn't like to blend in?"

Brooke pulled a photo from her wallet and handed it over with a sigh. It was of a beautiful woman with long, fluffy blonde hair, dressed in a bright pink tank top that hugged generous breasts, skin-tight pink shorts that emphasized a tiny waist and curvy hips, and strappy pink sandals that adorned feet with nails painted bright pink. Her lipstick, fingernail polish and hair barrette were also all pink.

"My mom didn't know how to blend in," Brooke said. "It just wasn't in her character."

She looked from the photograph to the house and shuddered slightly. "I hate pink."

"Were you embarrassed by her?" he asked.

Brooke faced him again. "Yes. Almost constantly. Even before I found out what she did for a living."

"You didn't know?"

"I thought I did. She told me she sold cosmetics. Which, actually, was true. But little did I know that selling lipstick doesn't bring home this kind of money." She gestured at the house.

He saw the change in her face. He couldn't really describe her expression, but he wasn't sure he was prepared to hear what she was going to say next. He asked anyway. "What did she do for a living?"

Brooke leaned toward him slightly and looked directly into his eyes. "My mother was a prostitute."

Brooke watched Jack's face. It almost, in that moment, didn't matter how he reacted. It was such a relief to have confessed. To him. Everyone else in town knew, and she wished they didn't. But somehow she wanted Jack to know.

She liked Jack. That was the simple truth. For a few days the idea of telling all had been brewing inside of her. In spite of—or maybe because of—his obvious disappointment with how she handled the patients and town, she wanted him to know. Then, if he ran, fine. She would know and her silly teenage fantasies about falling in love with him would go away and leave her alone.

If he didn't run... Well, he would still have to go away and leave her alone. But at least she would know her taste in men had improved.

Regardless, it felt good to tell him.

He blinked a few times as if thinking over her statement.

"A prostitute?" he finally asked.

"A very highly paid call girl. A hooker. A—"

"Okay, I got it." He looked back at the house in front of them. A long moment of silence passed. Then he said simply, "She must have been good at it."

Brooke stared at him. She wasn't expecting that. She let the comment sink in. Then she felt a smile begin as she glanced back at the house. Well, he had a point.

"Yeah, I guess so. In San Antonio most of her clients were millionaires. My mom loved men with money."

"Did she do…that…here?" he asked, stumbling over the words as if unsure how to exactly ask.

Brooke could easily recall the sick feeling that started in her chest and spread to her stomach when she'd come home early from school one day in San Antonio and caught her mom "at work". She'd confronted her mother about what was going on and Dixie had refused to lie. At least Brooke could respect that. From then on Dixie had been far too open about it all.

She shook her head. "We moved here to be near the man who wanted her as his mistress. Just his. They'd had an on-again, off-again relationship for a few years as he traveled for work, but finally he wanted her just for himself."

"He asked her to move here?"

"No. He wanted her to sit in San Antonio and wait for him to come to town here and there. But mom thought that wanting her to himself meant that he was in love with her. She loved him too and wanted to see him more often."

"She didn't think that might be a problem with his wife and the town?"

"You have to know my mom. She thinks about five minutes ahead. She's incredibly spontaneous. She just figured she'd stay out of the way but be right here whenever he wanted her."

Jack sat quietly, and Brooke wondered if she'd scared him off. Well, she'd gone this far. If she'd lost him, she'd lost him. He hadn't exactly been hers in the first place. She might as well tell him everything so at least he would understand what was going on with her and Honey Creek.

"She was Walter Worthington's mistress."

Jack jerked and looked at her with shock. "Walter?"

Brooke felt bitter and tired whenever she thought of her father-in-law. Walter had been a weight on her shoulders for so long. She wondered if she'd ever be out from underneath his pressure.

"Yep. And she ruined his life. Well, most of it. I finished off the rest."

Jack's eyebrows arched.

"I overheard them one night talking and arguing. Walter had been over, as usual, and was getting ready to go home. I heard my mother tell him she loved him." Brooke felt the years-old resentment rise up even now with the retelling of the story. "And he laughed at her."

She felt Jack's fingertips rest lightly on her shoulder. She leaned into the contact slightly and went on. "I'd never seen my mother cry until then. She was the most upbeat person I'd ever known. I'd also never seen her embarrassed or humiliated. We were close, then anyway. My mom is so fun. She would order pizza and have it delivered at school for lunch. She would wake me up in the middle of the night to watch an old Broadway musical on TV. One time she took me out of school early and we drove ten hours straight for a Bon Jovi concert. She was spontaneous and outgoing and made an impression everywhere she went."

Talking about her mom made Brooke's chest ache. She hadn't seen Dixie in nearly two years. Dixie sent her a text message every other week. Brooke responded to about half of them. They stayed connected, but just barely. She hated thinking about it. She blamed her mom for things in Honey Creek being uncomfortable and unwelcoming for her. She could be honest about that.

Dixie didn't know how things had been for Brooke after

she'd left and she had, after all, given Brooke the chance to leave too. In fact, at any time she could have called her mom and Dixie would have come to get her. But she wanted more than life with her mom could offer.

She didn't approve of how her mom had come by her money, but without a man supporting her, Dixie wouldn't have been able to afford having Brooke live with her or go to college. College had been the biggest issue. Brooke was determined to go, to make something of herself so she didn't have to depend on someone else. Dixie wouldn't have been able to afford it and Brooke was not going to take money, even indirectly, from Dixie's next guy.

"I assume your mother stopped seeing Walter?" Jack's voice broke into her memories.

Brooke nodded. "But that wasn't enough. She only knew one way to get back at him and she used it. She seduced his biggest client, became that guy's mistress, and married him after he left his wife. Then she convinced him to drop Walter as his supplier completely."

Brooke couldn't help her smile. It had been the most devious thing her mother had ever done. Most people, of course, judged her harshly. Brooke didn't necessarily approve either, but she couldn't fault Dixie for standing up for herself.

"Wow," Jack commented, looking down at the picture of Dixie. "She really got him back."

"Yeah. But it affected a lot of people. Like I said, my mom wasn't a big forward thinker. Because Walter lost his biggest contract he had to downsize, which meant he had to lay a bunch of people off, which affected the town's economy. They definitely haven't forgotten that my mother almost single-handedly ruined Honey Creek."

That sounded melodramatic, but wasn't entirely untrue.

"That must have been strange for you and Mike."

"How so?"

"Well, being in love like you were, having your parents involved, then having them hurting each other like that had to be hard."

Right. That would have been hard. If she and Mike had actually been in love.

She needed out of the close confines of the car suddenly. Partly it was the nearly overwhelming urge to throw herself into Jack's arms and ask him to hold her. But she was also feeling claustrophobic with all of the old memories crowding in and the emotions that seemed to constantly fill the space between them.

"Want to take a walk?" she asked as she wrenched her car door open and slid from the seat.

Jack got out of the car on his side and, without a word, came around the car to stand next to her.

It was strange how the house seemed to grow bigger without the windshield between her and it. As if sensing her tension, Jack took her hand. She was amazed at how good and calming it felt. They stood like that, looking at the house, each lost in their own thoughts for several minutes.

She couldn't remove her hand from Jack's, though in a corner of her mind she wanted to. The less he touched her, the less he looked at her like he cared, the easier it would be for her to ignore her heart screaming for more.

Finally she looked down at their joined hands, not wanting to see his face just then. "Mike and I were never in love."

She felt his whole body suddenly go rigid.

"What did you say?" he asked softly.

"Mike and I were friends. We got along great. Mike was angry at his dad for what he did to my mom. But we were never in love."

"You married him."

Jack's voice sounded tight but she didn't dare look up at him.

"Yeah. We made a deal." She sighed. She had never, ever, even once betrayed Mike's secret or their arrangement. But she had to with Jack. For some reason she needed him to know everything.

"A deal?"

"Walter ran Mike's life. He'd decided what school Mike would go to, what he'd study, he'd even decided—assumed—that Mike would marry Amanda. He had it all planned out. But Mike didn't want any of that. During high school he went along with it because it was easier, but he wanted to go to med school not business school, he wanted...not Amanda. We were seniors in high school when all this went down with my mom and Mike saw a chance for he and I to both get something we needed."

She felt Jack's grip tighten on her hand.

"Brooke."

His voice was low, laced with emotion but she still couldn't look at him. She had to finish this story first.

"The deal was, if I married him, Mike would make Walter pay both our tuitions and a living allowance for college. I didn't want anything more than to go to college and didn't have any better options, so I agreed. We got married by the Justice of the Peace in Amarillo before we even approached Walter. Once we were married there was nothing he could do—we were legal adults who'd entered marriage willingly and knowingly. Mike told Walter that he had to pay for both of us or Mike would cut himself off from the family for good."

"And Mike got away from Amanda and you in his bed every

night. Pretty sweet deal."

She couldn't help but glance up at that. There were so many emotions in Jack's eyes that she couldn't identify just one. In general, he looked worked up.

"Let me guess," he went on, almost angrily—the first time she'd experienced that emotion from him since meeting him. "He'd always had a crush on you but no chance until suddenly you needed something he could give you. Paying to sleep with you was better than not sleeping with you at all. Besides, it was daddy's money."

Brooke stared at him, feeling like he'd just slapped her. She jerked her hand from his. His assumption hurt. Which was stupid, because it was what everyone in Honey Creek thought. And it was what she and Mike had let them think. That was the plan from the beginning. Mike professed a long infatuation with her and everyone knew Walter was giving them money. They added two and two together. Her end of the deal was to never let on that the last thing Mike actually wanted from her was sex.

"I was never in Mike's bed."

Jack didn't say anything to that.

"He didn't marry me because he'd had a crush or to get away from Amanda. I was his cover, his protection."

"Protection from what?"

"Being disowned."

Jack scowled. "Being disowned for what?"

"Being gay."

Several seconds ticked by as Jack clearly processed the new information. Shock, then confusion and finally understanding crossed his face. "Walter would have disowned him for that?"

"In a heartbeat. And Mike was still coming to terms with it.

Being married, to a woman, helped him in a lot of ways."

Jack focused on the horizon instead of her face. "You did it for the money?"

She swallowed hard. "Yes. Kind of. I was eighteen, the daughter of the most hated woman in town. She left for Vegas and I knew if I went with her college would never happen. Mike was absolutely my best option. I could have gotten loans but this was a chance to go to college *and* be debt free. Plus..."

The rest didn't paint her as a very nice person and she hesitated.

"Plus what?"

She sighed. She'd already come this far. "The idea of getting to spend Walter's money without my mom having to sleep with him was appealing. And a Donovan woman got the Worthington name after all." It had seemed like sweet justice at the time.

And it was a great deal. Until they finished undergrad and wanted to go on to med school and PA school. Walter had put his foot down then. Unless Mike was pursuing his MBA, Walter wasn't footing the bill anymore. Hence the deal with Honey Creek to pay their student loans back.

"You stayed married after college though," Jack pointed out.

She shook her head. "Actually, no. We got an annulment as soon as everything settled down. We had to actually get married because we knew Walter would check for the license and everything, but once we were in school with the tuition paid, we annulled it. We lived together, as roommates, but that was it."

"So why'd you come back here?" Jack seemed weary suddenly.

"I didn't intend to. I was already working for the Girls Home. Mike and I were still living together because it was easier, but we were just friends and he was in love. I figured as soon as he finished med school, he'd move on. But..." she sighed, "...he had a gambling problem. He got in way over his head and needed to be bailed out. He finally went to his dad who agreed to help, but only if he came home. Mike arranged it to have his school loan paid off too if he worked in Honey Creek for two years."

"How'd you get dragged into it?" Jack was scowling again.

She shrugged. "Everyone here still thought we were married and Mike was afraid to tell his dad the truth. Mostly because he didn't want to let his dad think he'd been right about me, but he was also concerned his dad would try to bully or manipulate him into staying. Married to me there was no fear—Walter didn't want me to stay. I remind him too much of my mom."

Jack nodded. "A lot less flashy though."

"Thanks," she said sincerely.

She'd always hated how weak Mike had been with his dad and how easily he sucked her in to helping him. But he'd been the one person who hadn't judged her because of her mom. He knew firsthand what it was like to have a parent he wished he could divorce.

"So after Mike died, why did you stay here, with all of this..." he seemed to struggle to find an appropriate word, "...stuff?"

She frowned. "Because they expected me to go back on my word. They assumed I would take the easy way out. That's the kind of person they think I am. I'm here to prove them wrong about everything they think about me."

She saw Jack's jaw tighten. He looked angry. "You've been living this life with—for—Mike all this time and now you feel stuck here. That's not fair to you, Brooke."

She couldn't help herself any longer. She moved forward, wrapped her arms around Jack and held on.

Jack wasn't stupid. He immediately pulled Brooke closer.

They stood like that for several minutes. Finally, she pulled back out of his hold and gave him a wobbly smile. "Thanks for saying that."

He tucked a strand of hair behind her ear without saying a word. He was so torn. Part of him hated the idea that Brooke had been unhappy and unfulfilled. But part of him—an admittedly much bigger part—was thrilled that Mike Worthington had not been the love, or lover, of her life.

"I feel like maybe I should just put this out there—you know, just in case," she said.

"Okay."

"I can't sleep with you."

He felt his eyebrows rise. "Just in case?"

"In case you were thinking about us having sex."

"I can assure you," he said, pulling her closer. "I've definitely been thinking about us having sex."

She nodded, as if she'd expected his answer. "Not gonna happen."

He wouldn't smile. "Because...?" He knew exactly why but he wanted to hear her say it. So he could tell her she was wrong.

"That's also what they expect. Hell, it's what *I* expect, Jack. I don't want to be that person."

"The one with the healthy sex drive and a guy who can't keep his hands off of you?" he asked. He ran those hands down over her butt and then up to her low back.

The corner of her mouth curled. "Don't forget the reputation."

"Do you really care what they think?"

She looked a little sad as she nodded. "Kind of."

"You know that the reputation isn't deserved. Let it go."

She shook her head. "Can't."

She needed to.

Okay, that sounded like a great excuse to get laid. But he did believe that Brooke needed to let go. It wasn't about physical release—well, it wasn't *only* about physical release—it was about being herself and not apologizing for it.

She wanted this. He knew that. And there wasn't a damned thing to be scared of or sorry for.

Enough with the talking.

His held her face between his hands and claimed her lips.

Her surrender was immediate. When she opened her mouth and moaned, he softened the hard, I-will-possess-you kiss. Her hands tangled in his hair, holding him in place, though he had no intention of stopping for the next year or so. He cupped her butt, drawing her up against him.

He made love to her mouth for several long, delicious minutes before they finally came up for air.

She let out a long breath and pushed her hair back from her face. "There are moments when I can almost see why my mom chose her profession."

He squeezed her, chuckling and groaning at the same time. "You have to stop saying stuff like that if you want me to stop thinking about sex."

"I know." She stared up at him. "And it looks like you'll have to be the one to stop thinking about it, because I sure can't."

He took a deep breath. “I think you need to know that chivalry only goes so far.”

“I’m pushing it?”

“Badly.”

Her lips curled. “I have to admit I kinda like it.”

“Messing with me?” And she was. It was quickly becoming critical that he have her—taste her, touch her, learn everything about her.

“The idea that maybe the good consequences can outweigh the bad,” she said softly.

Well, hell. He’d never been that good at chivalry anyway. He leaned in just as a shrill beeping erupted from his pocket. Less than a second later, the same noise spurt from Brooke’s jacket.

It seemed to take her a few seconds to recognize the sound as well, but professional instincts finally kicked on and they reached for their pagers at the same time.

“It’s Carla,” she said, checking the number.

He nodded. “Me too.”

“Damn.”

Yeah.

He pulled his cell phone out and hit the number two. The clinic was already on his speed dial.

“It’s me.”

“Is Brooke with you?”

He glanced at the woman already sliding into the driver’s seat.

“Yeah. What’s up?”

“Get back here pronto. There’s been an accident.”

He slid into the passenger seat as Brooke started the ignition.

"Where?"

"Fifth and Main. Car-pedestrian collision," Carla told him. "I'll meet you there with supplies. Hurry."

Chapter Six

For a brief instant Jack felt as though he was trying to swallow a tennis ball. The bike was crumpled, one wheel bent nearly in half.

The woman, who he assumed to be the driver of the car, stood leaning against the back door of the Cadillac, getting her skirt and jacket dusty. Two other ladies were there, clearly fussing over her, while the woman held a cloth against her head. The cloth was bright white, so she was obviously not bleeding profusely, and she was talking and gesturing with her free hand. A man brought her a glass of water, and when she smiled her thanks, Jack knew she could wait.

He was out of the car before he knew for sure where he was going. His eyes flew to the small crowd that had gathered and immediately located the owner of the bike. The little boy's helmet was on but tipped precariously to one side and he was unconscious. Jack's throat tightened, making airflow to his lungs impossible. In seconds he was kneeling next to the child. A small bloodstain was beginning to seep into the torn denim that once covered the boy's knee and there was a thin ribbon of blood trailing from the gash on his right temple.

Jack took a deep breath and prayed that his hands would be steady. His fear and adrenaline rush would do nothing to help this kid. "What's his name?" he asked the crowd.

"Rico Castro." Brooke's voice answered and Jack glanced up over his shoulder.

"Hey, Rico," she said softly to the child, moving beside Jack to kneel next to the boy. "Rico, can you hear me? It's going to be okay. Dr. Silver is going to take really good care of you." She touched Rico's head tenderly before turning her eyes back to Jack. "He's a hemophiliac." She said it softly and calmly but he heard the underlying tension. "We have to get him stabilized and to Amarillo immediately."

Jack swallowed hard. This was more than a bicycle-car collision. Rico was prone to excessive bleeding. His body would not cause his blood to clot normally. The potential for serious internal bleeding from this accident was real and life-threatening. The sooner he was taken to the hospital, the sooner the clotting factor could be given and the sooner the risk would be under control. Every minute counted.

Jack nodded, struck by the commanding note in Brooke's voice. She appeared composed but he could see the emotions swirling in her eyes. Fear and concern and protectiveness were all there but the defensive, reserved woman he had been working with at the clinic was gone.

"Carla!" Brooke called, waving the nurse over to her side. Carla brought the Philadelphia collar and the backboard as well as blood pressure cuff and stethoscope from the back of the Explorer. "Get the helicopter right now," Brooke said, positioning at Rico's head to apply the stiff collar that would keep his neck stable.

"Already on its way," Carla reported.

"You ready for the backboard?" Jack asked Brooke.

She nodded and together they gently rolled Rico to one side, slid the hard board under his body and rolled him onto it, keeping his spine straight, and secured him with Velcro straps.

Brooke knelt next to Rico's head and touched his cheek. "Rico? Can you hear me? Rico, I want you to open your eyes." Nothing happened. She patted his cheek and tried again. Still, no response.

Jack felt for Rico's pulse at his wrist. "Pulse is steady and strong," he told her, applying the blood pressure cuff to Rico's left arm to further check his vital signs.

She carefully lifted the little boy's shirt, examining his skin and joints, looking for further damage. It was difficult however to move the clothing out of the way, especially the jeans, with Rico on his back and their hesitancy to move him too much before knowing that his spine was stable.

She felt through his clothes for bumps or signs of fractures along both arms and legs, then stripped off his right shoe and sock and dug her fingernail into the sole of his foot. Rico's face flinched and he pulled his foot away. "He's responding to pain."

They checked his blood pressure regularly, relieved it stayed fairly stable over the next few minutes. Jack felt confident they'd found all the external areas of bleeding. Between him, Brooke and Carla, they were able to keep pressure on all of the sites at once.

But it was only a few minutes later that Brooke checked his blood pressure again. Her eyes found Jack's and she said hoarsely, "It's falling."

He nodded his understanding and looked down at the little boy. "Carla," he said, taking charge. "We need to get that IV started. I think his spine is stable enough to move him to the clinic."

They began to move as a unit just as they heard the faint sound of the helicopter's propeller beating in the distance.

"Where are his parents?" Brooke asked Carla.

"Bruce at the hardware store called them right away. They

should be here soon."

"Send them on to Amarillo—we can't wait." The helicopter put down in the field about four hundred yards from where they were standing.

"You've got this, Brooke," Jack told her, stretching to his feet. "I'll get this one covered." He gestured toward the woman who had been driving.

The woman was now standing next to the front of her car, watching them work on Rico and looking very scared.

Brooke glanced down at Rico. "You sure?" she asked.

"Definitely. I'll handle her."

The paramedics were there and all she could do was give him a quick nod. The woman, Johanna Gardner, was a friend of her ex-mother-in-law. Likely, she would prefer Jack's help anyway. Rico moaned slightly as the paramedics lifted the board and her attention was immediately back on the situation at hand.

She helped the paramedics carry the backboard to the helicopter as she filled them in on the situation and Rico's condition. Once inside the copter, one EMT continued applying compression to the injuries on Rico's head, knee and arm while the other took his blood pressure and then cut off his shirt and jeans to inspect for further injury. Bruising was beginning to show on the little boy's ribs.

The paramedic near the door grasped Brooke's hand as she jumped lightly to the ground.

"We'll take good care of him," the young man told her.

"I'm counting on it," she told him. She didn't have a smile to give. Rico was hardly out of the woods yet.

She turned away from the copter, ducking as she hurried

far enough away that she could safely watch their departure.

"You're not going with him?"

She turned to find Rico's father, breathing hard, as if he'd run the ten miles from work.

"Arturo," she said, stepping forward and taking the big man's hands in hers. "They have everyone and everything they need to get him safely to Amarillo."

Arturo's eyes were strained with fear and concern. "But what if he wakes up in the air?"

The chance was unlikely, but she wasn't willing to share that information with the worried father. "The staff on that flight are highly trained professionals," she assured him.

"But Rico doesn't know them." Arturo watched as the third paramedic jumped on board the helicopter and adjusted the tubes they'd hooked up to Rico. "I want you to go with him. They'll let you?" he asked.

She pressed her lips together, then nodded. "I'm sure they would let me."

"Please." Arturo tightened his grip on her hands. "Please go."

"Dr. Silver should go then." She tried to turn to find Jack.

"No," Arturo said firmly, tugging on her hand until she looked at him again. "You."

"But Dr. Silver is an emergency physician." She wanted to go with Rico, but Arturo was beside himself and wasn't thinking clearly. He was scared. He obviously didn't remember that there was a doctor at the scene. "Dr. Silver is very good," she insisted.

"Fine," Arturo said, squeezing her hand. "But I want you. Rico will recognize you and won't be so scared when he wakes up."

She looked up at the tall Hispanic man, slightly perplexed.

He really did want her to go.

"You were the best student in school. You're smart," Arturo said. "And you're sweet. You know us. You'll take care of Rico."

She knew that he knew that she was smart. That was no secret. She'd been Valedictorian and had helped tutor Arturo through Biology and Chemistry. But what echoed in her head was that he thought she was sweet.

And that was why the paramedic slammed the helicopter's door behind her a few moments later and she waved to Jack and Carla as they lifted off on their way to Amarillo.

She watched as Arturo and his wife, Marie, headed for their car. They would be behind the copter, of course. She could understand them wanting to send someone to watch over Rico until they could get there.

And she was touched that they'd chosen her.

Brooke couldn't quite describe the feeling it gave her, in fact. Arturo had wanted her. And not just because she was the only one there. He'd chosen her to take care of his child.

She frowned as the helicopter turned east. She'd assumed that no one in Honey Creek trusted her. Could she have been wrong?

The question plagued her all the way to Amarillo as she held Rico's hand and talked nonsense in soothing tones, hoping the little one could hear her voice if not understand the words. And it gave her the chance to let her mind wander a bit.

She *was* sweet, dammit. And smart and caring and genuinely concerned for the people who needed her.

Could she have been so caught up in hating Walter, concentrating on his hatred for her, and wrapped up in paranoid assumptions that she hadn't noticed that not everyone felt as Walter did? Was it possible that there were people in town who would accept her, trust her, come to her if she was open and genuine as Jack had encouraged her to be? She had been so busy pushing them all away before they could push her away. Was it possible that there was only a handful who would have tried to shove her back?

Jack watched the helicopter lift away from the ground, kicking up Texas sand, churning it much like his emotions at the moment.

He'd seen Brooke's face as she'd talked to Rico's father, Arturo. More importantly, he'd seen her face and heard her voice when she'd run over to tell Carla that Arturo had asked her to accompany Rico to Amarillo.

She'd been happy. Nearly ecstatic. She seemed to be having trouble believing Arturo's request even as she was embracing the chance the man was giving her.

Good for her, Jack thought.

He meant it. He really did.

He viciously kicked a swell of sand created by the whirling copter blades and fought the urge to swear loudly.

His entire dammed trip to freakin' Honey Creek was about that woman being happy.

But once she was happy, adjusted and confident she wouldn't need him anymore.

Which was the whole point. Supposedly.

She'd have everything she needed.

Except...

Would she respond to another man the way she did to him? Would she let someone close enough to make her respond? And would that man appreciate what getting close meant? Would he understand that being in Brooke Donovan's bed meant he was truly special, someone she was willing to take a risk with and that he better live up to that?

Hell no.

Brooke needed to finally let go with someone who understood that she needed more from him than just a mind-blowing orgasm.

Not that she didn't need that too. She did. Badly.

Yeah, maybe his work here wasn't quite done after all.

"What the hell do you mean you're thinking about staying?"

Jack held his cell phone away from his ear slightly. His brother's reaction to his idea was expected, though the volume was a surprise.

"Why not?" he asked.

"Because that's ridiculous," David announced. "There's no reason."

"There's more to do. That only I can do."

"Well, of course there is," David said. "Superman never said, 'I think I'll let Batman take this one today'."

Jack rolled his eyes. The superhero comparisons got old sometimes.

"Seriously. I've done some good work here. I've built the clinic up, gained their trust…"

"No wonder you like it there," David interjected. His tone wasn't nasty, but it was definitely condescending. "So, you've found a place where you can be an even bigger hero than in the ER. These people actually know you and remember you. And you've realized that it makes you feel even more important, right? But are you sure you're ready for it to be more intimate? To know these people? What about the times when you can't save someone?"

"Having me back in the ER would probably make you feel better, huh, Dave?" Jack said sharply. "It would be easier to be assured that everyone was mentally balanced, no one was going to go crazy, right? In the ER, I'm at a distance. I don't get hurt."

His brother was quiet for a moment, and Jack tried to regret his harsh words. But dammit, this was about Brooke. And the fact that Jack was happier with her than he had been in as long as he could remember.

"You're right," David said quietly. "I don't like seeing the people I care about get hurt."

"Well, until I called you, I felt better than I have in a long time."

"Because you're assuaging your guilt. But when does it end? It sounds to me like *she's* doing well."

"Meaning I'm not?" Jack asked.

"You tell me."

The conversation was, thankfully, interrupted by a knock at the door.

Jack cradled the phone between his ear and shoulder, anticipating the taste of Vi's tangy spaghetti sauce and buttery garlic bread. But instead of Vi's teenage delivery boy, Brooke was standing in front of his motel room.

Every thought flew from his mind, except for the niggling reminder that his judgmental, psychiatrist brother was on the other end of the phone.

She gave him a shy smile and he forgot what he was about to say. Something like, *Hi. Could you come back later?* Or *I was just about to call you* or *Don't tell my brother that as soon as I hang up with him I'm going to start kissing you and I'm not sure I'm ever going to stop.*

"Hi," she said when he continued to fail to add anything into the silence.

"Hi," he managed.

"Can I come in?" she asked, stepping forward and over the threshold before any invitation was given.

He wondered if David could hear her voice. If he could, surely he could hear how adorable and vulnerable and sexy and seductive she was. How was he supposed to resist that? Whether he was subconsciously staying because of his hero complex and whether or not he believed he could save her or not, his subconscious was also reminding him of all his fantasies and the fact that blondes with green eyes were very much his type.

"Jack?" he heard his brother ask in his ear.

"Yeah?" he asked gruffly as he watched her look around his room with curiosity but without being nosy. It was cute the way she inspected everything, but refrained from touching—

"Jack!"

"What?" he asked sharply.

He turned his back to Brooke to shut out her distracting presence. It didn't work, of course. He was conscious of every noise she made as she moved about his room.

"I believe we were in the middle of a conversation," his brother said.

"I believe we were in the middle of a session," Jack corrected him. "And I think I've had enough."

"So you're going to stay anyway?" David asked. "In spite of the fact that it isn't good for you. Or for your life. Or your—"

"I don't know," Jack cut in. He didn't want to finish this

discussion at all. But he certainly didn't want to do it with Brooke, one of the direct subjects of said discussion, only a few feet away. Especially when he wanted to narrow that distance considerably.

When he turned to find her, she was standing next to his bedside table looking over his collection of CDs. It must have been seeing her so close to his bed because the heat, and the force with which it hit him, nearly made him drop the phone.

She was dressed in a white cotton sleeveless dress that was simple, almost plain. The neckline was slightly scooped but otherwise it was fairly formless as it fell to just above her knees.

It still made him hard.

In fact, there was nothing actually sexy about the summer dress or the flat leather sandals or the way she had her hair pulled up as always. Everything about her was cool and reserved.

But he knew there was heat there. For him. And that was a bigger turn-on than even skimpy black lace and red satin sheets.

In spite of everything David had said, and reminded Jack of, and tried to get Jack to accept and admit, Jack wanted Brooke. And it wasn't just for her sake. It was as much about him in that moment. It was his body that was heating and hardening and imagining all kinds of things that would likely shock Brooke Donovan down to the very soles of her sensible, arch-supported, water-resistant leather sandals.

He watched her pick up the copy of *Newsweek* he'd been thinking about reading. She flipped to the table of contents, then just as nonchalantly tossed it back on the table. She glanced over his collection of soda and microwave popcorn, yesterday's *San Antonio Times* and his laptop computer. She seemed restless. Yet, she was obviously content to occupy herself until he was available to talk. He took the chance to study her, giving David an occasional non-committal *uh-huh* so both David and Brooke would think he was still paying attention to the conversation.

She moved between him and the bedside table. The light from the lamp shone softly through the skirt of the dress silhouetting her legs and hips.

"Dave, I've got to go," Jack said, interrupting whatever it was that David had been in the middle of ranting in his ear.

"I really think—"

"Far too much, brother dear," Jack said.

Suddenly he felt lighter. Brooke was here now. She was in his motel room looking sexy in spite of herself and Jack was unconcerned about what brought her here—only about what she would be doing while she was here. "You know, Dave," Jack went on, completely, blissfully ignoring David's indignant response. "I think you made a good point tonight."

David was clearly skeptical when he asked, "What was that?"

Jack laughed and felt it down deep where it really counted. "That I should think about what's good for me for a change."

"Okay," David said slowly.

"I know you're concerned about my mental health, little brother."

David sighed. "Yes, I am."

"What if I told you I'd thought of something that would be a considerable boost to my mental health and general well-being."

"As long as it's legal..." David said carefully.

Jack laughed again. He could tell that Brooke was trying not to look like she was listening. But the conversation had to be curious hearing only his end.

"Oh, it's legal."

"Is it addictive?" David asked.

"Likely," Jack answered truthfully.

"Jack—"

"As I said, I've gotta go."

"Okay." David paused.

"See ya." Jack was sure his affection was clear in his voice. Even if David did, ironically, drive him crazy, he cared a lot about his brother.

He was still watching Brooke as he hung up the phone. She was another person who drove him crazy. Though it was admittedly a different type of crazy.

And it was one he intended to do something about. Right now.

Brooke turned from looking over the short stack of novels on Jack's dresser as she heard him disconnect the phone call she'd been trying so hard not to listen to. It would have probably been polite to leave and tell him to call her when he had a moment to talk, but she didn't want to leave. She'd spent a great deal of time over the past few years being polite. She figured she was due for a bit of rudeness.

"Did you have these sent to you?" As she met his eyes, she completely forgot the question she'd just asked. He was watching her intently, one corner of his mouth curved into a smile, looking very pleased with himself. She raised her eyebrows quizzically. "You okay?"

He put his phone on the table next to the room phone, but he never took his eyes from her. "Absolutely."

She gestured toward his cell phone. "Everything okay at

home?"

"Yes."

He started toward her and her pulse sped up.

"Work? The hospital?" she asked, watching him approach. She licked her lips and prepared herself for what she sensed was about to happen.

"Fine. It's all fine."

He stopped in front of her and she tipped her head back to meet his gaze. His eyes traveled over her face as he stood so close that every cell in her body seemed tuned in to every thump of his heart. The heightened energy inside her was making her skin buzz with anticipation and it seemed that she could feel his body temperature rising.

"So, every—" She stopped and cleared her throat. "So everything is fine."

"Actually, no."

She blinked up at him. "No?"

"You look too perfect." He gently grasped either side of her head, unclasped the clip that held her hair up and then combed her hair out through his fingers until it settled softly against her shoulders. "I want your hair all messed up. Your perfect lipstick too. I want to put some wrinkles in that dress and some whisker burns on that perfect skin. In a variety of places."

She felt her eyes widen. Wow. She swallowed with some difficulty as all of those places, from her lips to her thighs, heated. "I came over here to tell you about Rico," she said.

"You can tell me about him later. Right now I need you naked."

Okay, *this* was why she'd come over here. She had intended to fill him in on Rico too, but yeah, getting naked had been part of the plan. Jack had been on her mind during the entire drive back from Amarillo, during her shower, as she'd gotten dressed and driven over here. She was here on purpose, to be with him. She'd come to him.

Yes, there was the risk that someone would find out, but she couldn't stay away any longer. She wanted him and he made her feel—among many other things—safe. She didn't have to suppress her desire or her true instincts with him. In fact, Jack encouraged her to be, say and do whatever she wanted. And she was going to. Right now.

"No foreplay?" she teased as she kicked her sandals off.

"We've been involved in foreplay since I set foot in this town," he said. "You want me as badly as I want you."

He had a point.

"Oh, good. I was afraid you were going to spend a bunch of time with kissing and stuff."

He gave her a lazy smile. "In fact, I'm guessing you're wet for me right now without me doing anything more than this." He ran his hand down her shoulder to her low back, nudging her closer.

He was cocky...but he was right. Completely right. She tipped her head to the side and looked up at him. "You know how you keep asking me what I need?"

"Yeah."

"You. I need you."

Heat flared in his eyes and he pulled in a deep breath through his nose. "Go wild, Brooke. Whatever you want. I'm here and I'm all yours for as long as you want me."

A surge of feminine power washed over her and once again she had a flicker of understanding for what may have drawn her mother to her lifestyle. Well, okay, not entirely, but having a man like Jack Silver willing to do whatever she wanted could be addicting.

The best part was that she didn't feel slutty—even contemplating all of the things she wanted to do to and with him. She felt wanted, desired, beautiful, confident and...as if she was exactly where she was supposed to be.

She wasn't going to waste a second of this.

She stepped back until he was just beyond arm's reach. "Take off your clothes."

He paused, then gave her a smile and began freeing the buttons on his shirt.

She backed up and sat on the edge of the bed, crossed her legs, leaned back bracing her hands on the mattress and said, "And take your time, sugar. I want to savor this."

"I'll give you something to savor," he growled and didn't slow a bit. He stripped the shirt off and pulled the soft gray shirt underneath over his head, tossing them both away.

Brooke let her eyes roam over him hungrily. He was perfect. Defined muscles, light hair dusting his chest and stomach, smooth tan skin. She licked her lips.

He watched her intently as his hands went to his fly, pulling the button open and lowering the zipper. It was clear that he was as aroused as she was and she felt her chest grow tight anticipating seeing all of him for the first time. The denim parted and slid over his hips then dropped to the floor. He kicked the jeans out of the way but her eyes were riveted on the white cotton briefs and the amazing length of the bulge they contained.

Then he dropped them too and she had to take a deep breath.

She finally lifted her gaze to his. He was just watching her. "Now what, *sugar*?" he asked.

She knew exactly what she wanted. She'd been with a handful of men but she'd never been free to explore, free to follow her urges, free to use him to satisfy all of her curiosity and desires.

With Jack she felt free. No guilt, no consequences, no fears. She stood. "Sit down."

He raised an eyebrow but followed her direction, taking a seat on the edge of the bed. "Your turn. I need a little more skin from you."

"Not yet."

His cock stood straight up, ready for her, and she knew which urge she was going with first. She wasn't undressing right now. Instead, she went to her knees in front of him and ran her hands up his thighs. He shuddered. "Brooke..."

"This is what I need, Jack." She studied his cock—the color, the shape. She hadn't had a chance to really take her time like this with anyone before, and she was enjoying being up close and personal.

"I don't—"

She leaned in and licked the tip.

Jack swore, his hips jerking. She looked up at him. The expression on his face was almost pained. But she knew better. She did it again, taking more time, running her tongue around the tip and then sucking slightly.

He groaned and his hand came up to cup the back of her head. She took more of him in, running her tongue down the front surface, sucking as she came back up.

"Brooke, God, I can't—"

She wasn't listening to him. He could and he would. He was here for her. He'd said so. And she wasn't nearly done with him yet.

She wrapped her hand around the base of his shaft, sliding up and down, watching his face. He was breathing raggedly, one hand still on her head, the other fisted in the bed's comforter.

Eyes on his, she slid her hand down and cupped his balls. He stared into her eyes as his hips lifted and his breath escaped with a hiss.

Oh yeah, she loved this. She took him in her mouth again, moving her hand and her tongue, making him moan. Finally she lifted her head. He looked like he was having a hard time sitting still. But he was doing it. For her.

"Don't move," she told him. She got to her feet and reached back for the dress's zipper.

She felt the touch of the room's air as the fabric separated over her shoulder blades then fell forward from her shoulders and down to her waist.

The heat in Jack's eyes made her heart pound as he looked at her. He didn't say anything and definitely didn't seem to be in a hurry. She glanced down, wondering what he found so fascinating.

She blushed as she realized that a white bra wasn't very sexy. She had on white panties too. But Jack didn't seem to care. He was watching her as if he had never seen anything so beautiful. Her nipples responded, tightening and straining against the silky cups. She wasn't as ample as her mother, but she was far from flat-chested.

She wiggled her hips and the dress fell to the floor.

He sucked in a quick breath and she smiled. The panties had lace and were high cut on the legs, but they dipped below her belly button and were simple white satin.

"Brooke," he said hoarsely.

"Yes?" she asked.

"Come here."

The bra hooked in the front and she undid the clasp as she put a knee on the mattress beside his thigh. He was watching raptly as she peeled back first one cup, then the other. He seemed to hold his breath as she slipped the thin straps from her shoulders and dropped the bra on the floor. Then she braced a hand on his hard stomach, lifting her other knee onto the mattress and sliding up until she straddled his hips.

Lord, she didn't even bat an eye, Jack thought. She just climbed on. In this position, without panties in the way one good thrust would have embedded him fully right where he was aching to be.

"You're gorgeous," he told her before letting his eyes drop and fully drink in the sight of her bare breasts.

She just let him stare too. There was no uncomfortable shifting or trying to cover up or blushing. She just watched him watch her.

He didn't realize she'd been holding her weight up off of him with her legs until she relaxed and her pelvis settled fully on his. They both groaned as her soft, hot center met his hard flesh.

That was it. Enough playing around. He wrapped his arms around her to keep her where he wanted her, then took one of those teasing little nipples into his mouth. He reveled in her surprised gasp, which turned to an aroused moan as his tongue ran over and over the turgid tip.

His thumb mimicked his tongue's actions on her other nipple and her head fell back. He felt her hair brush the back of the hand he had splayed between her shoulder blades, supporting her body against his mouth.

"Jack," she whispered and her voice caught on what sounded like a sob.

He took in her flushed skin, the dazed look she gave him and her panting breaths and knew he couldn't wait much longer.

He wanted her wild and wanton, begging for release. She was getting close.

He separated his knees slightly, bringing her thighs apart enough that his hand could reach between them.

The silk of her panties was hot, her response to him obvious and enough to make him grow harder, nearly to the point of pain.

He watched her face as he traced a finger along the edge of the panties that rested against her left cheek. She was holding her breath, but also his gaze. She watched him, unabashedly, shuddering as his hand moved closer to her wet heat.

He steadily pressed his finger inward and as his finger slid into her silkiness she let out the breath and shifted her hips, drawing him deeper.

Damn.

She rocked her pelvis against his hand, wordlessly asking for more.

Gladly.

He caught her mouth in a kiss that quickly turned carnal as he stroked her intimately, harder and faster, following her body language. She gripped his shoulders and lifted herself, then lowered her hips again against his hand. She repeated the motion and he ripped his mouth from hers. He wanted to watch her orgasm.

Instead she surprised him again by reaching for his erection and pressing toward it.

"Move your hand," she said through gritted teeth.

He didn't. "You still have panties on."

"Don't care." She stroked him and he groaned.

"Condom," he managed, pointing toward the bedside table.

"Birth control for cramps," she said.

That worked for him. He withdrew his fingers and she immediately sank down on his cock, taking him deep.

They gasped together and paused, just feeling, adjusting, soaking it all in.

"Lie back," she instructed.

He did, propping on his elbows, the shift causing him to surge deeper.

"Like that," she breathed. Then she moved.

She lifted and lowered herself on him again. The sight was erotic to say the least. Her hair was free, her lipstick definitely smudged, her breasts bounced as she moved and her body held him in a tight, hot glove that seemed to be trying to pull everything from him at once.

He concentrated on breathing and fighting the urge to thrust. He let her ride him, loving that she was taking charge, loving the look on her face. She set the pace and he just held on, relishing every slide and glide. The friction was perfect, the heat was amazing, the fit like it was custom-made.

Heaven.

He held back from arching up into her, but barely. He let her dictate the rhythm until she moaned, "Jack," and he knew she needed more.

With one hand he pulled her panties out of the way and with the other took her hand and guided it to her clit. "Right here, honey." Her middle finger pressed and circled above where their bodies were joined and her breathing grew more ragged.

"Just like that, Brooke. I want to feel you come." How he was holding on, he had no idea, but it mattered. He wanted her to let go on him, with him.

"I need you Jack. Do...something."

He smiled in spite of the tension that had his entire body wound tight. He arched slightly.

"More. Of. That," she breathed. She lifted her hand to her breast, circling the nipple.

"If you keep doing more of that," he said.

She focused on his face with a sexy smile. She tugged on her nipple and pressed on her clit. He thrust up again and they both groaned.

"I want..."

"I know." He gripped her hips, thrust up into her deep and perfectly.

"Yes. More."

He wanted to go forever but after six more thrusts they were already thundering toward the intense climaxes that swept over them a moment later.

When he slumped back he took her with him, her cheek against his chest.

They lay unmoving for several minutes.

Jack wondered if she'd fallen asleep, but as he stroked his hands down her back, she lifted her head and gave him a languid smile.

"So, you really are good at everything."

Surprised, he laughed. "I think that was more you than me."

"Hmm." She stretched and rolled to the side, reminding him of a contented cat who'd just been scratched under the chin. "Well, I'm no expert, but I can't see much room for improvement. That was awesome."

He grinned. She was as blatant in her appreciation as she had been in seeking pleasure.

She rolled to the edge of the bed and got to her feet as he sat up and watched her retrieve her bra. He appreciated the view as she adjusted her breasts in the cups before she stepped into her dress and turned to him, lifting her hair. "Could you zip me up?" she asked.

He stood and pulled the zipper up before truly registering she was now dressed. The exact opposite of how he'd intended to keep her all night.

"You better tell me you're going out for food," he said, keeping his voice mild.

She slipped on a shoe and laughed lightly. "No, I'm going home."

"Because you want to see if we're as good in your bed?" he asked, frowning deeply as he waited for her answer. That he was sure he was going to hate.

She smiled and shook her head. "It's after ten."

"What is going on?" he demanded. "You're leaving?"

She glanced at the clock next to the bed. "It's late. I need to go."

"Or your car turns back into a pumpkin?"

She slipped on her other shoe. "People will notice and talk."

"About what?"

"Us, and the fact that my car was here all night."

He ripped the sheet from the bed, not willing to fight with her while he was naked. He wrapped the sheet around his waist, tucked it securely and crossed his arms. "And what would they say?"

"That I spent the night," she said impatiently.

"And if you did spend the night, that would be true."

"And they would assume we slept together."

"Which we did—whether your car stays here all night or not."

She smiled a little sadly and reached up to touch his cheek. "Tonight was perfect. I'm happy for the first time in a really long time. Traditionally, Honey Creek ruins perfect and happy for me. I just don't want to share this with them. Not tonight. I can't risk it."

He caught her hand and pressed his lips to her palm. She sucked in a quick breath.

"Share it with me."

She rose up on tiptoe and kissed him firmly on the mouth. "Goodnight, Jack."

Then she was gone and he had to wonder, as he stared at his empty room and even emptier bed, if this was how Prince Charming had felt when he was left holding only a glass slipper and a memory.

Brooke glared at the dome light that came on, like a spotlight, as she unlocked her car. She rushed to get in and slam the door to shut if off. Once the interior was dark again she allowed herself one long, deep breath.

She'd managed to get out of Jack's room without blurting, *I love you.*

She leaned forward and rested her forehead on the top of the steering wheel.

It had been close. Really close. And how could she not love him?

But she couldn't tell him.

He had blown into her life like a refreshing breeze… Brooke frowned at the metaphor. He'd actually blown in like a tornado. But he'd come suddenly and she had no reason to believe he wouldn't leave just as suddenly.

Which would really be for the best. She had a crush on him because he made her feel things she'd never felt before. It was just simple infatuation. If she let herself act on it—well, beyond the actions she'd taken a little while ago in his room—she would look and feel ridiculous when he reminded her he was only here to help her out temporarily. And he'd helped her all right. He'd restored her belief that she really was still a woman, in every sense of the word.

And honestly—and in the dark solitude of her car she could be honest—that was what it boiled down to. Jack was the first man to make her feel lovable. So, she'd transferred that delight back to him and convinced herself that she loved him.

Brooke started the car and pulled out of the parking spot slowly, satisfied that she'd solved the mystery behind her sudden need to confess undying devotion to him.

She looked up and down the street carefully, praying that no one would see her, because, as she'd told Jack, she wasn't about to share the most special night of her life with the gossips in Honey Creek.

Chapter Seven

It was amazing to Brooke how fast a lot of money could get things done.

The pounding and banging started right at eight a.m. the next day.

She walked into the clinic waiting area and found Carla and Jack at the window. She calmly started restacking the magazines on the coffee table. The noise got Jack's attention and he turned. She pretended to not notice the way his eyes widened as they traveled over her new attire. She'd expected him to take note.

She hadn't, however, expected him to take so much time at it.

Her body reacted to his perusal as if his was physically touching her.

Though she kept her eyes on her task, she was very aware of how much leg showed beneath her short floral-print skirt and the strip of stomach that peeked between the waistband of the skirt and the hem of the sleeveless fitted yellow top as she moved.

She'd even taken time to paint her toenails a bright pink so she could wear the white leather sandals she'd retrieved from the shoebox on the top shelf in her closet. Not for Jack, she told herself. Sandals simply required toenail polish.

"I like where this is going so far," he said.

She smiled and straightened. "Good. This is just an estimate for now," she said, handing him a piece of paper. "I'll get you the actual bills when they come in."

He opened the paper and looked at the estimated costs for the redecorating. It was exorbitant.

She waited for him to comment.

"Looks good," he said. "But I don't see the cost of your new clothes here." His eyes dropped to the expanse of bare leg. "Because I'd gladly pay for that skirt."

He was impossible. And so was her reaction to him. Because she couldn't keep showing up in his motel room to scratch the itches he was creating. She also couldn't take him into her office and straddle him in her chair. At least she shouldn't do that. Probably.

Hoping her face wasn't giving away every emotion, she flipped her hair and her skirt as she moved around him. "I already had these clothes."

"You did?"

His question, and the amazed tone of his voice, stopped her. She turned back.

"These were in my closet."

He surveyed the outfit again. "I would have never guessed."

"I'm full of surprises, Dr. Silver." She really didn't mean it to sound as flirtatious as it did. At least, she hadn't done it consciously.

His eyes were back on her face in an instant. "I'm aware."

And just like that she flashed back to the night before and being on her knees in front of him. She resisted the urge to fan herself.

"Ms. Donovan?" a man called from the front door,

interrupting them. “We’re ready to hang the sign.”

Carla looked at her from the front counter. “The sign?”

“The new clinic sign, of course,” Brooke said flippantly.

Carla rolled her eyes again and sighed.

“I think I’ll go help with that,” Jack said.

“You’re going to help hang the sign?” Brooke asked.

“Oh, I’m very supportive of this whole idea. I want to do my part.”

He headed outside and she shook her head. Whatever.

Five minutes later, *whatever* turned into a definite something.

“Brooke! Hey! I need some help out here!”

Brooke and Carla both ran toward Jack’s voice. “What’s going...” Brooke rushed to Jack’s side. He was cradling his forearm against his stomach, the blood already soaking into his shirt. “Jack...”

“Get him,” he said, motioning with his head.

She turned and saw Carla kneeling next to one of the workers. He was lying on the ground next to the ladder, groaning and holding his shoulder.

“What happened?” Brooke asked as she helped Jack to his feet and they both jogged to the other man. The man had already sat up, but was holding his arm in a strange position.

“The sign slipped and grazed my arm, I jerked my end, made his ladder wobble and he fell,” Jack explained quickly.

“Grazed?” Brooke asked, looking pointedly at the huge bloodstain.

“It’s fine. Check him out.”

“I am,” she muttered as she felt around the man’s shoulder. “What’s your name?” she asked.

"Greg."

"Greg, try to relax a little and let me have your arm here."

He grimaced and sucked in a sharp breath when she tried to move his arm across his body. She could feel the ball of his joint more forward than it should be and her heartbeat sped up.

"Damn, it's dislocated."

"Damn," Jack agreed. "Okay, get him up."

"Let me at least look at your arm," Brooke said as she and Carla assisted the man up from the ground. She looked at her patient sharply when he leaned into her suddenly. He was pale and breathing shallowly.

"He's likely to go into shock. Don't worry about me."

"Get some ice on it at least. Elevate it. Slow the bleeding somehow," she instructed as they helped Greg into the clinic.

"Okay, Greg, we're going to help you lie down and Carla's going to give you something for the pain and a muscle relaxant."

Once the man was on the table and Carla had gone to get the medications, Brooke looked at Jack. "I have to stitch you up so you can reduce his shoulder," she said softly. Reducing a dislocation was a painful maneuver.

"I can't reduce it with stitches. You'll have to do it."

She glanced at Greg, who was lying with his eyes shut, moaning softly from time to time. "I've never done it before. I don't know if I can. I might not be strong enough..."

"Brooke," Jack broke in firmly. "Look at me."

She did, reluctantly.

"You have to do it. There's no other option. You'll be fine."

That helped. A little. Just trying to reduce the dislocation would be extremely painful and it was possible that the pain would be for nothing if she wasn't able to pull hard enough or correctly. If she didn't do it just right, she could injure him further. Butterflies kicked up in her stomach.

"I don't think he can wait. He's already faint. Check his pulse."

She did on both sides to compare and then turned worried eyes to Jack. "It's diminished on the left. And his fingers are cold."

"Then you have to do this, now."

She quickly checked Greg's sensation by pricking him slightly along the arm and hand with the tip of a paperclip. He reported that his sensation was equal on both sides.

"I should do an X-ray," she said to Jack.

"Quit stalling. You know what's wrong with him."

"Fine," she said crossly, wrenching a long bedsheet from one of the drawers to use in the maneuver.

Jack instructed them on what would happen. They looped a long bed sheet around Greg's torso and under his arm and Carla pulled on the ends, putting most of her weight behind it to hold his trunk in place. Brooke grasped his wrist, said a little prayer and slowly started pulling.

"That's it, easy does it," Jack coached softly from just behind her right shoulder.

She liked having him there. He steadied her. And she knew that if something went wrong, gaping wound or not, Jack would jump in to save her...and Greg.

"Keep balanced," Jack told her. "You'll feel it. You're doing fine."

Greg groaned, but the medications were helping and he mostly just gritted his teeth. Carla was doing the same thing.

Finally, after what seemed three lifetimes, Brooke felt the

joint shift and slide back into place. Greg gasped, but then quickly drew a deep long breath. As did Brooke. She let off the pressure and then helped Carla take the sheet off.

"Get him ready to X-ray. I want to be sure the joint looks good," Jack said. He bumped Brooke gently in the back with his elbow. "Good job."

"Thanks." She smiled at him, relief making her a little light-headed herself. "You're a good coach."

Then their attention was back on Greg. "We'll put you in a sling and give you some more pain medication for today, but we need to get you to Amarillo to see an orthopedist to make sure there's no soft tissue damage."

He nodded his understanding as Brooke once again checked his pulses, sensation and then asked him to move his arm. It moved much easier through the range of motion, though it was still painful, and the pulses in his wrists were equal right to left.

"Now, let's look at your hand," she said to Jack and led him into the next treatment room.

He seemed hesitant.

"What's the matter?" she asked. "You don't trust me?" She said it with a joking tone, but part of her feared it was true. What if he didn't want her to stitch his hand? He'd trusted her to reduce Greg's shoulder. Surely he wouldn't...

"It's my forearm, not my hand. And I might need you to look at my shoulder too," he finally said, a bit sheepishly.

"What happened?"

"I fell off my ladder too."

She sighed and moved to the cabinets where the supplies she needed were stored. "That's why you should let the experts hang the signs up, Dr. Silver. What are you going to do without an arm to work with?"

"Let you take over."

She glanced over her shoulder at him. "What?"

He shrugged. "You could do it. It would show everyone that you're more than capable."

Brooke flushed at the compliment and turned to face him fully. "Was this some kind of plan of yours when you went out there today?"

His eyes widened. "You think I got hurt on purpose?"

She tipped her head to the side. "I don't know. Did you?"

"Hey, I'm dedicated to helping you out, but come on. This hurts. I could have tendon or nerve damage."

She walked over, took his middle finger between her thumb and forefinger and squeezed hard.

"Ow!" He jerked his hand back, and then moaned when the pain of the quick motion registered.

"Sensation is intact," she said calmly.

"I said I *could* have nerve damage," he said with a frown. "What I meant was that it would have been a risky thing to do just to prove this point to Honey Creek."

She accepted that without comment. "Let me see it," she told him, the supplies ready.

He pulled his hand away from his stomach and she began wiping the blood away. The gash went fairly deep into the tissue of his arm, just above the wrist, but the muscle was intact. The edges would be easily approximated with a few stitches and should heal quickly.

"You're going to be fine." There was no need for her to take over in the clinic. Thank goodness.

The irony wasn't missed on her either. She'd spent the last

few weeks resenting Jack's presence and his tendency to take over. Now she was unnerved to think about not having him able to step in.

This was not good.

He wasn't going to stay forever.

"Put pressure on it," she instructed, placing a large pad over the injury and pressing down harder than was medically necessary.

It was good that he wasn't going to stay, she reminded herself. That had been the plan all along.

But it wasn't good that she was starting to care about the patients, was feeling more confident, and was excited about the new paint.

Dammit. This was all Jack's fault.

The plan had been to just get through the next several months, not caring about the town, not getting attached to anyone, not doing anything spectacular so that when it was over she could move on with her pride intact and no regrets.

He had certainly never been part of her plan.

How dare he come in here and make her paint, make her like cappuccino, coach her in medical techniques that made her feel confident and show her what this clinic could actually mean to her?

Not to mention the sex. How dare he show her how good that could be too?

"Hey," he protested as she pressed even harder.

She pulled her hand back and moved quickly to the exam room door and yanked it open. "Carla!" she hollered.

"Yeah?"

"How's Greg?"

"Dozing."

"Then come in here and suture Jack's arm."

She could not hold Jack's hand, even if it was to put sutures in.

"You okay?" he asked.

"Of course," she said breezily. "Carla's just better at sutures. She does all that cross-stitching and stuff. I can't even sew on a button."

It wasn't very mature or professional of her to turn a patient over because she was falling in love with him, but right then all that mattered was getting some distance between her and Jack.

It was simply the biggest bow she'd ever seen. And it was red. The satin loops were the very definition of red...and big.

The ribbon wrapped around her office door as if it were a gift-box top. The center of the bow was actually wider than the door and stuck out from the surface nearly half a foot.

The note read simply, "I noticed you forgot to redo this room."

Obviously, Jack had something to do with it. Which made her contemplate opening the door with trepidation. Which was why she had been standing in front of the door, staring at the mammoth piece of satin for almost two full minutes, dumbfounded.

Finally, she reached out, as if reaching for a snake, and twisted the doorknob releasing the latch. She hesitantly pushed the bottom of the door with the toe of her shoe. It swung open and she paused another second before she stepped across the threshold.

And froze.

She felt like Alice must have after falling down the rabbit hole.

It was a different world on the other side of her office door.

The previously white walls were now a soft sea-foam green. Two high-backed wing chairs in deep turquoise and sapphire fabric sat on either side of a small, round glass-topped table. The two large windows were covered with wispy opaque draperies and the thin vertical blinds behind them blocked most of the sunlight, giving the room a calm, shaded look. The flat gray carpet had been replaced by a light, polished wood floor, and the center of the room was covered with a muted aqua-colored rug. The chair behind the new large oak desk was now covered in a peacock-blue fabric and a silver lamp with an opaque shade rested on the corner of the desk. The most astonishing addition to the room, however, was the collection of lush green ferns in heavy ceramic pots that circled the base of a babbling fountain.

Yes, a fountain.

It wasn't huge, but it filled the corner of the room near the windows. The base was a stone pool and a pump circulated the water from the cistern to the top of the four-tiered groupings of blue and turquoise polished stones. As the water tumbled over the rocks, Brooke found herself breathing deeply.

The entire effect was soothing, in spite of her whirling thoughts and confusion.

She felt strangely refreshed in here. In fact, she might never leave. She could easily hide herself away in this little haven.

Except that it was from Jack.

That was completely inappropriate...and completely tempting. Just like Jack himself.

She reluctantly left the office she knew she would have to un-decorate as soon as possible. The pale bare walls, gray carpet and thirty-year-old office furniture would have to do.

But she really did like that fountain.

When she got to the front desk, Carla looked up with happy expectation. Brooke's heart sank. How could Carla not see how ridiculous this all was?

Brooke sighed. This was so over the top she wasn't sure where to even begin.

"I need to see him," she told Carla simply.

Brooke had her elbows propped on the edge of her desk and was rubbing her forehead with the pads of her fingers when Jack's voice in her doorway made her jerk her head upright.

"The only way you're getting this office back to the way it was is if you're going to ruin your manicure and redo it yourself."

He strolled into her office, as if he had every right and reason to be there.

"And you really should wear your hair down," he added.

Before she could stop it, her hand flew up to touch the gold clip that was holding the large twist of hair on top of her head.

"And you really need to knock."

Jack didn't seem to take her irritation too seriously.

"This turned out nicely," he said casually, turning a full three-hundred-and-sixty-degree circle. He stopped when he faced her again. "What do you think of it?"

"It's beautiful," she admitted. "But, of course, I can't accept it."

"It's an investment in the clinic that I'm now a part of."

Her eyes narrowed. "You'd better explain that."

"Giving you an office where you can relax a little, get some real quality work done, feel a little inspired, makes the clinic as a whole better. It will benefit you and your patients."

"Are you implying that I'm not usually in a good mood?"

"Let's just say that I don't think it hurts to take every precaution against bad moods," he said tactfully.

She raised one eyebrow at him but didn't comment on him skirting the issue of her personal moods. Not that he would know about her moods anyway—she'd been avoiding him rather effectively for the past two days.

She knew he wasn't happy about it. He had been trying to corner her but she made sure someone was always with her so he couldn't catch her alone. She never went into her office—which made redecorating it rather easy, she supposed. And she didn't go home until late at night. In fact, she'd been spending some time at her mom's house. It was still fully furnished. Dixie had just packed a bag and left town. She hadn't wanted anything around her that would remind her of Walter—which was pretty much everything she owned at that point. So Brooke was hanging out in her old bedroom until it was dark and she was sure that Jack had given up trying to find her.

It was a chicken way to handle how she felt about him, but, well, she could live with that more easily than she could live with begging him to stay, or watching him leave.

"Anyway, it's not exactly something you can just give back," he said. "It's done. It's yours. You're welcome."

Her eyes widened at that. "Which actually brings up a very good point. Perhaps you should have asked me before you had my office redone. You basically defaced my property."

He laughed. "I don't think there is a single judge in this entire country who would agree that taking drab white walls and gray carpet and turning it into this—" he swept his arms wide, "—would qualify as defacing."

She sighed. It was hard to ignore the fact that she'd had sex with him—amazing sex that she wanted again—just three days ago when he laughed. Or smiled. Or breathed.

"I'm just saying that it would have been appropriate to ask."

He shrugged. "You usually say no when I ask you things."

"I do not." But she did. Except... "I didn't say no when you asked me to take my clothes off the other night."

She *really* wasn't very good at ignoring the fact that she'd had sex with him.

"Oh, you *do* remember the other night," he said dryly, coming around to sit in the chair in front of her desk.

"Yes, I do." In vivid, Technicolor detail.

"You haven't mentioned it, so I wasn't sure."

She narrowed her eyes. Was his ego bruised because she hadn't been begging on his doorstep again? Well, she wasn't going to tell him that the thought occurred to her pretty much hourly. "When did you think I would mention it? When you were swabbing Jerry Lader's throat for strep or when I was checking on Molly Hanney's rash? Or maybe I should have mentioned it when Amy was bringing you the brownies from Sharon Pearson or when Amy ran out to get you more ball point pens or when Amy—"

"Okay," he cut in. "Amy's got a little crush on me."

"And is very sensitive to what's going on with you. I can't let on that anything happened between us or it will be all over town."

"So?" he asked, scowling.

"I already explained this to you," she said. "If you can't respect that then it will never happen again." It really shouldn't happen again anyway.

"It's already not happening again."

She rolled her eyes but was pleased that he wanted more as much as she did. "You can't go three days?"

"Without you? After the other night? No," he said firmly. "It's making me crazy."

"Obviously," she said, gesturing to her new office.

He sat forward in his chair. "Go out with me."

"Out with you where?" They could have sex in her mom's house. No one would see them there...

"Anywhere. On a date."

She frowned even as her heart thudded in her chest. "A date?"

"Yes. Dinner, movies, a show, a walk, whatever."

She wanted to so much. "I can't."

"But then we'll be dating, that's different than just sleeping together, right? More respectable and all that."

She shook her head. She wanted to date him, but she was already half in love with him. And he was leaving.

It was all a really bad idea.

"I can't. I know I started it and you feel like I'm not finishing it but—"

"Dammit." He pushed himself up out of the chair. "It's not about getting laid. I want to spend time with you outside of this clinic. I want you to feel good. I want you to—"

"Be happy," she filled in. "Yeah, I've heard this a time or two."

He leaned onto his hands on her desk and looked into her eyes. "Tell me I don't make you happy, Brooke. Tell me and I'll drop it and not ask you again."

She stared up at him, knowing she'd never be able to lie about this.

"You do make me happy, Jack."

His eyes never left her face as he said, "Ever since I did CPR on my mother to keep her alive when she purposely overdosed on pain medication after my dad died, I've been into saving people."

She blinked at him. Where had that come from?

"I think you should know that about me," he said. "You should also know that I have a tendency to overreact, I'm incredibly stubborn—"

Like she didn't already know those two things. A certain ridiculous check came to mind. Not to mention the fountain currently gurgling away in the corner.

"—and I want you more than I've ever wanted anyone," he finished. "All in all that means you're going to have a hell of time getting rid of me. Consider that fair warning."

She wet her lips and nodded. Nothing about any of this was really fair, but what the hell? She was happy.

Then she took a guess that was based solely on a gut instinct. "You don't limit yourself to giving medical care in the ER, do you?"

"I've been known to help people find housing, work, given them clothes, money..."

"I'm not surprised," she said softly.

"You're not?" He looked calm on the outside, but she could see the emotions swirling in his eyes.

She felt the corner of her mouth tip up and she looked over

at the fountain he'd given her. "You certainly strike me as the type to go above and beyond."

He followed her eyes and she was relieved to see a small smile touch his lips as well. "You don't think it's nuts?"

The other corner of her mouth turned up. "Yes," she admitted. "But hey, join the club. I turned down two hundred and fifty thousand dollars to stay in a town I hate."

He pushed away from her desk with a smile. "You don't hate it here."

Well, hate was pretty strong...

"I'd rather be here than...at the North Pole without a coat in January," she conceded.

"Ah, see, you're coming around to Honey Creek." Then, "Are you coming around to going out with me?"

She shook her head. He was leaving Honey Creek. Of course, she could be back in San Antonio in a few months and they could...

"But you're keeping the fountain." It wasn't really a question.

It was important to him, and damn but making him happy seemed to be kind of important to her too. She sighed and nodded. "Yes."

And why not? Falling in love with Jack was far more ridiculous than having a fountain in her office, and she'd done that.

Saturday was beautiful. As was the Hilton Hotel.

This was going to do her a world of good, Brooke was sure. Carla's idea of getting away from Honey Creek on a shopping spree was going to save Brooke's sanity. Not just getting out of town and away from the clinic, but also getting away from Jack and the nagging feeling that she'd always regret saying no to dating him. She'd been preoccupied for two days wondering what that date would have been like.

And he hadn't asked again. She'd kind of hoped to have him try to convince her.

Yeah, she needed to get away.

She didn't see Carla as she walked into the hotel lobby where they were meeting for lunch and wondered if she should go into the restaurant or wait at the front.

A glass of iced tea sounded really good, though.

She turned a full three hundred and sixty degrees. If she could find the restaurant. She approached the front desk.

"Excuse me? Can you tell me where the restaurant is?"

The tall man behind the desk smiled. "I'm sorry, we don't have a restaurant, ma'am."

"Oh, I—"

"Are you Brooke Donovan?" the man asked.

Startled, her eyes widened slightly. "Yes, I am."

"I was asked to give this to you," the man said.

She took the red envelope hesitantly.

"Who is it from?"

"The party you are meeting here."

"What is it?"

The man gave her a smile. "I think it opens at the top."

Feeling silly for being so reluctant, she gave him a half smile and tore the envelope open. She wasn't good with surprises. But she was a grown-up. Carla was probably just telling her where they were meeting since the hotel didn't have a restaurant after all.

She recognized the handwriting immediately—and the little flip of her heart.

Go to room 526. Trust me.

A room key card was included in the envelope.

Brooke recovered from her surprise fairly quickly, but she couldn't decide. A hotel room with Jack? A weekend rendezvous? Was this a good idea? He thought it would be this easy to get her alone in a bedroom? Of course, it was a bedroom far from Honey Creek.

It took her two seconds to decide.

"Which way is the elevator?"

The man pointed behind her to the left.

Her heart was pounding as she stepped off on the fifth floor a few minutes later.

She couldn't have described the other people who rode up on the elevator with her if the survival of the world depended on it. She was going to see Jack today. Away from Honey Creek and the clinic, away from the pressures, and the busybodies and the expectations and the past.

He hadn't given up. He wanted her and he'd found a way.

She felt...giddy. It was a strange word for her, but it fit.

Smiling wider than she had in a long time, she inserted the key card and pushed the door open.

The room was empty.

No Jack. No champagne. No path of rose petals leading to the bed.

Just a huge piece of paper in the middle of the bedspread.

Big black letters read, *Go to the closet.*

Clutching the note tightly in her fist, she twirled toward the closet and pulled open the door.

A sexy little black dress hung in the center of the rod with black high heels on the floor under it. There was a note attached to the hanger.

Get dressed. I'll pick you up in an hour.

Her hand was trembling as she reached out and touched the silky fabric of the dress. It would feel amazing on her body. She pulled the hanger from the closet bar, wanting to see it closer. Then she noticed another note pinned to the back straps of the dress.

Quit worrying. This is amazing.

A big smiley face with its tongue sticking out took the place of a signature, but she knew the note was from Carla. She'd helped Jack plan this whole thing.

Brooke held the dress up in front of her in the mirror on the inside of the closet. Her eyes filled a bit at the thought of her friend's part in it all. And the thought calmed her. Carla thought this was a good idea. It was romantic and sweet...and fun. She thought again of the word "giddy". It felt strange...but good. Or at least like she could get used to it.

She wanted to laugh and yell and cry all at once. She wanted to run straight to Jack, while at the same time, running fast and far from him. She was completely overwhelmed and she loved and hated the feeling at the same time.

She replaced the dress and stepped back from the closet with her hand over her heart.

Wow. This reaction was just from him buying her some new clothes. Imagine what she would feel when they were actually together.

She could say no. Or say nothing at all. She could just go downstairs, get in her car and go back to Honey Creek. Or she could wait until Jack came upstairs to pick her up and then tell him that there was no way they were going on a date together.

She eyed the black dress again. It was a great dress. She had never had a dress like that. She'd never actually prepared for a one-on-one date with a guy she was truly infatuated with.

She took the hanger from the rod again and stared at it up close.

Or she could put the dress on, enjoy primping and wow Jack when he came to the door.

She was grinning as she turned on the shower. She had to give Jack credit. He'd found a way to date her in spite of Honey Creek.

The least she could do was dress up.

An hour later, she was nervous. Very nervous.

She'd never been to a fancy restaurant in a sexy dress.

Of course, she'd never been anywhere with a guy who made her feel like Jack did. Which was a lot of the reason for the butterflies jitterbugging in her stomach.

She curled a strand of hair around the curling iron that Carla, bless her heart, had included—along with hairspray and other miscellaneous necessities—in the hotel bathroom. As she waited for the curl to take, she studied the dress.

It fell straight to her knee and dipped low in back, the spaghetti straps running over her shoulders to crisscross over her shoulder blades. The silky material glided over her skin, moving with her, but hinting at every curve.

The last curl in place, Brooke sprayed the style and then turned to leave the bathroom, where she was confronted by the skimpy white lace nightgown Carla had hung on the back of the door. Pinned to the front of the nightgown was another big bright yellow smiley face.

The butterflies in her stomach picked up the pace when she looked at that nightgown.

A moment later, a sharp rap on the door nearly knocked the breath out of her.

One last glance in the mirror and she was as ready as she could be, torn between nervousness over how badly she wanted everything to be perfect and the anticipation born of waiting her whole life for this night.

The sight of Jack standing outside her door did knock the breath out of her.

He was dressed in a dark gray sports jacket with black pants, a crisp white shirt and a tie with gray and black geometric shapes. The jacket emphasized his broad shoulders and the whole thing made him seem taller and more powerful somehow. The clothing was something any man might have worn to a business meeting, even a funeral, but on Jack it was sexy. Or maybe it was just the incredible emotions coursing through her.

"Maybe I should have included a second option," he said, one corner of his mouth curving up in a lazy smile.

She couldn't help smiling in return. "A second option?"

"Staying in." His eyes toured over her slowly from head to toe and back. He clearly appreciated what he saw. And assumed she would have gone for that option.

She felt warm everywhere. How could the confidence that had initially driven her nuts be so attractive now?

She had to change the subject. "Did you pay for all of this too?" she asked spreading her arms to indicate her dress and accessories.

"Carla took my credit card," he said, taking another expedition with his eyes. "I hadn't seen any of it until now. But I can't remember ever being happier to spend money."

The warmth, which was more than physical, intensified. "Thanks."

"Thank you for staying after you found out what was going on."

She lifted a shoulder, though was not at all nonchalant about it. "You went to a lot of work."

"Funny, it didn't feel like work."

And suddenly she wanted to cry and kiss him all at the same time.

The nervous-tense-excited anticipation threatened to overwhelm her. She felt enough energy to run sprints up and down the hall and had the crazy urge to giggle, though she knew it would sound hysterical.

She also felt every bit of sexual energy and hormones that had been suppressed for—well, forever—suddenly surge through her.

She couldn't sit still across the table from Jack in a candlelit room. It would be too much romantic overload. She needed to get her emotions under control first.

"I'm not really hungry yet," she said as she stepped from the room and pulled the door closed behind her, shutting it harder than she intended.

"You want to do something else first?" he asked.

Though his tone was not suggestive, her imagination came up with several options to work up an appetite.

He put a hand on her back as they walked toward the elevators. His fingers touched her bare skin above the dip of fabric and Brooke sucked in a quick breath that she hoped he didn't hear.

This was nuts. She was just emotional over the effort he'd

gone to for her. Maybe she was a bit sleep deprived as well. Or maybe it was PMS. Something had her off-balance tonight.

But she could not beg Jack to make love to her just because he'd sent some flowers, given her a fountain and was taking her to dinner. This reaction was pathetic, a very acute reminder of how long it had been since she'd been attracted to a man.

"I was thinking a movie sounded good." She hoped her voice didn't sound as strained to him as it did to her.

A movie was good, she thought as the numbers above the elevator doors counted down. Other people would be around to keep her from doing anything stupid. Plus, they wouldn't be able to talk, so he couldn't say more sexy, charming things that made her want him.

"A movie?" he repeated. The elevator arrived and they stepped on. "Sure. Okay. Whatever you want."

They waited for the valet to bring the car around without speaking.

Her thoughts wouldn't stop though. Maybe she didn't want Jack. Maybe it was simply that he was an attractive man who was the first to give her attention and romance. It probably could have been any male over the age of thirty. She took a deep breath and felt a little better.

But she couldn't keep her mind from noting how large and strong Jack's hand was as he grasped the door handle to open it for her.

"What movie do you want to see?" he asked as they pulled out of the hotel's circular drive.

"Oh, anything." Her mind was only partially on the question he'd asked.

"So, you really want to see a movie, but you don't care

which one?" he asked, bemused.

"No." She really just wanted a distraction from Jack's bewildering presence.

It was all almost too good to be true.

She glanced at him. Was he nervous at all? Was it even a big deal to him?

Doubtful.

He'd probably been on millions of dates. They'd likely all been with beautiful, sophisticated women, too. Most had probably not ended until the next morning either, when they rolled out of bed, still with great hair and minty-fresh breath.

She couldn't live up to his standards anyway. She tried to take another deep breath, recognizing her hyperventilation as ridiculous. She felt like her thoughts were on a treadmill and someone had cranked the speed up to breakneck.

She pressed against the headrest and tried to calm down. It was dinner and a movie.

The movie would give her a chance to remember how to be rational and composed.

Jack was, thankfully, preoccupied with finding a parking spot.

"We're overdressed, you know," he commented as he finally pulled into a slot.

She managed to curve her lips into a smile. "A little," she agreed, her voice weak.

"Well, it will be dark." He got out of the car and came around to open her side. He took her hand to help her out, but didn't release her even as they started toward the 12-plex cinemas.

She tried to relax her fingers and arm. He would feel the tension, she was sure.

"You really don't care?" he asked as they stood perusing the listing of movies.

She seriously considered the question now. "No war drama or psycho thriller," she finally said. "But otherwise, I don't have a preference."

"Blockbuster action film it is then."

With tickets in hand the next stop was concessions.

"Do you want anything?" he asked.

What a loaded question.

She made herself study the food options, the candy in particular. She hadn't thought she could eat earlier, but this was chocolate—a whole different situation. Besides, she knew chocolate could cause an endorphin release much like sex did. Maybe that would be enough to appease her.

"I'll have Junior Mints and a jumbo peanut butter cup," she told the girl behind the counter. "Oh, and some chocolate-covered peanuts."

He looked at her with one eyebrow up, but simply paid the inflated price for her candy and his soda and popcorn.

He let her pick the seats. She stood in the aisle and quickly scanned the theater for anyone she knew. She hadn't thought of it until now, but this was the closest theater to Honey Creek. Her preoccupation with Jack was dangerous.

"Brooke?" He nudged her with the forearm he had wrapped around a huge tub of popcorn. "The lights are going down."

She hadn't even noticed. She started toward the steps leading to the top of the stadium seating. It seemed a more strategic position to be able to spot anyone she knew and hide before they saw her.

She stopped at the fourth row from the back and waited for the large man on the end to move so they could pass.

"You okay?" Jack asked near her ear.

All of her senses zeroed in on him—the warmth and size of him right behind her, too close for anyone watching them to assume anything other than that they were on a date. And Brooke felt the thrill, and another strong urge to giggle hysterically, shoot through her.

"I'm okay," she told him as they slid into their seats.

"You sure?" He didn't look convinced. "You seem jumpy."

Yes. She was most certainly jumpy.

"I'm fine." She even gave him a smile.

He grinned back and something in her that had previously been tight, melted and let go as a current of warmth swept through her.

Strangely, in spite of the relative relaxation, her desire to take off all her clothes intensified.

She turned from the sexy smile and tore open the king-sized package of peanut butter cups, eating all four before the previews were over.

When she'd swallowed the last bite, she sighed. She actually thought she felt better. Who needed men? Chocolate would only ruin her dress size...not her reputation.

Then Jack took her hand—now unoccupied by candy—in his. The warmth alone was enough to make her forget how to even spell chocolate. But then he started stroking the back of her hand with his thumb, and disquiet seemed a permanent state of mind for her over the next fifty minutes.

The caresses were not constant. Just now and then he'd run the pad of his thumb over the soft, evidently very sensitive, skin. Once or twice he rubbed along the outside of her index finger, or the inside of her wrist. And each time it was like turning up the gas on the Bunsen burner.

She lasted until the hero and heroine in the movie were locked in an embrace as their plane plummeted from the sky. They were sweaty, their clothes torn to near rags by their ordeal and they had only each other. The embrace turned into a kiss, which quickly turned erotic.

That was all she could take.

Chapter Eight

Brooke clamped her opposite hand over Jack's hand that had been tantalizing her with fairly simple, seemingly benign touches.

"Let's go," she whispered to him.

She tugged on his hand as she stepped over his feet on her way to the aisle.

Without question or hesitation, he rose and followed her to the door of the theater.

She stopped with her hand on the door. She didn't want to step out into the glaring light or the crowd that was on the other side the door. To the right was a space where a short wall separated the corner from the rest of the theater. Brooke didn't know what they usually stored in that corner, nor did she care. It was empty right now and semi-private.

She pulled Jack into the space then dropped his hand and faced him in the dim light.

"What's wrong?" he asked, leaning close so he could keep his voice low.

"Nothing. Everything." With no other even remotely satisfying option coming to her, she took the front of his shirt in her fist and pulled him forward. "Mostly, that I need to do this."

And she kissed him.

The relief was immediate, like the first bite of food after a long deprivation. But she immediately wanted, needed, more.

He didn't seem inclined to deny her.

She pressed close and his hands didn't just go around her, they cupped her butt and lifted her up against him.

Her arms went around his neck and the kiss deepened to the point that it was difficult to tell if there was any place they weren't touching.

She'd loved the delicious glide of the silky dress over her skin as she moved. But feeling the fabric sliding between her body and his warm hand made her tremble.

He began slowly walking her backward, his powerful thighs moving against hers, making her moan. Then she felt the wall against her back, which provided the support he evidently sought because he again deepened the kiss and increased the pressure of his pelvis against hers.

She moved against him, striving to be even closer. The ache for him had been present and growing, probably since he'd first walked into the clinic, but certainly since she'd checked into the hotel, and was now nearly unbearable.

His lips moved to her throat and she tipped her head back as her eyes slid shut.

She cupped the ass she'd admired since day one, slid her hands over firm muscles until she'd touched every inch she could reach without breaking lip contact. Then finally, without a trace of shyness, she cupped his erection.

He tore his mouth from hers with a sharp hiss.

She simply dropped her lips to his throat. He held the back of her head, his chest rising and falling quickly under her touch.

"Brooke," he ground out. "This is supposed to be about

you."

She lifted her head, her hand still holding and stroking him. "What do you mean?"

"I'll show you." His hand that had cupped her breast, slid down over her rib cage, and hip bone. Then, his palm flat against her stomach, his fingers pointed toward the very center of all of her desire.

He was watching her face as his hand slid lower over the front of the dress. She gasped and let her head fall back against the wall. His lips touched her throat as his hand cupped her where she ached.

"Jack," she moaned.

She felt the skirt being gathered up until his hand was resting against the silky front of her panties.

His fingers stroked over the black tulip that covered her and she felt dizzy. She grasped his forearm to steady herself and felt the muscles bunching in perfect rhythm with the sparks of sensation that were zinging through her.

The tension she'd felt all night knotted into a single ball directly under his hand and she felt like he was tying it tighter and tighter with each stroke. She struggled to press herself closer. "Jack," she breathed against his lips.

He lifted his head and she opened her eyes.

"Please," she begged.

Understanding dawned on his face and was then quickly replaced by intense desire.

"Oh, no you don't," he said his hand stalling as he pulled back. "At least let me look at you."

One hand lifted and pulled the strap of her dress down over her shoulder baring one breast. He shifted to let the other strap fall as well. "You're so beautiful," he rasped as he brushed his thumb over her nipple while the middle finger of his other hand pressed the sweet spot behind the black silk again.

She arched her back and suddenly the knot unraveled all at once. She felt the release, a sensational combination of pleasure and relief as she moaned his name. A moment later, she sagged against him, her forehead on his chest.

He wrapped his arms around her. He held her for several seconds as she struggled for breath.

Finally, she lifted her head, gratefulness and embarrassment washing over her in equal portions.

"Sorry, I just couldn't wait... I shouldn't have..." she blabbered.

"You damned well better not be sorry."

"Thank you," she said, without thinking. "I mean...that seemed appropriate, but..."

He lifted the straps of her dress back into place and covered her mouth with two fingers. "You're *very* welcome. I ...

The door to the theater burst open just then. Two teenage boys, evidently out for a popcorn refill, came in laughing. Then stopped short.

"Sorry, man," one mumbled with a big, knowing grin.

"Way to go, buddy," the other said, giving Jack a thumbs-up.

They proceeded into the theater but not without a glance back.

Brooke felt the skirt of her dress slip back into place over her thighs as Jack removed his hands. She hadn't realized how high her dress had ridden. The air-conditioning on her legs certainly hadn't registered. Nothing *cool* had registered.

He gave her a sheepish grin. "Got a little carried away."

She took a deep breath, trying to slow the heart rate that

was pounding so hard she could feel it in her head.

She wasn't sure if it was racing from Jack's influence or from the scare of being seen doing *that* in public.

Her lack of response made him bend slightly to study her face closer.

"It's too dark for them to have seen much," he said. "They were assuming a lot."

Her eyes widened. They'd seen the *position* she and Jack had been in. Even two teenage boys, who waited for the love scene to go for popcorn, knew what they'd been doing.

"They assumed correctly," she said. "Good grief, I must have lost my mind." She lifted a hand to try to straighten her hair.

"I'm glad to have that effect on you." He braced a hand on the wall next to her left ear. He looked like he was ready to resume where they left off.

She put a hand on his chest. "Whoa. Those were just two of a whole theater of people."

"I doubt they're all going to go for popcorn," he said.

Her face heated with the thought of how close the two boys had been to seeing a whole lot more than a little leg. "The way we were going at it I'm not sure we'd hear them if there was a fire alarm and they all stampeded."

He didn't reply, but his grin said it all.

"You don't have to look so smug."

"You've been itching to kiss me since I showed up at your door," he said smugly. "I'm just glad you finally did something about it."

Aching, more than itching, she thought. "Well, if I kiss you it's no one's business but mine." She sounded and felt cross.

He leaned forward, in spite of her hand on his chest.

"Honey, it's also very much *my* business."

That look in his eyes told her clearly that he didn't give a damn if they put it all on the Internet for the world to see.

That was dangerous.

The passion had fried his good sense. *She* had to take charge before they gave those teenagers, and maybe several adults, a real show for the admission price.

"We need to go," she said, ducking under his arm and turning to the door.

"You know," he said, right behind her, his hand pressing heavily on the door, keeping her from opening it, "you started this."

She grimaced, her back still to him. "I know."

"Just so we're clear. You wanted this too."

She wanted to ignore his words, or even deny them, or at least make an excuse. She turned to face him, but didn't meet his eyes. "It's hardly fair. You tricked me into going on this date. I've been confused since I got to the hotel."

"Brooke," he said calmly. "You knew about the date from practically the minute you got to the hotel. You certainly knew when you got dressed in that sexy dress and those skimpy panties."

She swallowed hard. "I thought you hadn't seen the clothes ahead of time."

"I didn't."

"How did you know about the panties?"

"I just felt them."

Oh, yeah. She took a deep breath. "These were the only option Carla left me."

He smiled slowly. "Remind me to give her a raise."

Brooke rolled her eyes.

"But I'm curious," he went on. "What about the white panties you were wearing when you got to town?"

"What... How... Did you..."

His smile widened. "Good guess."

She crossed her arms. "You think I'm a prude."

"You try to be anyway."

"Then why did you want to take me out tonight?"

His expression softened and he lifted his hand to her face. "Because you're real for me." He stroked his thumb over her bottom lip. "And you need that."

His words hit her right in the heart and she pulled in a breath to keep the sob back.

Dammit.

She had officially fallen in love...with the first man to give her amazing sex and some nice gifts.

Just like her mom.

But *unlike* her mom she was going to end it before she lost every bit of pride—before she confessed how she felt.

"If I ask you to take me back to the hotel will you settle for a handshake at the door or should I call a cab?" she asked. If she slept with him tonight, the whole night, there was no way she could keep from confessing it all.

He stared at her for a few seconds. Then he shook his head. "A kiss."

"Peck on the cheek?"

He shook his head again. "Full lips."

"But a peck?"

"At least thirty seconds."

"Ten."

"Twenty."

"Fine."

He dug his car keys from his pocket as he pulled the theater door open and she stepped through.

"And everything after that is negotiable."

She stopped. "*No*," she said firmly. "Nothing else."

He looked down at her, studying her eyes. "At least admit you *want* more."

She surrendered that much. "I do."

"You'll think about me in bed tonight," he predicted.

She sighed. "I'm sure you're right."

They walked to the car in silence, without touching. A few minutes later he pulled onto the street, changed lanes, then stopped at the stoplight.

"Kissing a guy who really likes you doesn't mean you're going to turn into your mother."

She gaped at him. "*What*?"

He glanced at her. "You heard me." He made a left turn and continued down the street, driving along as if they were discussing the weather.

She couldn't believe how close he'd come to the truth.

He pulled into the circular drive in front of the hotel, which was part of the nicest gift anyone had ever given her. He shifted into park and ignored the valet for a moment as he put an arm along the back of the car seat.

"Kissing you because you gave me a fountain and a nice dress isn't much better than the reasons my mom did what she did."

Out of the corner of her eye, she saw the one valet shrug at the other and lean back against a pillar to wait for them.

"I don't believe that's why you'd be doing it," he said, his voice soft and husky. "And neither do you."

"I believe I would be doing it because I'm genetically engineered to be a sucker for a hot guy who thinks I'm pretty."

"Thank you. And pretty is a mild word for what I think about you."

She shook her head. She would *not* tell him the real reason she wanted to kiss him—and more. She would not fall prey like her mom did to the sweet words, the sexy smiles, the idea that he wanted to take care of her. She would not be standing in the doorway watching him drive away. She would not cry over him.

If only she wanted to screw him for the sake of screwing him. Or if it was only for the gifts. That would be easier, more straightforward. Not exactly something to be proud of, but at least not heartbreaking when it was over. There were other guys who could buy her things.

But no, she had to be in love with him.

There was never going to be another Jack.

She slid toward the door and away from his hand.

"Goodnight, Jack." She opened the door.

"Goodnight, Brooke."

She turned back, slightly surprised by how easy that had been. "No arguments?"

He leaned toward her and wrapped an arm around her waist, pulling her across the seat and into his arms. "I don't want to *argue* with you," he said just before his mouth took hers.

What they'd agreed would be a twenty-second touching of the lips quickly became an erotic takeover of every nerve ending in her body. He pulled away a few minutes later.

She was still breathing hard when she climbed from the car

on wobbly legs and managed to remember which room was hers—after asking the front desk.

Jack wasn't exactly sure when it hit him but he'd narrowed it down to the time between Brooke inhaling two candy bars and her orgasm by the movie theater door. He'd liked her before that, he'd cared about her before that, he'd wanted her before that. But somewhere between the peanut butter cups and her coming apart so easily for him, he'd realized that he was in love with her.

And he really wished he hadn't booked two hotel rooms.

If she was stuck in there with him in her space she'd have to face him, she'd have to realize that ignoring this wasn't going to work.

She thought she was turning into her mother. He got that. Kind of. She'd been programmed to think that relationships were about being with someone because of what you could get from them—her mother's entire lifestyle had been like that, Brooke's marriage to Mike had been like that.

But he knew she didn't want to believe that.

She was trying to rationalize how she felt about him in relation to what he had and could give her. The stronger her emotions got, the more she was afraid she was using him.

It looked like David had rubbed off on him. That was a hell of an analysis.

Jack paced his room. He had to find a way to show her that she was falling for him *in spite* of what he could give her.

And she was falling for him. She had to be.

Maybe he should just go to her room and tell her he was in love with her.

That was something different from what her mom had ever had. It sounded like she'd never been with a man who had truly loved her or appreciated her.

Maybe he should just propose. That was something else her mom hadn't had until she'd seduced Walter's client.

He couldn't buy her anything. *That* was the last thing that would prove she felt more for him than gratitude. He couldn't just march up there and sweep her off her feet and into bed either. Sex and gifts were the whole problem here.

Maybe he should just leave her alone.

But he really hated that idea.

He was startled when there was a knock at his door.

He made it across the room in three strides, yanking the door open. Brooke stood on the other side, still in the black dress. She looked like she'd been crying.

Pulling her into the room he asked, "What's wrong?"

"Turns out, I'm going to be crying no matter what at this point so I thought I should at least take you up on your offer."

He couldn't take his hands off of her. He ran his palms up and down her bare arms. "Absolutely. Which offer?" It didn't matter. He'd do anything for her.

"The offer to go wild, let loose, do whatever I want with you."

Heat and lust surged through his body. No woman had ever affected him like this and it nearly took him to his knees. He cleared his throat. "Why are you crying?"

She wiped her eyes. "Doesn't matter. Can you just take my dress off and put your mouth on me? All over?"

He could almost taste her now. "Brooke, there's no way in hell I would ever say no to that. But maybe we should talk—"

She stepped close until they were belly to belly. "Not unless the words we're using are fuck and cock and deeper and harder and—"

Fine. They could talk later.

He reached down and stripped the dress up and over her head, tossing it somewhere behind him.

She was naked underneath.

He started on his shirt but she took his hands. "I want all of that too. Eventually. But right now all I need are your hands and mouth."

She headed for the bed and sat, watching him. His eyes roamed over her body, knowing he would never get tired of it. Thirty pounds, wrinkles, sunburn, scars—nothing would make her less beautiful to him.

"On your knees, Jack," she ordered.

"Whatever you say." He sank to the floor in front of her. It was like every fantasy coming true. She was taking charge even more than she had the last time. She was not only willing to ask him for what she needed—obviously—but she seemed to have a really good idea of what she wanted.

He ran his hands up her thighs as she had done to him the night in his motel room in Honey Creek. "Just tell me what you want."

She lay back and parted her thighs. "I'm thinking you can take it from here."

Okay, well then. He couldn't take his eyes from the wet, pink folds on display for him. And yeah, he knew exactly what to do.

"Thank you, Brooke," he said sincerely. He slid his hands up and under her ass, pulling her hips closer to the edge of the bed. "Making you scream will be a pleasure."

She smiled and lifted a hand to her breast, playing with her nipple. "No one's ever done this to me."

He stopped halfway there and looked up. "What?"

"I've read it in romance novels, but never actually done it."

"That," he said sincerely—thanking God that the men she'd been with were total idiots—"is the best thing I've heard in a long time."

He kissed his way up her inner thigh, adding little flicks of his tongue, running his hand up and down the other thigh at the same time. She shifted restlessly, her breathing uneven.

When he was sure she was ready, he put his mouth over her clit and breathed. The hot air made her arch toward him.

"God you smell good," he told her gruffly. "You're so beautiful, so amazing."

She moaned and wiggled.

He brushed a finger over the soft hair on her mound, preparing her for the more intimate touch, then slid the pad of his index finger to her clit.

"That's good." Her head pressed back into the mattress, arching her neck.

"Oh, you have no idea." Good was going to be an understatement. Then he put his lips on her, kissing softly. His hand under her butt lifted her slightly and he kissed her again with more pressure. Her gasp spurred him on and his tongue flicked out to lick her.

The touch of his tongue against her clit made them both moan. She tasted like everything good he'd ever had. Tracing his finger along her hot cleft, he forced himself to go slow, to work up to more but she arched up.

"Please."

He loved having Brooke need him.

He slid a finger inside of her and lifted his head slightly.

She was spread open on the bed, offering herself up to him, and he had to taste her fully.

Withdrawing his finger he replaced the touch with his tongue, licking long and boldly.

Her fingers gripped his hair. "Jack. Oh, my…"

He did it again, then sucked her clit into his mouth, sliding two fingers into her. Flicking her clit with his tongue he pumped his fingers deep, curling them into her G-spot.

She came apart a moment later, crying out his name.

The tremors subsided slowly and he lifted himself from between her legs. "What do you think?" he asked, stripping out of his shirt.

"I can't believe I went that long without that."

He undid his fly. "Anytime you want more just say the word."

She slid her legs up and down on the slick sheets and gave him a sexy grin. "More."

Well, he was dedicated to her happiness. He started to kneel again when she laughed.

"Keep undressing. I want more of everything."

He stripped his clothes off. "Whatever you want, Brooke."

"You. Deep and hard."

She was still on the edge of the mattress, she was wet and hot, and she'd just said two of his favorite words. "I can do that."

She bit her bottom lip and looked unsure for a moment.

He didn't like that look at all. "What is it?"

"I just… I wanted…"

"Anything."

"No judgment?"

"Absolutely not."

"Well, I'm in the mood for trying new things."

He was more and more interested. "Such as?"

"New positions."

He swallowed hard. "What haven't you done?"

Her gaze wavered, her eyes going to his collarbone instead of his face. He knelt on the mattress next to her and gripped her chin between his thumb and finger. "Never be afraid to say anything to me. I want you. In every way. Nothing you could say could change that."

She nodded. "Okay."

"So what do you want?"

"Hands and knees."

He almost came right then. He breathed deeply to slow himself down. When he had some control back, he slid his hands to her hips, bent and kissed her, then flipped her to her stomach. He ran his hand up and down over her spine, then gripped her hips again and pulled her ass toward him. She went up on her knees, bracing her hands flat on the mattress. Goose bumps erupted down her back and he bent to lick the base of her spine.

"God you're beautiful," he said gruffly. "In any position."

She wiggled her hips. "Show me how much I like this one."

Hands on her hips, he thrust forward, sinking deep. Her breath hissed out while he groaned. He felt the heat and friction all the way to the soles of his feet. Unable to stay still for even a second, he moved immediately.

It only took a few thrusts for her to match his rhythm, pushing back, meeting his strokes. His release built quickly and he wanted her with him. He reached around and found her clit, but it wasn't necessary. She was right with him. She bent, lowering her head to the pillow and pushing her ass higher in the air, taking him even deeper.

"Brooke," he groaned.

"Yes," she answered.

They went over the peak together a moment later.

"Yep, definitely in the top three," she gasped as they sprawled on the mattress together, her butt against his groin.

He laughed into her hair. "Duly noted."

After she fell asleep, Jack couldn't relax. He ran his hand through her hair over and over. This was a breakthrough. She'd come to him—again. She'd asked him for what she wanted, even things she'd been hesitant to admit she wanted.

She trusted him. She wanted him. And he was staying here, with her, for good.

"I love you, Brooke," he whispered, kissing the top of her head. "You're all mine now."

Brooke was, not surprisingly, in a great mood the next morning as she drove home from Amarillo, in spite of the early hour. It was Sunday, but she wanted to get back to Honey Creek before everyone was up and going to church—before anyone could notice that she'd been gone overnight. Or worse, that Jack had been too.

Still, even with only a few hours of sleep, she was happier than she'd been in a long time.

She was also famished.

Of course, that wasn't a surprise considering how she'd burned the calories the night before.

Jack had awakened her twice more in the night,

encouraging her to tell him about her fantasies, try new things. She was quite fond of hands-and-knees but also found that with him even missionary was damned good.

She'd shown up at his room when she realized that being without him was going to hurt no matter when or how it happened. She was already in love with him. She was already going to cry. In fact, she'd been crying alone in her room before deciding to have one amazing night, one night where she let go and gave him everything.

It didn't matter that she might end up like her mom. It didn't matter that he was going to leave.

If this was how her mother had felt about Walter, Brooke couldn't blame her for risking it all.

Then at one point, as they'd been drifting in that delicious dream-like place between conscious and unconscious, she could have sworn he'd said he loved her.

It might have been a dream but lying there in his arms and when he'd made love to her the next time...she'd felt it.

And finally she'd whispered that she loved him too.

How she was going to manage when he went back to San Antonio, she wasn't sure but she only had a few more months in Honey Creek. Then they could be together. Just a few more months.

In honor of her newly optimistic attitude, and to show Jack that she appreciated being able to be herself, she chose to wear a shirt in a deep red that had been relegated to the back of her closet.

She was actually humming as she stood at the counter in the kitchen preparing to slide two pieces of bread into the toaster. She wondered if Jack was similarly ravenous. She'd worked him hard last night. He'd probably be at Vi's now, ordering a large breakfast.

Brooke paused with the first piece only partially in the slot.

She'd always heard that Vi made great muffins. In fact, the rumor was that Vi made great eggs, pancakes and coffee too. Brooke didn't know firsthand, but suddenly all of the above sounded great. Her stomach rumbled in approval.

After her workout last night, she needed something more substantial than toast, she reasoned as she put the bread back. She knew that her decision to brave the diner had more to do with seeing Jack as soon as she could rather than filling her stomach, but she *was* hungry, and with him there it wouldn't be nearly as intimidating to walk into Vi's.

She hoped.

She was proud of how confidently she approached the front door of the diner seven minutes later. The morning sun glinted off the huge front windows making it nearly impossible to see anything inside. She kept her chin high and her smile firmly in place in case anyone was watching her from inside.

And she kept repeating to herself, "There's no reason you shouldn't walk right in there like you belong. There's no reason you shouldn't walk right in there like you belong."

The bell tinkled above her head as she pushed the door open, halting her mantra...and, evidently, the conversation near the door.

She *felt* the heads turn in her direction even before she saw them.

More conversation quieted, like dominoes tipping over one by one from where she had figuratively started the cascade.

It was as if it had been scripted.

She hesitated, for just an instant. And was immediately annoyed with herself. This was a public place, it was during business hours. She wasn't brandishing a weapon, she didn't have two heads, she wasn't carrying a banner that declared *Down with Diners*. She was prepared to give Vi money in exchange for some of her muffins. Nothing strange, nothing funny, nothing to worry about. There really was no reason that she shouldn't walk through that front door as if she belonged there.

"Hi, honey," Vi greeted, breaking the strange, uncomfortable silence. "What can I get ya?"

"A dozen muffins." Brooke stepped to the counter.

She was in a great mood, Brooke reminded herself. She took a deep breath as Vi retrieved a box from under the counter and moved to the bakery display case.

"You want a little of everything?" Vi asked, her smile friendly and her eyes a little sympathetic.

"Sure. Thanks," Brooke answered, glad her voice didn't waver. But she kept her eyes firmly on the muffins Vi was choosing from the case. She couldn't even make herself look for Jack.

While she waited on her order, she tried to boost her confidence. Speaking of Jack...

She'd had the best sex that anyone on the planet had ever had. And so had he. She was *not* going to let these people ruin her mood.

But she still couldn't pull her eyes from watching Vi fill the white cardboard box.

Vi was almost finished when Brooke heard, "Interesting that you would come in. Jack just finished telling us the news."

She closed her eyes as her ex-father-in-law's voice penetrated the thick silence. Two more minutes and she would have been free.

She should have known better. Walter was at the diner

every morning and he would never think of letting her escape unscathed.

Of course, Walter had never, ever been afraid to say anything anywhere. *He* had certainly never hesitated at the front door to an establishment he wanted to go into, public or not.

But as she turned to face him she wished that she had opted for a conservative navy pantsuit and had put her hair up rather than wearing it down the way Jack liked. Her usual appearance was like a suit of armor. And she needed as much protection—even that which was mostly in her head—as she could get with Walter.

"Really. The news?" she asked innocently. If Walter was going to make idle conversation with her, fine. She could be an adult and participate...for the one minute it would take Vi to finish her order.

Walter laughed. "Well, there's really no way you could keep it a secret."

Oh, no. Brooke jumped from resigned to panicked in two seconds. She felt her face heat and her breathing quicken alarmingly.

There was no way that Jack had told anyone about them, she told herself.

Was there?

"I, um," she stopped and cleared her throat.

Seemingly out of nowhere, Jack appeared at her side. "After our meeting last night how could I not tell everyone?"

She'd been so excited to see him. She'd been anticipating that first smile between them, a knowing wink, a covert touch. Now all she could do was barely resist grabbing him and shaking him and yelling, *What were you thinking? You ruined everything!*

"Tell them what?" she, somehow, asked instead.

"That I'm staying."

He was looking at her like he was concerned she might throw up. Which she was seriously considering.

She knew exactly how this was going to go. "Staying," she repeated.

"Maybe we should let her negotiate all of the contracts for the City Council," someone said.

Scattered chuckles met the comment.

Yep, exactly how it was going to go.

"I'm not sure we can afford her rates," Walter said, with a mild smile. "But then maybe you're giving him a break. Professional courtesy and all."

The light laughter died and the tension in the room heightened.

"After all," Walter continued, typically pleased with the rapt attention his words were getting. "Jack has helped you out a lot around here."

She met Walter's gaze directly and hoped he wouldn't see her bottom lip tremble. "Are you insinuating that Dr. Silver has agreed to stay for other than professional reasons?"

Walter shook his head. "I would never say you aren't a professional."

And there it was—the you're-a-prostitute-like-your-mom comment he always managed to get in. It still stung.

Brooke felt Jack move in front of her before she could recover.

"Be careful, Walter," he warned, his voice low.

The stunned numbness that had filled her since she

stepped into the diner lifted with Jack's words.

Anger and defensiveness took over, though neither emotion was for her. Walter had insulted Brooke a number of times. Now he'd included her mother *and* Jack. She wasn't going to let Walter drag Jack through this.

And she wasn't going to hide behind anyone anymore.

She used her elbow to move him as she stepped forward, putting her directly in front of Walter.

"Dr. Silver and I are professional colleagues, in *medicine.* If he stays, it will be to practice medicine."

Walter's eyes narrowed at her unusual show of backbone. "Are you implying that neither of you need *practice* in any other area?"

She was braced for something like that, so hers was not one of the gasps heard in the room.

"Dr. Silver is a wonderful physician. Rather than denigrating his character, you should be happy he would want to stay."

"I'm trying to thank *you* for convincing him," Walter said.

Uh-huh. Walter's tongue would probably shrivel up if he said something nice to or about her.

She ignored his tone and turned to look at Jack, simply because she couldn't stand to look at Walter another second. "I'm sure his decision had nothing to do with me. This is obviously the kind of practice he wants to be a part of."

"Actually you were a very large part of my decision," Jack said.

Brooke frowned at him. How did he miss this? No one had dared ask for a refill on their coffee, not to mention actually trying to get up and leave. How did Jack miss what was going on? He was just making things worse.

"Well, of course, I was part of the decision since we'll be working together, but it was a professional decision." She kept her tone pleasant, but she was absolutely positive that he could not misinterpret the look she was giving him. He *had* to go along with this.

Jack did nothing of the sort. Instead, he moved closer to her, too close for there to be any doubt that there was more than business between them. He put his hand on her shoulder and slowly slid his palm down her arm, in an obviously intimate gesture, until he held her hand. She tried to unobtrusively tug free, but he held her firmly. He pinned her with an intense stare, but before he could say anything, Walter had to speak. Of course.

"And then there are the fringe benefits."

Brooke couldn't take her eyes from Jack's even as she heard some of Walter's cronies chuckling.

Jack didn't flinch with Walter's words. He also didn't deny what Walter said. In fact, his eyes seemed to be daring *her* to deny it.

"I need to get going," Brooke said, hating how scratchy her voice suddenly sounded. She had no problem pulling her eyes away from Jack's gaze now as she shrugged out of his grasp.

"Here you go, honey," Vi said as Brooke turned toward the door.

She glanced back and then gave Vi a shaky smile as she accepted the forgotten box of muffins. Her hand was on the metal handle of the door when Walter spoke *again*.

"Careful, Jack. If you upset her, you might not keep getting it for free."

Brooke said nothing as she pushed on Vi's front door. A moment later, she stepped out into the morning sun and fresh air, proud that she'd fought the tears and won.

Chapter Nine

"You know what you and Walter both need?" Jack was right on Brooke's heels. There was no way he was going to let this go. "For you to tell Walter to fuck off."

When she rounded on him, the emotions on her face were numerous. "Excuse me?" She stomped back to where he stood.

"I want to know why you denied we're together." He held his body tense, frowning down at her.

She didn't look especially intimidated, or inclined to be agreeable.

"Because this is what they expect of me," she nearly shouted. "They think sex is the only thing I can offer someone, even a business partner. I can't prove them right after I've fought so hard to change my image."

"So you would choose to protect their opinion of you over publicly acknowledging what we have together," he accused.

He had stood in that diner staring at the woman in front of him now, feeling like she was a stranger the morning after they'd been as intimate as two people could be. Even now, close enough to her that he could see the individual strands of hair naturally highlighted to a pale blonde, he couldn't believe it.

"Yes! If they think that we slept together…"

"We *did* sleep together."

"And it's none of their business."

"But it's *my* business. They don't need details, but if they ask if we're involved, then I don't intend to deny it. And I don't like hearing you deny it."

She tipped her chin up and crossed her arms. "So it's an ego thing? Everyone has to know you scored?"

"No, dammit." He advanced on her again and she backed up, further infuriating him. "I didn't announce it to the diner but I don't mind them knowing. I'm not ashamed of it."

"You're *proud* of it then?"

What the hell was she doing? "That a beautiful, smart, funny, sweet woman let me get so close to her? Hell yeah, I'm proud of that."

The compliment seemed to further irritate her for some reason. "And why didn't I know that you were thinking about staying?"

"You didn't think that after last night I might be thinking along those lines?" How could this be the same woman he'd held last night?

"So it does have to do with last night," she said. "It's not about the clinic, or your own professional development, or even about our professional partnership. It's about the sex."

He clenched his jaw and stepped forward again. She started to move back, but he caught her, holding onto her upper arms. "Stop moving away from me!"

"They're going to think something is going on!" She struggled against his hold.

"Something *is* going on!"

She stopped squirming and met his eyes directly, pain, confusion and anger in her gaze. "So Walter was right. This is about me offering better *benefits* than they do in San Antonio."

Anger rose up hotter than the hurt. Walter was right? The man who had made her miserable for years? She believed Walter over him? The guy who had supported and encouraged her?

Jack pulled her up until they were nearly nose to nose. "I can get sex, and lots of it, anywhere, any time in San Antonio," he ground out. "I think you need to remember that. I don't need to come all the way to the middle of nowhere Texas for a piece of ass. That is *not* the reason I'm staying."

"Good," she shot back. "Because if you stay here, last night was the last time."

He let go of her then, suddenly, and she stumbled back.

"Is that right?" he said, his jaw so tight his temples throbbed. "Are you sure you want to make a promise like that? I might hold you to it."

She narrowed her eyes. "What does that mean?"

He wanted to make her admit that she couldn't just walk away from it all. The woman who had been in his bed last night had not come for a one-night stand. She was *glad* he had come to Honey Creek and not just because of the physical pleasure he had given her for the first time in her life but for *all* that he'd done for her and given to her.

Dammit! She was trying to discard him for *them*, the people who had never appreciated her and certainly wouldn't start just because she managed to keep herself closed up, miserable and celibate.

Suddenly, despite his most heroic efforts, he wanted to hurt her like she was hurting him.

"Like I said, I can have plenty of sex," he said, struggling to keep his voice calm. "You were the one lacking in that department from what I understood."

Her expression was shocked. “So you were doing me a *favor* last night, is that it? You did it out of the goodness of your heart? You took pity on the poor widow woman who married a gay guy?”

He crossed his arms and nodded. “Are you gonna say thank you real nice?”

For a moment he thought she was going to lunge at him and scratch his eyes out. There were likely a million not-so-complimentary things on the tip of her tongue. But at least she seemed to have forgotten about the people watching from the diner’s window.

“So sleeping with me made you feel important?” she asked, her voice controlled. Too controlled.

“You mean when you were demanding I put my mouth on you, when you were begging for my touch and calling out my name like the ‘Hallelujah’ chorus? Yeah. I felt a little important.”

She sucked in an angry breath and held it so long he began to wonder if she would pass out. Then instead of blasting him with a tirade, she spun on her heel and marched toward her car.

He was right behind her and stopped her with one hand on the top of the driver’s side door when she attempted to open it. He couldn’t stop. He couldn’t accept that she could dismiss everything between them like that.

She yanked on the car door, but he held it firmly shut.

“I don’t need to sleep with you to feel important,” he told her. She spun to face him and his voice dropped low. “The sex might be the best thing I gave you but I’ve been feeling important since I got to town.”

She pushed against his chest to back him up, but he held his ground and instead, leaned in closer.

"You consider buying me a cappuccino machine important?" She propped her hands on her hips.

He laughed, but he was anything but amused. "Oh, I think you can count higher than that."

"Excuse me?"

He held up a finger, "Money."

"Which I didn't accept."

He ignored her interruption and raised his second finger. "A supervising MD just in time to save your butt." His third finger came up. "A bigger case load than you've had since you've been here." His fourth finger rose and he held his hand close to her nose. "And let's not forget, not just one," he said as he lifted his fifth finger, "but *six* earth-shattering orgasms." He dropped his hand. "Not that I'm keeping track."

She opened her mouth but nothing came out except for a little squeak. Suddenly, he stepped back. The anger left him in a rush, until only the hurt remained. He couldn't do this anymore. Hurting her was the last thing he wanted to do and his own heart felt like it was in shreds. He should have left Honey Creek, and Brooke's life, when he'd been ahead.

Maybe David had been right. He was too addicted to the hero thing. He had to just keep pushing and doing more and more. Maybe this was his own fault.

He should have bought her the cappuccino machine and called it good.

There was just one more thing that needed to be out in the open between them. Then he could pack his bags and go back to San Antonio.

"You know," he said. "Now that I've counted it up, I think I've paid what I owe you."

He didn't know whether she was surprised he'd finally

moved back, or by what he'd just said.

"What you owe me?" she repeated dumbly.

He swallowed hard and nodded. "I came to Honey Creek to help you, to make your life better. And I've tried my damnedest. Hopefully some of it will stick after I leave."

"Why?" she asked, her eyes suddenly wary. "Why did you come to help me? Why did you try to give me all that money?"

"To make up for something I'd done."

"What?" Her voice was quiet, hesitant now, as if she could read in his eyes that the answer would change everything.

And it would. But it was time she knew.

"Killing your husband."

While Brooke tried to wrap her mind around Jack's words, he dug in his pocket, then flipped his wrist and something dropped from his fingers to the concrete at her feet.

Numbly she watched the plastic hair clip bounce against the cement.

Hair clip?

More than slightly detached from reality at the moment, she realized it was the hair clip she'd worn to his motel room the first night they'd made love.

She looked up to find him already two blocks away. What the hell was he talking about?

She started running after him, but even with a sensible, not-too-high heel, her pumps were a hazard. She stopped and hopped on one foot to remove first one shoe, then the other. Then she started after him again.

Her bare feet were quiet against the pavement and he didn't

hear her coming, especially over the muted swearing he was doing.

"Hey!" She grabbed his arm, yanking hard enough to stop him. "What am I supposed to do with *that*?" She asked gesturing back toward the sidewalk where he'd dropped the bomb.

He swung to face her, his expression stormy. "You heard me."

"Just that you're all paid up?" she asked. "For some debt I don't even understand. And then I'm supposed to just let you walk away?"

"Yes," he said firmly. "I would very much like for you to just let me walk away."

"You said you killed my husband. Don't you think I have a right to ask a few questions?"

He stood staring at her for a long moment, his breathing uneven, a large crease between his eyebrows. "Didn't you ever wonder why I was here?" he finally asked.

"You were..." She trailed off, letting herself actually consider his question. "The money," she eventually answered. "You came to give me the money."

"And I stayed."

He had. Beyond the cappuccino machine and the fountain. He'd stayed to keep her from having to close the clinic. He'd stayed far beyond anything that made sense.

"You were determined that I either have the money, or the equivalent in equipment, supplies...or service," she said, thinking out loud.

He didn't affirm her statement, but he didn't deny it either. He just watched her.

"You seemed so determined," she said, watching his face

for any tiny indication of what he was thinking or feeling.

He still stood just looking at her, as if he knew she was figuring it out.

A coldness settled near her heart. "Edward Movey killed Mike," she said softly. "Drunk driving. You said it yourself."

"He was my uncle."

She digested that for a moment, but it didn't make things much clearer. "He was alone," she said. "You weren't there."

"No, not when he got in the car I wasn't," he said bitterly.

She bit her bottom lip, seriously considering letting it go. Did it matter? She wasn't sure.

But in the end, she couldn't. "Why do you feel responsible?"

"He'd been drinking. I knew it. I tried to talk him into letting me give him a ride. But when he got stubborn and refused, I got frustrated. And walked out."

The coldness now encased her heart and lungs, making it hard to breathe. But she shook her head. "So? That doesn't mean you're responsible. Things like that happen."

"He'd done it before. I knew it. But I still left."

She was still shaking her head. Jack stepped close and his hands went to either side of her head to stop the movement. He looked deeply into her eyes.

"I would have saved his life if I'd stayed with him. I would have saved Mike's life."

"And you feel obligated to *me* somehow?" she managed to ask when all she really wanted to do was throw herself into his arms as he released her. Though she wasn't sure if she would be seeking comfort or giving it. The pain in his eyes tore at her heart.

"You were the one left to pick up the most pieces."

"You thought the money would help me pick up the pieces?"

"I'd hoped it would."

She took a long shaky breath. "It's pretty hard to put a price on something like that, isn't it?"

"Extremely."

"Especially when the person won't take the money."

"Yes."

She hated how her stomach kept drawing tighter and tighter and the coldness in her chest spread outward.

"In lieu of the money, you thought you could give me *things*."

He nodded.

"No one needs that many cappuccino machines though"

"I would have thought of more."

"And when I wouldn't take stuff, you thought you could substitute service."

He nodded.

"You thought you would work off what you believed you owed me?"

He didn't say or do anything.

"I know you're a good doctor, Jack, but that's a year's salary. Not something you can earn in a few weeks or months."

"No."

His voice was flat, his expression suddenly neutral and the sick, cold feeling now filled her completely.

"So you thought throwing in a couple of orgasms could help even things up a bit."

"*No.* Brooke—"

Now she stepped back from him, shaking her head quickly. "No wonder you thought you'd stay for a while. I mean, the sex was good, but it would take some time to work off that kind of price tag. Even my mother didn't get that kind of money for just one night."

She turned on her heel quickly, feeling her skin scrape against the rough cement, but she kept moving as she prayed that Jack wouldn't follow her.

He didn't.

"I got a replacement." Jack settled himself on the corner of Amy's desk as he spoke to Carla.

Carla looked up from the computer monitor with wide eyes. "Already? You were only on the phone twenty minutes."

"Alex, a past medical student of mine. He owed me a couple of favors." Thank God. Jack was definitely not above cashing those in. The blow up with Brooke had happened just yesterday but he already knew he couldn't stay. It was too hard.

Carla whistled. "He must have."

"That and I offered him a lot of money."

Carla gave him a smile as she rose and went to the file cabinet. "So if it was that easy why didn't you just call him in the first place?" she asked as she opened the second drawer.

Jack frowned. "The first place?"

She pulled two folders from the drawer. "When you first found out we needed a new doctor."

He started to reply. Then realized he didn't have an answer.

"He wouldn't have..." He stopped. Alex would have come. Jack had proved that just a few minutes ago. "I mean, he couldn't have..." But Alex could have handled everything just fine. He was a great physician, a friendly, warm, natural people person. He would have done well in Honey Creek.

"You okay?" Carla's expression turned worried and curious as he fumbled with his thoughts. "You look...weird."

He felt weird. Why the hell *hadn't* he called Alex right away? It would have been a perfect fit. He knew Alex was looking for something new, a change of pace. He had been staring the perfect opportunity for Alex right in the face. And he'd taken that opportunity for himself. In spite of the fact that it turned his life upside down, upset Brooke and put tension between him and his brother. He'd completely ignored what would have been great for Alex, and Brooke.

When the truth hit a moment later, it was like a hard jab to the chin.

"You know," he said slowly. "You've got a point."

"Yeah?" Carla asked.

"Bringing Alex in, introducing him to Brooke and Honey Creek, covering his salary for a year or so, would have been very charitable, wouldn't it?" he asked, his speech gaining speed as he put thoughts and words together.

"Charitable?" Carla repeated, obviously puzzled by his choice of words.

"I mean, if my intention was only to help Brooke, to ease my guilty conscience, I could have called Alex right away."

Carla tipped her head to one side. "Seems that way," she said slowly. "But *you* stayed instead."

"And why did I do that?" he asked her, coming off the corner of the desk, the realization full in his mind and a thrill humming in his veins. "If my original intention was to just drop off a bunch of money and then beat it out of town, why didn't I do the same thing with Alex when I had the chance? Dump a replacement physician on Brooke's doorstep and then get going before I could get too involved? *That* would have been the perfect, charitable thing to do."

Carla was watching him with a look than swung between worried and amused. "I don't know why you didn't do that."

"I do." He felt the huge grin stretch his mouth. "I know exactly why."

He stood grinning at her like an idiot for several seconds, until Carla prompted, "Why?"

"Because by that time, I *wanted* to be involved."

"You did?"

"I didn't just want to make things a little better for Brooke. I wanted to be *involved* with her."

It was a relief to feel the understanding wash over him. He'd let David's nagging questions about his motivations get into his head and overpower his emotions. But his relationship with Brooke wasn't, and hadn't been, about his guilt. Guilt brought him to Honey Creek, but it hadn't kept him here.

Happier than he'd been in a long, long time, he crossed the space to where Carla stood and gently gripped her upper arms in his enthusiasm.

"Don't you see?" he said, his eyes intent on Carla's. He had to practice making a woman understand all of this. "I was fascinated with her from the moment she refused my check." He knew he was grinning stupidly but he couldn't seem to stop. "After that, I wanted to get to know her. As I got to know her, I started to care about her. And then..." He stopped and took a deep, cleansing breath.

"Then?" Carla asked, smiling.

"I fell in love with her." He let go of Carla and stepped back, spreading his arms wide. "I'm in love with Brooke Donovan," he proclaimed. He dropped his arms, "*That's* why I stayed."

Carla grinned back at him. "I know."

"I can't leave," he added as that realization also hit.

Carla sighed and turned her eyes toward the ceiling. "Thank God."

Jack's thoughts were coming almost too quickly to keep up with now. He began pacing. "I can't leave. But I also can't just stay. I can't force her to put up with me."

"You've been forcing her to do that since you first set foot in this town," Carla reminded him.

He acknowledged her comment with a slight inclination of his head. "Okay, but that was different. My motivation was different. I just wanted her to take my help, in some form, some way. Now she has to want *me*, not just what I can give her or do for her."

"She never did want what you could give her or do for her," Carla said with a small laugh.

He shook his head. "She didn't want to *admit* it, but I think she did want my help. So I found something she couldn't say no to. She *had* to agree to let me be her supervising physician. She didn't have a choice."

"So now she gets to choose between you or Alex?"

Something tightened in the pit of Jack's stomach at the thought of Brooke being faced with a choice between him and...anything else. What if she didn't choose him? What if she was that angry? That hurt? How could he convince her that it *wasn't* charity that kept him in town and in her life?

He couldn't stay here and continually try to make things better for her and fix things and help her if she didn't want it. Maybe even if she did. Both of them needed to realize that Brooke could be in charge of her own life...and her own choices.

She missed her fountain. And the cappuccino.

Brooke was hiding out at home because her house was the only place in Honey Creek she went where Jack had never been. It was supposed to be a haven from memories and desires.

But it didn't have a fountain or good coffee. Or any coffee. She hadn't bought new coffee grounds since the machine had come to the clinic.

Ironically, the noticeable lack of some of her favorite things was as much a reminder of Jack as anything.

Passing the mirror over the dresser in the bedroom also made her think of him. She was dressed in boring colors—gray sweat pants with a gray hoodie over a black T-shirt—with her hair pulled up the way he hated.

She stopped in the middle of the room and looked around, suddenly aware that it wasn't just her clothes that lacked color. Her bedroom was decorated in mostly cream. There were a couple of pale blue throw pillows and some blue flowers on the valances, but everything else was neutral, from the carpet to the paint on the walls to the bedspread.

The living room was decorated in tan and brown. The kitchen was white.

Was this really what she chose to surround herself with?

Brooke leaned back against the living room wall and numbly stared at her belongings. What belongings there were. She owned the furniture, but had gone for practical, rather than expressive. She had surfaces to sit on, eat at and sleep in. Beyond that, there was nothing special or unique about her furniture, house or décor. She didn't have photographs displayed, no knick-knacks, no keepsakes. She hadn't invested anything physically or emotionally in this place because she hadn't planned on staying.

Much like the clinic.

Until recently.

Suddenly she wanted to be there sipping a cappuccino and sitting next to her fountain. She wanted to talk to Carla, even Amy. And yes, of course she wanted to see Jack. She even wanted to see patients.

Yes, her house was the one place where Jack hadn't been. But it wasn't better for it. It certainly didn't give her the peace she wanted. In fact, it made her crazy. The blandness of her environment, and her life, was obvious here and it made the changes Jack had brought all the more obvious and appealing.

She headed into the kitchen, feeling a thickness her throat that could easily give way at any moment to sobs. She yanked the freezer door open and sighed, instead, in relief.

There was a small tub of Ben and Jerry's Cherry Garcia ice cream right in the front.

At least *that* had some color to it.

The cappuccino didn't taste as good as she remembered.

Brooke stirred the cup, frowning at the contents. She hadn't come to the clinic yesterday. One day. How could anything actually be different already?

She pushed the cup away, disgusted—with herself. Coffee didn't taste bad because Jack wasn't in love with her. That was stupid. The cloudy sky, running out of shaving cream and her headache also weren't because he didn't love her.

Well, the headache probably was. But not the other stuff.

She had to get a grip. So Jack didn't love her. So what?

He'd just felt guilty. Really, really guilty. Big deal.

The shock of his confession had definitely faded. It actually all made sense now. She had wondered why he'd stayed, why he'd been so persistent about being there and making changes. Now she knew. Guilt was a powerful emotion, especially for a self-proclaimed hero. Jack wasn't used to making mistakes. And he did tend to overreact. So he'd overcompensated for this one.

Fine.

Now her life could go back to where it had been.

Boring, lonely, depressing and frustrating.

Great.

A knock at the door jolted her from her thoughts.

"Yes?"

Brooke expected Carla, but instead Jack strode through the doorway. It was the first time she could remember him actually waiting for an answer before coming in.

She'd missed him.

It was such a strange thing to feel with him standing right in front of her. She stubbornly denied herself the sob that wanted to escape.

He came to her desk and handed her a folder. "I got a replacement," he told her simply. "He'll be here Monday."

"Monday?" she repeated in surprise. "As in three days from now?"

"Yes."

"A replacement for..."

"Me."

Her heart banged against her ribs. "I see." As if anyone could replace him.

“You have a choice now. Me or him.”

You. But she held back. She still wanted him, but she was angry he’d kept the truth from her for so long. She was hurt that she didn’t know what he’d done for her because of guilt and what he’d done because of more, if anything. But she still wanted him.

She picked up the resume and scanned it. Dr. Alex Carter was a young doctor with three years’ experience in family practice in San Antonio at the hospital where Jack worked. Dr. Carter’s resume was perfect for the Honey Creek clinic.

“Looks great,” she commented.

“Great.” With that he turned and headed for the door.

She stared after him, stunned. He’d found a replacement. Just like that. As if all he’d been to her was a supervising physician.

Yes, he’d seen patients. Yes, he’d bought the frickin’ cappuccino machine. Yes, he’d encouraged her to redecorate. But he’d done a hell of a lot more than that. And that was even before she’d gotten in his bed.

He had never acted charitable toward *her*. He had never acted like he felt sorry for her.

He’d certainly never coddled her. There hadn’t been any *Poor baby* from him.

He’d pushed her to let go, be real, to be happy with herself.

He’d invested even more time, patience and energy into Brooke herself than he did the clinic he was now attempting to cover with this new doctor.

That had to mean something.

She started after him, thoughts and emotions swirling. She had one idea about how to find out his real feelings for her.

“So he’s a full replacement?” she asked.

Jack turned. “What do you mean?”

“He can tell enough stupid knock-knock jokes to keep Mr. Willis laughing and can eat enough cookies to keep Thelma happy and can talk with some authority about Sponge Bob with Christopher? Because if not, he’s not the right guy,” she said, watching Jack’s face carefully.

His eyes narrowed. “I’m sure he can do all those things. I’ll be sure to prep him.”

“And don’t forget to tell him that bringing Amy a Dr. Pepper on Monday morning will keep her on his good side.”

“Right. I’ll make a note.”

“And I’m sure you filled him in on all *my* needs.”

Something flared in his eyes. “What are you talking about?” he asked in a near growl.

“Well, you know that there’s more going on here than just a clinic in need of a doctor. I mean you stepped right in. If you really want me taken care of you’ll have to be sure Alex is willing—”

“If Alex so much as gets you a cup of cappuccino, I’ll break his neck.”

Her eyes widened at his fierce reply, even as her heart did a happy flip. “But I thought the idea was to fill in for what I lost with Mike.”

“I know exactly what you lost with Mike Worthington.” He took another step closer and his voice dropped further. “Carter can very adequately replace what your husband did for you. Including sleeping with someone other than you.”

She probably should have flinched at his blunt words, but she actually found the comment amusing. He was right. “So what have *you* been doing all this time? I thought the whole point of all of this was filling in for Mike because you felt sorry for me."

He seemed actually unsure of what to say for a moment. A rare occurrence indeed.

There had been so many opportunities and reasons for him to leave and very few for him to stay. Unless he had a really good reason.

"You could have given up when I didn't take the money in the first place," she went on. "You could have at least washed your hands of it all after patients were coming in and I was more confident or after the clinic was remodeled and I finally took some of your advice."

His eyes narrowed as he finally said, "I didn't think of any option other than staying myself."

"Exactly." She stepped closer and grasped the front of his shirt in her fist. "There's just one more thing I need to know." She went up on tiptoe, put her other hand at the back of his head and pulled him forward to meet her lips.

His arms went around her as he dipped his knees to bring her up more firmly against him. He groaned deep in his throat as she buried both hands in his hair and molded herself to him. As they poured their feelings into the kiss, Brooke ached all over for him and it went so far beyond the physical she couldn't have put words to it anyway.

When the kiss finally ended, she felt a little dazed. Jack was breathing raggedly, his hands still on her. Neither of them said anything, but she knew what she needed to know.

That was *not* a goodbye kiss.

"If Carter comes to practice here there will be rules," Jack said. "One, he won't touch you and two, he won't buy you anything. The rules if I stay are, I will touch you all the time, even in public and two, I will buy you things—inappropriate, over-the-top things that you'll love. Pick."

The door slammed loudly behind him before she could tell him her decision.

But that was okay. She knew she needed to *show* him.

Even though Brooke had shunned outrageous behavior and over-the-top sentiments for a very long time, that didn't mean she didn't recognize when a situation called for them.

So the only question she had was—what would Dixie do?

Jack made himself stay at the diner smiling, chatting and accepting free cups of coffee and two pieces of pie as the town learned of and expressed their happiness over his decision to stay in Honey Creek. He couldn't tell them his decision lay with Brooke.

He listened to a few friendly suggestions about the clinic, he politely declined an offer to be set up on a blind date with someone's niece and he happily accepted an invitation to Sunday dinner.

But all the while his heart was screaming at him, *Go get her!*

What was Brooke thinking, feeling, *doing* right now? Should he have stayed and convinced her they were supposed to be together? He was a doer by nature. He took charge, made the decisions, told others what was going to happen. But he'd put it all in her hands. And he had to wait.

He forced the last bit of free chocolate-cream pie into his mouth and chewed even as his emotionally knotted stomach protested.

He pushed his plate away a moment later as the group of men he was sitting with burst into laughter. He had missed the entire joke, but was saved from admitting it by the sudden hush that fell over the entire diner.

Along with the rest of the back section of Vi's, he swiveled to see what was going on.

And he nearly choked on his pie.

Brooke was coming directly for him.

The first impression he had was that she was wearing her hair up—the way he *hated.*

"Jack, I need to talk to you."

He wanted to gather her into his arms, stiff white lab coat, sticky hairspray and all. But she looked so serious, so damned *professional,* he knew his heart would be in even smaller pieces if he tried to hold her and it was a medical issue or something equally benign that she needed to discuss.

He folded his arms. "Yes?"

"I've been thinking and...I want to discuss your rules in more detail."

He couldn't seem to get any of the rest of his body to do anything.

She kicked off her black pumps and reached back to unclasp her hair. She shook her head better than any model in any shampoo commercial in history. She began speaking as she opened the top button of the lab coat.

"The thing is," she said as the second button released. "I not only accept your rules but I understand them. When you touch me and buy me things it's not to get me to do something for you, it's because you love me."

His brain registered her words at the same moment he glimpsed bright pink satin.

Pink.

Satin.

Both concepts sunk in as the third button parted from its hole and the jacket gapped further showing how the pink satin hugged the inside of her right breast then dipped below the lapel.

"But I have a couple of rules of my own that you should probably hear."

The truth slammed in to him all at once. She had a *pink* bra on under her lab coat. And that was all.

"Rule one, if it's lingerie, I prefer pink and number two, I intend to touch you a lot too, publicly and privately, and it will be wonderfully inappropriate some of the time. So we should probably get married to avoid any scandal."

The lab coat fell open and Jack saw nothing but a lot of smooth tan skin and pink silk.

He swallowed hard. She wore pink well. Her shoulders moved and he realized that she was about to shrug out of the jacket.

Unwilling to share the rest of what was about to happen with anyone else, he lunged for her.

He gathered the front of the lab coat in one fist and gently turned her toward the door with his other hand on the back of her neck.

"See y'all later," he told their audience.

"Wait, just one more thing," Brooke said, digging her heels in as they approached the door.

"Wha—"

She'd stopped beside the booth where Walter Worthington was sitting with two other men. "Walter," she said calmly.

Jack's body tensed, ready to pull her behind him if necessary, but he didn't stop her.

Walter turned slowly to face them. He was the only person

in the diner not already looking at the spectacle she'd created, but Jack knew that the other man was as aware as Jack was of what Brooke said and did. Walter met her gaze directly, unblinkingly, but said nothing.

"There's something I've wanted to say to you for a long time," she told him.

"I can hardly wait," he replied.

Brooke took a deep breath and let it out, then said calmly, "Fuck off, Walter."

A stunned silence followed her words.

Then a spattering of applause erupted from several tables.

A surge of pride and desire for her coursed through Jack and he stood, amazed, when she started for the door again.

"You're just like your mother," Walter called after her.

She paused and again Jack tensed. If Walter made her cry, he'd punch the older man without hesitation or regret.

But when she turned she was smiling. "That's the nicest thing you've ever said to me, Walter."

Head high, she left the diner, and Walter Worthington, behind her. Finally.

Jack was two steps slower, but caught up to her quickly. And took over from there.

He put his hand on the back of her neck again and didn't stop steering her until they were a block from the diner and its huge front window. He ducked around the corner of the hair salon where it threw a shadow on the sidewalk beside it and stopped her, then dropped the handful of jacket.

"Okay, go ahead."

"Go ahead?" she asked.

"Let's see what you've got for me." He gestured at the front of her jacket.

He fully intended to enjoy every inch—and the truth that it really was all for him.

She looked like she had something to say but she must have thought better of it because she pulled the lab coat open and then let it fall to the pavement.

His mouth went dry.

The bra and panties were definitely pink—what little there was of them.

"I have to say something before you act on that look on your face," she said quickly.

"Okay, but hurry up," he growled.

They definitely had some talking to get done first. But it could be short and sweet.

"I don't blame you for Mike's death."

That enabled him to tear his eyes from her body and focus back on her beautiful, though concerned-looking, face.

"Brooke, I—"

She stepped forward quickly, covering his mouth with her hand. "I understand how you feel. But *I* don't blame you. If you blame yourself, all I can do is love you and hope that you will eventually be able to forgive yourself too. I'm not saying it's good Mike died. But people die and the rest of us have to pick up, regrets and all, and go on. And sometimes we get a chance to be happy again." She took a deep breath. "Or for the first time."

He couldn't speak. So he pulled her into his arms, a bit roughly, and held her against the heart that was full, for the first time, because of her.

"I love you, you know," he said against the top of her head.

"I know," she said quietly. "I love you too."

She could almost feel the relief shudder through him.

"And this *isn't* charity."

She pulled back to stop him, but he gave her a look that halted her words.

"Let me finish," he said.

She nodded.

"Charity is giving and sacrificing, and I intend to do that with you. But true charity is not *taking*," he said, looking directly into her eyes, "and there are some things I definitely intend to get out of this deal—love, time, your secrets, your dreams and mine, your body, your devotion—"

She hugged him tightly, interrupting his words. "It's all yours, sugar. Everything I've got." She couldn't believe how great it felt to say that. How *right*.

He squeezed her ass. "Hey, the clinic's closed, right?"

"Well, yeah." Since they were both right here rather than there.

"Good. I think those cabinets up front could use a good dusting."

"You want to bring us full circle, huh? I think your shrink would approve."

"Yep." He grinned down at her. "And this time I have no intention of having *any* morals about what happens. Just to warn you."

She giggled. "Ah, now I know why you bought me that new big, *sturdy* desk."

"Let's go see if I got my money's worth."

Epilogue

"Amazing."

Jack turned to look at his brother. David sat in one of the white wooden chairs they'd brought in for the outdoor wedding. He had one foot crossed over his opposite knee and a glass of champagne in hand.

Jack followed David's gaze and his mouth curled up.

"Which one?"

They were seated on the lawn under the huge white tent that had covered the ceremony and now the dinner and reception. David was looking at the back patio of Brooke's pink house where she stood with her mom and Carla.

"The house, my wife or her mom?"

All three required at least a second look.

They'd chosen to have the wedding at the house because it had gorgeous grounds, plenty of room—including a kitchen—and allowed Dixie to avoid the town and anyone she didn't want to see. Jack suspected that Brooke was also accepting the fact that the house was a part of her, for better or worse. He thought it was quickly becoming better. Dixie Donovan-Kotes was also a sight to behold. Dressed in head-to-toe pink, including a huge hat, she was hard to look away from. She was a beautiful woman with an infectious laugh. Jack liked her a lot.

But he did prefer things just a bit more muted than Dixie. His gaze hung up on Brooke.

His wife.

They'd only waited four months to get married and he was still getting used to the term. Every time he heard it his chest and throat felt tight. He hoped that never changed.

She was still dressed in her wedding gown and he still wore his tux. Her dress was simple and elegant—sleeveless with a deep V in front and an even deeper V in back. It was a shimmery smooth silk that reminded him of the black dress he'd bought her in Amarillo. It hung just to her knees, showed a lot of skin and there wasn't a button or white jacket in sight. And her hair was down.

The best part, though, was that the dress was a pale rose color. So pale you had to look close to be sure, but it was there.

"Actually I was talking about her." David gestured with his glass to Brooke's maid of honor.

Carla was scolding one of her boys.

Jack swung back to face his brother. "Yeah?"

David grinned. "She handles those boys like a pro. The perfect amount of praise with the discipline. They know they have boundaries but that they're loved. Impressive. And as a single mom, often tough to do. I'm intrigued."

Jack chuckled. "I never realized what turns a shrink on."

David shrugged. "Well, she's got a great ass too."

Jack laughed outright at that. He started to tell David that was how things had started between him and Brooke but their mother approached just then.

She dropped into the chair next to him and kicked her heels off with a sigh. "I just had the strangest conversation with Brooke's stepfather."

Jack liked Phillip Kotes. Even if he had cheated on his wife and had almost ruined the town Jack loved, Phillip seemed to genuinely love Dixie and it was clear he wanted Brooke to like him.

Jack figured he and Phillip had a few things in common as two men who'd fallen hard for Donovan women—in spite of the complications it seemed to cause. "What did he say?"

"Apparently he offered Brooke a huge amount of money for the Girls Home," Ann said.

Brooke had decided to turn her mom's pink house into a second location for the Mary Elizabeth Girls Home. There were already six girls planning to move in at the end of the month. Brooke and Jack would provide the medical care along with their work at the busy clinic in town and they would be hiring locally for housekeeping, cooking, counseling and the other needs.

"But she turned the money down?" he guessed.

"Yes," his mother answered, clearly shocked. "So he asked if he could give *me* the money and then have me give it to her but not tell her who it was really from."

"*No*," Jack and David said at the same time, emphatically.

Ann's eyes widened. "Okay."

"I'll talk to her," Jack said. He was getting good at talking Brooke into things. It was still a knee-jerk reaction to not want to take help, especially money, from men. But she had to ignore that Phillip was sleeping with her mother. This money had nothing to do with that. It was about the girls they could help. She'd see that eventually.

Just as she was coming to believe that plenty of people in town liked and trusted her. She and Amanda Cartwright would never be friends, and Walter Worthington would never set foot in the clinic, but they were both a lot slower to voice their opinions about the woman who was quickly becoming a Honey Creek favorite.

Ann leaned in, looking at her oldest son closely. "I've never seen you this happy," she said honestly.

He found Brooke through the crowd and caught her watching him with a smile.

"Brooke's awesome, Jack," David agreed. "I'm really glad you came to Honey Creek."

Jack looked at his brother trying to decide if he should thank him or slug him.

"You're not worried about my mental stability anymore?"

David finished off his champagne. "Oh sure I am. I worry about everyone's mental stability. And I'm thankful daily that we're all a little crazy or I'd be out of a job."

"You don't think staying with Brooke and Honey Creek is bad for me?"

David shook his head. "Not anymore. Not since *you* realized they're not bad for you."

Jack stared at his brother. "I never thought they were bad for me."

"Yes, you did," David said, his eyes on Carla as she danced with Billy Perkins. "You told yourself you were only here to be a hero because you were afraid that's all she really needed or wanted from you."

Jack frowned. "*You* said I just wanted to be a hero."

"I was putting words to your thoughts and feelings so you could better face them and deal with them," David said. "And once they were out you could realize that there was a lot more going on."

Jack looked at his mother who just shrugged and took a drink of her champagne. His brother was full of shit.

"I suppose you expect me to thank you then," Jack finally said.

"Seeing you so happy is thanks enough," David returned with a grin. He stretched to his feet. "Now I believe I'm going to dance with a hot Honey Creek girl."

"I think that's a great idea," Ann said, watching David cut in on Billy Perkins—and Carla let him. "You should do it too."

"You can read my mind almost as well as David can." Jack got to his feet.

Ann laughed. "Sure. It takes a trained professional to see how much you want to be with your wife."

He bent and kissed his mom's cheek. "Love you."

"Love you too." She put her hand on his cheek. "You deserve all of this, you know."

He straightened, his heart full. "I do," he agreed.

A minute later he took Brooke's hand. "'Scuse us, Dixie," he said.

His new mother-in-law smiled at him and he absolutely knew why she'd caught Walter Worthington's eye.

"About time you came to get her." Dixie smiled at her daughter.

"You don't mind then?" He pulled Brooke up against his side.

It didn't matter if she minded, but he wanted to be polite.

"Mind?" Dixie laughed. "You're not supposed to spend your wedding night with your mom." She winked at him.

Phillip arrived at her side just then and she snuggled up against him. She might have seduced him out of revenge, but it was clear she'd married him for more.

Jack folded Brooke into his arms on the dance floor.

She grinned up at him. "I can't believe how many people came."

Most of the town had turned out for the wedding. "They love you."

"And *you*," she said with an eye roll.

"Well, sure, Thelma's here for me, but the rest are for you." He squeezed her butt as she laughed.

"Oh, by the way," she said as she wiggled closer. "Dixie gave me lingerie as a wedding present."

His eyes widened. Lingerie from Dixie? He could only imagine what it looked like. And he suddenly was imagining just that.

"And...they're pink," she added.

He groaned. Of course they were. "My new favorite color."

"Yeah?"

"Definitely."

"I'm glad you feel that way."

"Oh?" He wondered if he dared kiss her. It would turn into a lot more very quickly and they were technically in public with both of their mothers watching—one of whom would care.

"Yeah. Because I think the baby's going to be a girl."

"What bab..." He pulled back to look down at her.

She had that mischievous smile he loved on her face.

The truth sank in quickly. "A baby girl, huh?" That sounded just about perfect.

"I have a feeling," she said with a nod.

Gathering her close and tucking her head under his chin, Jack sighed happily. Little girls always thought their dads were superheroes, didn't they?

"You ready for this?" Brooke asked.

"Nope. But I haven't been ready for most of what's happened here in Honey Creek."

She chuckled. "Me either."

It was going to be great.

About the Author

Erin Nicholas has been reading and writing romantic fiction since her mother gave her a romance novel in high school and she discovered happily-ever-after suddenly went a little beyond glass slippers and fairy godmothers! She lives in the Midwest with her husband who only wants to read the sex scenes in her books, her kids who will *never* read the sex scenes in her books, and family and friends who say they're shocked by the sex scenes in her books (yeah, right!).

For more information about Erin and her books, visit:

www.ErinNicholas.com

www.ninenaughtynovelists.blogspot.com

www.twitter.com/ErinNicholas

www.groups.yahoo.com/group/ErinNicholas

Suppose the solution to all your problems
is the one thing you never wanted...

Anything You Want

© 2011 Erin Nicholas

It figures the one time Sabrina Cassidy is determined to do the responsible thing, karma kicks in. After four years on the road chasing her musical dream, she's stranded six hours from home with no money, a ruined credit history—and morning sickness.

Out of options, she swallows her legendary independent streak and calls the only person who won't hang up on her. Luke, the man she left behind.

Marc Sterling's first instinct is to protect his business partner and best friend from another broken heart. That means letting her think she's talking to Luke, then finding a way to send her in the opposite direction.

When he shows up at her hotel room, there's something in the air beside their customary insults. Sure, her rebellious attitude, smart mouth—and purple panties—still drive him crazy, but now it's a different kind of crazy. The kind that has him driving her home instead of to the nearest airport.

And when Luke offers to solve all her problems if she'll only say "I do", Marc realizes he's just crazy enough—about her—to forget whose heart he wanted to protect.

Warning: Contains two people who don't like each other very much, a Toyota that can't quite handle the road trip home, and a spontaneous proposal. Or two. Or three. And foreplay with—what else—pie filling.

Available now in ebook and print from Samhain Publishing.

SAMHAIN
PUBLISHING
www.samhainpublishing.com
Green for the planet.
Great for your wallet.
OK

CPSIA information can be obtained at www.ICGtesting.com
Printed in the USA
BVOW011024100912

300028BV00006B/2/P

9 781609 287955